Haven Strong

Jessica Rakus

FIRST EDITION

ISBN 978-8-9939107-0-3

Dedication

To John, Alec, & Maddie.

Acknowledgements

Teamwork makes the dream work, so team shout outs:

Michelle Rascon, Jeni Chappell, and Miranda Darrow all provided editorial services that made every word of this book better.

Beta reads, feedback, and critique came from the group at Cicada Books in Huntington, WV, Dawn, Amanda, James, Brent, Kim, and anyone else I forgot, I can't thank y'all enough. Amanda also made my stunning book cover, and has been the most supportive human possible about this publishing journey.

Sara LaFontaine was the first to encourage me to figuratively kill my darlings, which in this case was flashbacks, which live on in my drafts folder, but weren't helping the story. She was one of many members of the Women's Fiction Writers Association who helped this book become what it is.

The Stubborn Hearts, Frani, Merida, and Nicole, for every word of their feedback and support. In a lot of ways, you made this book happen.

My literal Team, Christine, Marisa, and Meg, who have been the best friends for the last eight years, even without seeing each other in person. There aren't words for the ways you've changed my life, and all because someone called us a word I can't repeat in print.

My mom and sister, who are amazing, strong women, and have shown me how to be the same.

My perfect children, who blindly love this book they are probably not old enough to read yet.

My husband, ever present. Without knowing it, he's been there while I worked through this story in my head, while I grieved with my characters.

CHAPTER ONE

I handed my husband his sneakers, shoes he should have been able to keep better track of, given how often he wore them. At least he didn't leave them where I'd trip on them, like the kids did.

"Thanks, Jo, you're a lifesaver." He cupped my face with his free hand. My shoulders relaxed and I melted against him, forgetting all the things on my to do list. My eyes drifted shut as he kissed me, the lingering kiss we were rarely allowed, with three kids running around the house. Our daughters were spending a few hours with their grandparents, and our son was upstairs ignoring us. And even without the kids interrupting us, Steve's cell phone pulled us apart, ringing incessantly from his pocket.

"Ignore it, Steve," I murmured against his lips.

"It's Reston, and we have to leave anyway." He stepped away from me and answered the phone call before sitting down to tug on the sneakers, grubby with constant wear. "We're on our way, I swear. Walking out the door as we speak."

A lie. Despite multiple reminders we needed to leave, Matt was still in his room. Matt and Steve were due at school in ten minutes to catch the bus to this evening's basketball game. And if the head coach was calling, we had to leave the house now.

Still, I snickered when Steve ended his phone call. Game Day Reston was a lot to deal with, but by now, we were used to this call, the faux urgency. We weren't late in reality, only late in Reston time. Placating Reston was fifty percent of Steve's job. They were like

1

brothers, bickering, sparring, but balancing each other, each one the other's perfect foil.

"Do you find Reston's antics charming?" Steve glanced at me, looking not quite as amused as I was. No chuckling or eye rolling by him, but also not as annoyed as he'd sounded on the phone.

"It's comforting that he hasn't changed in forty years," I replied. It was soothing to have something in my life that always played out as I expected. I turned toward the staircase. "Matthew!" I yelled up the stairs. "Hurry up. Coach Tucker called to complain that we're late."

Matt slumped down the stairs, earbuds lodged in place, backpack slung over one shoulder. Matt was a twenty-eight years younger carbon copy of his dad, both of them, collectively simply "my boys," sandy-haired and freckled and taller than everyone around them, even when they were with the team. He didn't bother to grab his jacket, even though he couldn't possibly be warm enough in just his sweats over his game uniform. He kept his green eyes on the ground as we walked outside to the decade-old van, the ice melt on the path to the driveway crunching under our feet. Matt liked to stay focused before a game, and interacting with his mother supposedly broke that focus. I was used to it, after all these years of him playing ball. Still, I missed the little boy who couldn't stop talking about how excited he was about the game, how much he was looking forward to playing with his friends, how he was going to score "a million billion points." Every game moved us further away from that kid. He still loved it, but now it was too important to be a game.

The roads were mostly plowed after a recent snow, but small patches of ice kept me on my toes as I navigated toward the school. Steve's phone continued to chime, more texts from Reston. On game days, he was always keyed up to the point of annoyance, for Steve at least. I'd known Reston all my life, and his pregame anxiety was beyond routine. I glanced in the mirror a few times, checking on Matt, still silent in the back row of seats.

With school out for the winter holidays, the parking lot was almost empty, just Reston's well-loved beige sedan and a small bus they'd take to the game a half hour drive away.

I wasn't surprised that the rest of the team was absent, given that we were still early, despite Reston's texts. He was taking his anxiety out on our family, which was par for the course, had been from almost the first season he and Steve had coached together. He couldn't control everything in the lead up to the game, but he could control us. Or at least we let him think so. There wasn't much I'd deny one of my oldest friends, especially when his texts sounded perfectly reasonable, like: "Can you show up early so I have one less thing to worry about?" It got a bit less reasonable when one text turned into thirty texts plus a phone call.

Without bothering to greet Reston, Steve snagged an errant basketball from the back of the van, and he and Matt wandered a few feet away before beginning a game of keep away. Basketball season meant putting my boys on buses, sitting in stands watching my husband and his best friend direct the action, and watching my son flit around the court. Basketball was their love language. It was almost impossible to keep them from playing whenever they had the chance.

I ambled over to Reston, hoping to catch up for a few minutes.

"Hey, it's Matt's mom," he said warmly, putting his arm around my shoulder and tucking me against his body.

I rolled my eyes. "If you, of all people, think of me as my kids' mom instead of as, you know, Jo…"

Reston held up his hands. "Sorry. I was teasing, but I'm sorry anyway. How are you doing, Jo?" he asked, putting an unnecessary emphasis on my name.

Of course I'd known he was joking. "I'm hanging in there. This time of year is exhausting."

I'd barely recovered from serving Thanksgiving dinner to twenty people before it was time to prepare for Christmas. With only four days left until the big day, I'd had to send my daughters, eight and ten and still believing in Santa, as far as we knew, to my mom's house. Otherwise I'd have no secrecy to buy, wrap, and hide Christmas presents. Steve couldn't help much. He'd just finished a semester and had midterms to grade and report. And the boys had this game tonight, the only thing standing between us and our family of five being at home together for over two weeks. We were so rarely all together, and these were my two favorite weeks of the year, time where the house was full and yet quiet, all of us there but no one else, our friends and family having our attention straight up until Christmas was over.

"I forget that the holidays are the worst time of year for moms. I probably should have had someone else manage the pancake supper for the team. Do you need help with your holiday stuff?" He paused, pulling his eyes from the pickup game happening a few feet away to regard me. "As if you'd accept help even if you needed it."

"And as if you have a ton of time to volunteer."

"Same end-of-the-semester problems Steve has, yeah," Reston replied with a laugh.

I wrapped my arms around myself, as if that would work any better than my coat at keeping out the cold. "Are you still coming for Christmas morning brunch? I'm grabbing the last of the groceries once I'm done here."

"I'll be there. I wouldn't miss it."

"Are you ready for this game tonight?"

Reston shrugged. "How is he?" he asked, nodding toward my husband and son. Steve had never been as fast as Matt on the court, and his height advantage was quickly being erased by a boy who couldn't seem to stop growing.

"Matt?" I asked.

"Yeah."

"He's better. Still not quite himself, but not as bad as it was when he and Landon were having...whatever it was they were having."

Matt and Landon had been best friends since birth, but this year had started with a dustup between them. It had caused friction on the team. While Reston would never say so, I suspected he blamed Matt and Landon for the team's loss in the state championship back in the spring. They'd stayed distant over the summer, but this school year, and a new basketball season, had seemingly brought them back together. They were talking again, texting each other far too late at night, spending time at each other's houses. Their usually flawless silent communication on the court still wasn't what it had been, a pass occasionally bouncing wide, but they were back to status quo enough that I no longer needed to have long conversations about what might have gone wrong with my longtime best friend, Amanda, who was Landon's mom.

"The season's going okay, right?" I asked. It was early days, only the fifth game, and their only loss had been a last-second buzzer beater. Still, Reston was a perfectionist on the court.

He shrugged, frowning, and I knew instinctively what he was about to say.

We should be undefeated.

"We took that loss that we shouldn't have," he grumbled.

"You can't win them all."

"I absolutely can."

I couldn't help but smile. Same old Reston.

An SUV pulled in beside us, Amanda behind the wheel. She waved toward us as Landon tumbled from the backseat. He called a distracted hello over his shoulder at his coach before joining Matt and Steve in their game.

Like Reston, I didn't remember a time when Amanda hadn't been in my life. A natural blond, she had monthly visits to the hair salon to make her blonder, and wore fake eyelashes to drop her son off at school. We'd been friends through major and minor catastrophes for close to forty-five years. When Matt and Landon had first seemed to be drifting apart, we'd worried we would drift apart as well, because parents whose kids don't get along don't get to be friends anymore. We'd grown up together, gone to college together, where we were roommates for four years, and stood up in each other's weddings. I couldn't imagine where I'd be without her.

Amanda wouldn't be coming to the game tonight. She rarely made it to the away games anymore. She'd burned herself out, overscheduling Landon and her younger son Elliott for years. By the time Landon started basketball at age five, he was already doing swim, soccer, tee-ball, and karate. "We want to keep his options open," Amanda had insisted. Why a five-year-old needed options was beyond me.

Now Landon only did basketball, all other extracurriculars falling away. Amanda's and my pregnancies with our oldest kids overlapped, the boys arriving weeks apart. Landon was born ahead of schedule, but somehow they both came home from the hospital on the same day. We decided they were fated to be best friends.

Amanda's window slid down.

"You sure you don't mind dropping him back at home after the game?" she asked.

"It's practically on my way," I replied. "It's not a problem."

"Thanks. See you later then. 'Bye, Reston."

We waved goodbye as Amanda backed out of the parking spot and drove out of the lot.

Landon's arrival negated the need for Steve's presence, Matt shooing his dad away in favor of his friend. Steve loped over to us, more out of breath than I would have expected. The three of us watched the boys playing together, something we'd seen the two of them do countless times.

"They seem better," Reston said after a few minutes of watching.

"I told you."

"What's Reston worried about now?" Steve shot Reston an amused glance. "What isn't Reston worried about?" I replied.

Reston frowned toward the teenagers passing the basketball between them. "Yes, how ridiculous of me to care about my job and my team."

"Your job and your team are fine." I nudged him with my shoulder.

"Well. We'll see."

I glanced at my watch, knowing I had things to do before picking up my daughters. "Do you need me to bring anything when I come to the game?"

"Just the usual stuff," Steve replied.

"Okay. I'll see you guys later."

Steve wrapped me in his arms and kissed me goodbye, a brief peck, not the promise our kiss at home had been.

I squeezed Steve before stepping back. "Have a good game. Drive safe, Reston."

"I always do."

"I know."

He'd gotten his CDL and bus driver training in an effort to make himself necessary. Before he'd taken over coaching the team, he'd wanted to make sure he had every possible advantage over any other candidate. It was helpful that the school never needed to find someone else to run the team to and from their games. And he would never let anything happen to the kids on his team.

I pulled out of the parking lot.

The grocery store was crowded, full of people stocking up before the holidays. It took longer than expected to get what I needed, making me late getting to my mom's to pick up the girls. I only had so much time before the sitter was coming over so that I could head out to the game.

I didn't take the time to walk up to my mom's door, instead texting her to tell her I was waiting outside. My girls burst out of their grandmother's house, bundled in their winter gear.

Eight-year-old Olivia climbed into the van ahead of her sister, tugging off the pompom-ed hat that left her sandy blonde hair flying in all directions. Addy, two years older, removed her hot pink jacket before climbing into the van, shooting a longing glance at the passenger seat she wasn't yet old enough to occupy. Her hat was likely crammed in a pocket, her dark hair smooth, her ears pink with the cold. It had been an ordeal to get her to agree to leggings under the dress she insisted on wearing despite the late-December chill in the air and the snow still on the ground.

"Hey, girls," I said. "How was Gran's?"

They'd had a good day, they reported. Gran had spoiled them with sweets. Par for the course at Gran's. My mom spoiled her grandkids, partly because she knew Steve's parents, who lived an hour away, couldn't indulge them as easily. And frankly partly because that was my mother's nature. She was a giver.

The girls were out of the van as soon as I put it in park in the driveway.

"Could you please help me with the groceries?" I asked, but when I turned toward them, they had already disappeared into the house. Classic.

I grabbed as many bags as I could manage and started toward the house. I heard a car pull to the curb behind me and turned. It was a state police vehicle, no lights or sirens, and I glanced up and down the street, curious who was having a problem. Nothing seemed out of the ordinary, so I continued into the house. I maneuvered around the discarded winter gear the girls had left behind on their way to the TV and dropped the grocery bags on the kitchen counter. Hopefully only one more trip out into the cold.

The police car was still parked in front of the house, but no one had gotten out. Maybe he was lost? Did cops get lost?

With the last grocery bag in hand, I slammed the back of the van shut, echoed by the closing of the door to the police car. I didn't want to look toward it, refusing to acknowledge why a state police officer would be parked at my house.

"Josephine Grant?"

The grocery bag in my hands threatened to fall. He was here for me.

I'd known it since I first saw him, and praying I was wrong had done nothing.

I swallowed hard before turning. "Yes?"

He didn't speak again until he'd navigated the driveway and stood in front of me. I set down the bag of groceries; my shaking hands and knees had rendered holding things impossible.

"Could we step inside for a moment to speak?" he asked.

I glanced toward the door. "My daughters are inside."

He nodded, seeming to understand my concern. Whatever he had to say, he didn't want them to overhear any more than I did.

"Mrs. Grant, I'm so sorry. There was an accident earlier today involving a bus. Two of the people on the bus were identified as Stephen and Matthew Grant."

No. No no no.

"We're still trying to figure out exactly what happened, but emergency personnel at the scene did everything they could for everyone. I'm sorry to tell you they passed away at the scene."

My legs gave out and I collapsed to the ground. Cold seeped through the knees of my jeans, but I didn't care. My head dropped, my forehead settling into the gray slush that lined the driveway.

The officer crouched beside me as a sob burst from my throat.

"Is there someone who can come stay with you?"

Crumbled on the ground, I struggled to extract my cell phone from my back pocket, but I lacked the strength to pull myself up. Finally I got it. Through the blur of tears, I fumbled to find the button to make a phone call. Instead I landed on random apps, frustration adding to the crush in my chest.

The officer took my phone gently from my hand. "What name?"

"Esther Franklin," I replied. "My mother."

He stepped away, and without someone standing over me, I could no longer stop the tears. I sobbed into the cold gray concrete, praying my daughters wouldn't come looking for me.

CHAPTER TWO

I was still wailing into the driveway when my mother arrived. She pulled me from the ground, rubbing the raw red spot the snow had made on my forehead before gathering me in her arms.

"Oh, Jo," she murmured. "I'm so sorry."

I heard the police car start and turned toward it in a panic. "What if I need more information?"

"I have his card," Mom said.

She nudged me toward the house, toward the moment when I'd have to tell my daughters that their father and brother were dead. I pulled back against her gentle guidance, not prepared to go inside. The cold had numbed my body, and I wanted to slip into a pile of slush and disappear.

"You have to do this."

I shook my head at my mother's words. "I can't."

It wasn't just telling my daughters. It was figuring out how to live without the boys. That would be impossible, and I refused to consider it.

My mom pushed me forward again, her arm around me. "I'm here with you. I'll stay with you as long as you need me."

She opened the front door and all but shoved me inside.

"What took you so long?" Addy called from the living room.

When I didn't answer, Olivia came running into the hallway, shouting, "Gran!" before registering what I must have looked like. She paused, leaning back toward the living room.

"What's wrong?" Olivia's chin wavered.

I swallowed hard. "Let's go to the living room." We'd be sitting under a portrait of our family when I told the girls that our family was gone.

Olivia snuggled close to me, clinging to my side. Addy stayed on the floor, looking up at me with wary eyes. I was about to ruin their lives, and I didn't know how to start.

"There was an accident," I said finally. "The bus crashed on the way to the game. Daddy and Matt died."

Olivia began sobbing, while Addy stared at me, shaking her head slowly.

"I'm so sorry, girls. I'm so sorry."

Addy crawled up onto the couch, joining her sister in my lap. We clung to each other, crying, melting into tears and grief. We'd gone from five to three in an instant. I'd never let go of the girls.

From somewhere in the room, I heard my phone ring. I didn't remember getting it back from the cop, but my mother must have, because she handed my phone to me. Amanda's name was on the screen. Oh, God, Landon.

"They're airlifting Landon to Raleigh," she yelled into the phone, a rush of wind behind her. "We're on our way. Are you going too?"

"No," I said softly. Landon had survived the accident. Was it only him? Had it only been my boys?

"He's got a head injury. They don't know what it means yet, but they said as long as he's still alive, they'll keep working. Where are Steve and Matt going?"

"They're dead, Amanda."

She fell silent. I could hear road noises through the phone. She was on her way to be with her son.

Her volume dropped, the panic that had tinged her voice gone. "Jo, I'm so sorry. I didn't know. They didn't say anything."

My knee-jerk reaction was to tell her it was okay, but it wasn't. How many times would I tell people it was okay, that I was okay?

"I don't know when I'll be back," Amanda said. "I'll come see you as soon as I can. You're not alone now, right?"

"Mom's here." My voice was flat. I no longer wanted to be part of this conversation. Her son was alive, doctors were doing everything they could to keep him that way, and a random police officer who didn't know me had ruined my life in my driveway.

I ended the call and handed my phone to my mom. "No more calls."

I picked Olivia up, even though she was probably too heavy for me to carry, and grabbed Addy's hand. We climbed the stairs together. All three of us crawled into the bed I'd shared with Steve and now would sleep in alone. The pillows smelled like him. I pulled the blankets tight around us. This was where we lived now. I tucked the girls into my sides, squeezing them to me while they cried themselves to sleep. I didn't know what to do for them. I didn't know what to do for any of us.

As they drifted off, I brushed hair back from damp faces. Like Matt, Olivia resembled her father, her nose dotted with freckles, her sandy blonde hair always wild. She'd been our bonus child, the one we didn't know we needed or wanted until that unexpected second line on the pregnancy test. I'd been overwhelmed. Addy was barely two when Olivia rolled in. Steve had been overjoyed, especially when she'd turned out to be another girl. We'd assumed the kids would align with their parents along gender lines, but that hadn't worked out. I'd taken to being a boy mom, whatever that meant, like a duck to water, always ready to show up to games and organize the other parents and never missing a chance to jump into the play when I could. And Addy, while the girliest of girls, had gravitated toward her dad. Once I'd taught him to do her hair for dance, she didn't need me anymore.

Olivia had no use for either of us, preferring Matt from the first time he'd held her. She'd always calmed for him as a baby, always run to him with a skinned knee as a toddler. Even with the seven-year age difference, when girls and cars and basketball vied for his attention, he'd been the perfect big brother.

How were we going to do this? How were we going to live our lives without our boys?

The girls' deep breathing soothed me, reassuring me that they, at least, were here with me. Still I couldn't shut off the worries in my head.

I hadn't worked outside the home since Matt was born, and now I'd need to figure out how to support us. How was I supposed to do that, when I also needed to be at all the girls' things, dance and sports and school events? How was I supposed to be everything the girls needed, when I was missing my teammate? How was I supposed to raise my daughters if I wasn't raising my son along with them?

My mom tapped on the doorframe with a knuckle.

"Jo? You have to take this phone call."

I tried to roll away from her, but the girls had me pinned. "I said no."

"It's Amy at the hospital."

If we lived somewhere else, she'd probably be Dr. Michaels, even to my parents, but this was Haven and we'd known Amy forever, attending the same schools, joining the same teams and clubs. I knew Amy, and I liked Amy, but I didn't want to talk to a single person right now.

"I don't care," I replied, still trying to turn away.

"It's about Reston."

"What about Reston?"

"They need you to make medical decisions for him. He can't consent, and you're his proxy."

Wait.

"Reston's alive?"

"Yes."

I looked at the girls sleeping beside me and eased my way out of the bed. As I reached my mom, she set my phone in my outstretched hand.

"Amy?"

I kept moving down the stairs, gathering what I needed to get to the hospital.

"Oh, my God, Jo, I'm so sorry," Amy said in a rush.

"Thanks," I replied after a moment, not knowing if it was the right thing to say. What does one say to condolences?

"Did your mom tell you? I need you to come deal with some medical stuff for Reston until he's able to do things for himself."

"I'm on my way," I replied.

"Avoid the front entrance," Amy said. "Reporters."

The grocery bag I'd abandoned in the driveway was still there. I kicked it off the concrete and onto the grass. Groceries were pointless now.

I started the car and the radio blared. I reached to turn press the power button, then stopped.

"...we know there are survivors, at least one of them here at the medical center in Haven," the radio said. "Based on information gathered at the scene, it is believed that most of the fourteen on board lost their lives, as well as the driver of the other vehicle involved. Police are still investigating the cause—"

I jabbed at the button. I couldn't hear any more right now.

News vans crowded the front of the hospital. I parked a couple blocks away and walked, skirting the back entrance, avoiding the spotlights illuminating the front. It was loud here, voices swirling together, the smells of bleach and blood overwhelming, my head spun. Were the boys' bodies here? Would they let me see them?

I heard my name over the din. Amy waved to me from across the room, her light blue scrubs stained rusty. The things Amy must have had to do today. I hurried over to her.

"I'm sorry about Matt and Steve." Amy walked over to me, her hand wrapping around mine, squeezing my fingers.

I knew they wouldn't have told me they were gone if they weren't positive, but still the hope that somehow they were wrong stuck with me. She walked quickly, and as I caught up to her side, I grabbed her arm, desperate. "Are you sure...have you seen them? Who identified them? Could they be wrong?"

Amy stopped, meeting my eyes as she shook her head. "I haven't had a chance to see them, no," she replied. "Reston did that. He did that for the whole team."

The whole team. Oh, God, poor Reston, to have to do that. To be responsible for looking at the bodies of his team and name them...I blinked back tears, swallowing hard.

I swiped at my face, trying to keep up a façade of composure. "Reston's well enough to have been able to identify them?"

"He's in decent shape."

"Decent shape?" I repeated. "Then why did you need me here?"

"He's been in and out of consciousness, and he's been...combative. He'll need to consent to surgery, and given how he's behaving, I don't know that he's aware enough to make a choice. I assume you can keep him in check, make him listen to us. He's not bad off enough that I think we need to transfer him. We'll get to him," she said, opening the door to a hospital room.

We'll get to him. He was basically fine then, wasn't he?

How was that possible? My boys had died, and Reston was...fine?

He didn't look fine, his face barely recognizable under the cuts and bruises, his hair matted to his forehead with blood. I cried out when I saw him, then clapped my hand over my mouth. If this was what it looked like when someone was "in decent shape," what did Matt and Steve look like? Was that why I couldn't see them yet?

She puttered around his bed, looking at machine displays, listening to his heart and breathing, being a doctor.

"Is he conscious?" I asked softly.

"We're treating his pain right now. There isn't much else we can do for him, and that's keeping him more or less asleep. He's been pretty with it when he's up. Not fighting exactly, but definitely not appreciating the state he's in."

"Will it hurt him if I touch him?" I asked, my voice barely above a whisper. Could he hear me?

"It could, so be gentle. He has a lot of broken bones. I'm going to have a nurse come in to get some info from you, and a social worker will stop by. Thanks for coming." She paused. "There are no words, Jo, I'm so sorry."

I placed my hand on Reston's chest, feeling the rise and fall of his breathing. I had been surprised when Amy said I was his medical proxy, but who else would be? We'd been inseparable as children, until he'd gone out of state for college, wanting to escape the place where everyone knows your name. No one else seemed to make it further than NC State before wandering home four years later. When he finally returned to Haven more than a decade after he'd left, he'd been Matt's first coach, his only coach, as it worked out, essentially a member of our family, since he no longer had his own. Reston's dad had never been in the picture. When breast cancer took his mom six months post-diagnosis not long after he'd moved back, I'd been his first call. At the funeral, Steve and I had flanked him, the boys he coached sitting in the row behind us. We were Reston's people. Of course I was his emergency contact.

Reston awoke with a start, and a guttural cry of pain. I pulled back, afraid that my feather-light touch on his chest had caused this pain. He didn't seem to know I was there. His screams echoed in the tiled room, and I winced, needing it to stop.

"Reston."

He stilled at my voice, and I could breathe again in the silence.

"Jo?"

His voice was rough, raw, but it was unmistakably his, proving that it was indeed Reston Tucker under all those bruises.

"Yes, I'm here."

"Jo. Oh, God, Jo, I'm so sorry, I'm sorry, I lost the team, I'm sorry, Jo."

CHAPTER THREE

He was sobbing, and I cried along with him, trying to keep from clinging to him, for fear of crushing his already broken body. I didn't know which bones were broken, which ones were merely bruised, but I knew everything must hurt. I wove my way around tubes and cords and wires to reach him, needing the comfort and familiarity of him, and knowing no one understood how I was feeling in this moment the way Reston did. I rested my head on his chest, ignoring the metallic scent of blood and the rattle in his chest with every breath. My husband and son were gone, along with I didn't know how many others, and while I needed to cry, I also needed to believe with everything I had that Reston was going to be okay.

"I was supposed to keep them safe," Reston managed between sobs. "I failed them."

"No, of course not. You loved those boys like they were your own. This wasn't your fault."

Oh, God, what if it was? My body reflexively recoiled from him, but I fought to stay in place. What could have happened to the bus that my boys were gone and Reston looked like this? Had Reston run a light, or sped around a curve, or…. Had Reston taken them from us? If he'd been responsible in some way, would I ever be able to forgive him?

"What happened?" I croaked.

"I don't know. There was this car. She…she had to have seen us, but she didn't…I don't know."

I wanted to feel relieved, but how could any of this bring me comfort? My husband was dead, my son…. My throat closed, and I

17

struggled to breathe. What was I going to do without them? How was I supposed to keep going?

"Amanda says Landon is alive," I said, trying to give us both good news to latch onto.

"I'm pretty sure Isaiah is too," Reston said, his voice raspy, grating across my heart. "He talked to me while we were waiting for help. The rest of them…none of them made it. Not Steve, not Matt, not Zach, not Ashton--"

He was going to list them all, and I couldn't hear it. I couldn't handle the tally of human life, of boys I'd known most or all of their lives, gone. I fought the urge to clap my hands over my ears to drown him out.

Instead I held up my hands in front of me, warding off his words.

"It's…we can't do this. Not right now."

"I promised I wouldn't let anything happen to them. It was the most important thing, and I failed."

"I'm sure you did everything you could do for them, Reston."

He grabbed my shoulder, his grip light, barely there, but his intention clear, fixing his eyes on mine. His eyes were bloodshot, the left one swollen nearly shut. He looked crazed.

"I should have died with them, Jo," he croaked.

I nearly collapsed under the weight of his sorrow. I wanted to hold him and tell him that everything would be okay, that he'd get better, but it felt like lies. We'd never feel whole again.

"No one wants more lives lost." I gently removed his grip on my shoulder.

His hand flopped onto the sheet, the small cuts smearing the fabric with blood. "I do. I want to be with my team."

"Isaiah and Landon need you. My daughters need their Uncle Reston." I took a shaky breath. "I need you to be okay, Reston."

"Do the girls know?"

I nodded, wrapping my arms around myself. Trying not to picture their faces as they absorbed the news. Blocking the memory of their cries.

"Are they okay?"

"Of course not. They lost their dad and their big brother, and they're little. They have no idea what it means."

"You should be with them."

I no longer had the strength to comfort my daughters. I needed to refill my energy stores, and being with Reston was doing exactly that. I didn't have to be as careful as I would with my daughters. With Reston, I could swear and cry and question how this could happen to us. The girls were asleep, had no idea I wasn't at home with them. They were fine.

"Have they told you what's wrong with you?" I asked.

"Broken ribs. Broken arm. Broken leg. Cuts from the glass."

People were dead and Reston had a broken leg? He was going to wear a cast for a few weeks, and then everything would be normal? I shook my head, unable to understand.

"How is that possible? It seems like so little."

"I was wearing a seatbelt, Jo."

Of course he was. The driver always did. Keeping one person safe on the bus and leaving everyone else to hope they didn't crash.

The nurse Amy promised arrived, too young to be one of our classmates, but the right age, apparently, to be one of Reston's kids. He called Reston "Coach" as we went through stacks of paperwork, paperwork required because Reston was…fine, I guess. He was angry, feisty, and that let me believe that he was going to be okay. He was probably concussed. It would explain a lot. Reston Tucker was not this defeatist. He was a coach, an encourager, and I didn't know what to make of this man who wished he'd died. He was going to recover, and he was going to be able to go back to his normal life.

Except he wasn't, I realized. Reston's normal life was coaching those boys. If they were gone…what would he come back to?

The paperwork complete, Reston dismissed me, but how could I leave him? For now, the only connection I had to Steve and Matt was this broken man in the bed in front of me.

"I'm glad to stay, Reston."

"Go home to your daughters. They need you."

I should have. He was right. But if this is what Reston's grief looked like, how bad would it be with the girls, who had never experienced death before? I wasn't sure how to explain it to them, let alone to allay their fears or make them feel better.

"The girls are sleeping," I needed an excuse other than running away from them. Only a terrible mother would abandon her children after something like this. I hated myself for being scared to face them.

"Go home, Josephine."

His pain, physical and emotional, was etched on his face, swollen and purple with bruises. I wanted to fix it, wanted to somehow erase this day that had taken so much from so many. I wanted my family back, wanted all those kids to be okay, and would have given anything to make it better. Especially for Reston.

Before there was ever a Stephen Grant, there was a Reston Tucker. Barely-eighteen-year-old me had understood why he wanted desperately to get out of Haven, where everyone knows every bit of your business, but that didn't stop me from feeling abandoned when he left. I'd loved him the way only teenagers love, as if nothing could possibly go wrong, and had ignored how sure we all were that he'd leave Haven the first chance he got. It wasn't that I didn't believe he'd leave. Reston kept his promises and went after what he wanted. He was always going to leave. I assumed it wouldn't matter. We'd always be friends. Even if he never came back, we had these bonds, and bonds don't break because you're a plane ride away instead of down the street. There was a point as a teenager when I'd expected we'd get married and have a life together. That was what happened in Haven. You had to pick the right person in high school. Your fate was already sealed. When he left, I was hurt because what we had didn't matter to him. But our relationship had mattered very much to me. To my surprise, he finally returned to Haven after years of no contact with anyone here.

Reston left a week after high school graduation. By the time he came back, it had been too long for things to be remotely like they'd once been. Steve ended up being everything Reston wasn't. Steve loved my tiny hometown and relocated there gladly with me after college. Steve wanted me, and a family, and those were things I would never have had with Reston.

Reston and Steve became friends, coaching Matt's club teams together until Reston took over coaching at the high school. Steve changed careers to follow him. They were the inseparable ones now, each other's right arm. I didn't know how Reston was going to manage without his other half.

Which explained why Reston wasn't managing right now.

I squeezed my eyes shut against the realization that I, too, was going to have to manage without my other half. I wasn't ready to contemplate what that looked like, what it would feel like to wake up in the morning and remember that they were gone. For now, I'd pretend that Reston was the only one suffering, and I would do my best to take care of him. When I thought I could face a future without the boys, then I'd allow myself to worry about how I was going to manage.

My house was dark, save for a lamp in the living room, and I gravitated there, looking for my mom. She was reading a book, or at least pantomiming reading, but she looked up when I entered.

"How is Reston?" she asked.

"Good, but not." I took a seat next to my mother on the couch.

She stroked my hair as I recounted the time at the hospital, the noise, the bustle, Reston's injuries. The same way I knew every kid on Matt's team, Mom knew Reston inside and out. She'd grown up with Reston's mom. She latched onto his needs right now the same way I did, focusing on something remotely positive, because we couldn't begin to comprehend anything else.

I needed to plan a funeral.

It was there in the back of my mind, the logistics that came with death. I needed to find a place to put Steve and Matt, needed to decide where their bodies would lie, needed to gather everyone together to mourn. I needed to face all of that.

But I couldn't. I couldn't comprehend a life with half of my family missing, my boys, the collective unit that was my six-foot-four, towheaded son and my six-foot-seven, greyer-every-day husband.

I lay on my couch, with my head on my mother's lap, and received her comfort the best I could. She let me distract myself with the thought of things that would get better, and for a time, we both ignored reality.

"What am I supposed to do now?" I finally asked, tears stinging my eyes.

"I don't know," she replied. "I don't know how any of us will go on, Jo."

Thirteen families were in the middle of this, but dozens of others were on the outskirts, mourning along with us. Friends, co-workers, girlfriends. Everyone in town knew at least one of those kids, because that's what happens when there are fewer than a thousand people in a town.

"What if this is a mistake?" I asked. "What if we wake up tomorrow and this never happened, and the boys come through the door, asking why everyone is so sad?"

"That's not going to happen," Mom said gently, stroking my hair. "I'm so, so sorry, Jo, but they're gone."

I swallowed hard, trying to dislodge the lump in my throat.

"I want my boys back," I croaked, my tears streaming now.

CHAPTER FOUR

Daylight was harsh, streaming through the bedroom windows, waking me and the girls. I pulled them to me, the three of us wrapped in a blanket that had the faintest scent of their father. I never wanted to leave this bed. We'd be safe here, able to ignore reality, to pretend that the world hadn't fallen apart. Yes, we'd stay in bed for the rest of our lives. We could pretend the boys were simply at practice or a game, the way they so often were.

But soon they demanded food, television, toys, needing the distractions that I'd given myself the night before. I sent them to find their grandmother, determined to stay in this cocoon.

Mom brought breakfast up to me, but I ignored it, the way I planned to ignore everything. From here on in, ignorance would be bliss. It wouldn't bring my boys back, but it would let me believe that they could come back.

Sticky with the syrup from the pancakes Mom had made them, the girls returned to the bed, neither wanting to be away from me for long. They wanted cuddles and reassurance and answers. Part of me wanted to return to the hospital, to distract myself with Reston and learn more about what had happened to everyone else. But I couldn't take the girls there. I couldn't let them see Reston looking the way he did. I couldn't let them hear what had happened to all the boys who had spent so much time in our house.

"I saw online that everyone didn't die," Addy said, nestled beside me.

"When were you online?" I asked, shocked and annoyed that my mom hadn't been keeping them away from any news.

"They didn't say any names. Who's alive? Is it maybe Daddy and Matt? Were they wrong when they said they died?"

I wanted to be able to reassure them. I wanted to take all the pain away. If only that was possible.

My throat was tight when I responded. "No, baby. It's Landon and Isaiah and Uncle Reston."

Olivia began to sob, and I pulled her closer. "That's not fair."

"I know," I said, my vision blurring with tears. I nuzzled the top of her head, trying to comfort both of us. "But I am so thankful that some people are going to be okay."

"What happened? Why did the bus crash?"

"I don't know, Addy. Uncle Reston said there was another car, but the police are still figuring things out."

I assumed so, anyway. Surely they were investigating, and someday soon we'd have answers. Answers weren't going to bring back the boys. Pointing fingers and assigning blame wasn't going to make this any better. We'd have somewhere to focus our negative emotions, and that would only help so much.

"I want to see them," Addy said.

"Daddy and Matt?"

"Yes. Did you get to see them?"

"Not yet."

I said yet as if it was something I was sure I could do. Part of me wanted to see them, final proof they were gone. But part of me knew seeing what had happened to them, their broken bodies, would destroy me.

"Then how do you know it's true?"

There was nothing I wanted more than for it not to be true. I wanted it to be a lie, a horrible prank, a nightmare we could wake up from.

"No, Addy. They're not okay," I said softly, tucking her against me. "They're gone."

"Forever?" Her bottom lip quivered.

"Forever."

"I don't want them to be gone forever, Mommy."

"Oh, sweetheart. Me too. I want them back so much." My throat tightened as I tried not to cry.

"Is Uncle Reston going to be okay?"

"Yeah, I think so."

I didn't know, but that was the impression I got when I was with him, from Amy telling me that surgery could wait, from his own behavior.

"Can we see him?" Olivia asked.

"When he's feeling a bit better. He's hurt very badly."

"Then how do you know that he'll be okay?"

I paused. "I guess I don't. But the kind of hurt he is, usually people get better."

I had better not get to the hospital to find out that he was worse off than they'd thought. What if they finally got him into surgery, and it turned out he had a ton of internal damage, his insides destroyed, but his exterior hiding it?

"Does Uncle Reston know what happened? Does he know that Daddy died?"

"He does."

"And Matt?"

"Yes."

"Gran says we can't stay in bed all day."

"We can stay in bed all day every day if that's what we want to do."

"What will happen on Christmas?"

I couldn't think past today, but oh, God, I had three days to figure out how we could possibly celebrate the merriest day of the year when I was sure that we'd never be happy again. The presents were bought and wrapped, the tree was decorated, but I wanted nothing more than to tear everything down, to bury my head under the blankets on my bed and ignore it. I had two little girls who still believed in every bit of magic the season had to offer, and I needed to give that to them. I had a dozen people coming for Christmas morning breakfast, except I didn't anymore, because some of them were gone and some were barely hanging on. Fake it 'til you make it, I thought, but faking it could only get me so far. Christmas might be forever ruined, the lead-up clouded by what we'd lost. I could only do so much to make the day about fun and festivities and not...the loss.

"I don't know," I replied. "We'll figure it out together. All of this. We can be like the three musketeers, the three of us sticking together and keeping each other safe."

"I don't want to be three musketeers," Olivia said. "I want to be five."

I pulled her closer, cuddling my girls, wishing I could take this hurt away.

"Me too, baby."

My mother appeared in the doorway. I hoped she hadn't heard me contradict her edict that we get out of bed.

"You have a phone call, Jo," she said.

"Take a message."

"I've been taking messages. This is important."

I sighed, heaving myself out of bed. Every time I climbed into bed, it got harder to get back out.

"Jo, it's Amy."

"Is everything okay?" I asked.

"There's been no change here," she replied. "They're ready for you at the morgue. There's some paperwork so that they know what to do with...with Matt and Steve."

"I can see them," I said softly.

As soon as the option was in front of me, I knew what I wanted.

"I think they'd let you, if you asked, yes."

"I'm on my way."

I hung up my phone and turned to grab my coat from the closet.

"You should get dressed first," my mother said from behind me. "If you're actually planning to leave the house."

Fair enough.

The girls were at attention when I returned to my room.

"Who was on the phone?" Olivia asked.

"Doctor Amy." I pulled a sweater and some jeans from my closet.

"What did she want?"

"They need me to come to the hospital to fill out some papers."

"Can we come?"

I ducked into my bathroom to swipe on some deodorant and comb my hair. "I'm filling out papers. I'll be back soon. You aren't missing anything."

Even if I was allowed to see Matt and Steve, there was no way I wanted the girls to see that. I couldn't imagine what they looked like, how obvious their injuries would be. I wanted the girls to remember them how they'd been in life.

"I promise I'll be back in a little bit." I kissed each girl on her head. "Gran's in charge, be good."

I blinked against the sunlight as I walked to my car, somehow surprised that the sun had the audacity to shine while I grieved. The roads on the way to the hospital were dotted with puddles, the last indication of the recent snow.

I'd forgotten Amy's recommendation from the previous night to avoid the front entrance, remembering only when I saw the throng of reporters between me and the door. I took a deep breath, steadying myself, and started forward.

"Mrs. Grant!"

I ignored the voice, stunned that they recognized me. How did they even know who I was? Had someone given them my name?

They pressed closers, cameras, phones, and recorders in hand. Flashes popped around me, and I ducked my head, trying to push through.

"We're sorry for your loss, Mrs. Grant."

"Could you talk to us about your son and husband?"

"People around the country are praying for you, Mrs. Grant."

"Mrs. Grant, do you have an update on the survivors?"

I paused, trying to figure out what I could possibly say to these people. Sure, it was news, it was a story, and people were paying attention to our small town, the same way we had noticed small towns affected by floods and fires and guns. Tragedy on a large scale always brings the eyes of strangers. But it was my life, I was a real person mourning a real loss. This wasn't some "reality" show where my friends and I had scripted fights over nothing.

"No," I said finally. "Excuse me."

CHAPTER FIVE

I expected the morgue to smell like death, like decay, but it was still that antiseptic hospital smell from the rest of the building. It was colder and grayer, and void of the noises that came with the lives upstairs. My footsteps echoed in the hallways, bounding off the once-white tile of the floors and walls.

"We're so sorry for your loss, Jo."

This from the morgue attendant, Tom, who had been a year or two ahead of me in school, but still we knew each other, because everyone did in Haven. He peered at me with watery eyes behind owlish glasses, and I looked away from him quickly, not wanting his imminent tears to bring on more of my own.

"Can I see them?"

It was my only thought, my goal in coming here, a desperate need to see with my own eyes that it was them. I knew they'd been seen by people we knew, that everyone in Haven could have identified them fine. Still, I had to do this, or I'd never stop wondering. With all the chaos and all the death, could there have been a mistake?

"I don't recommend seeing them. Their injuries haven't been repaired."

"I understand, Tom," I replied, trying to move past him. "I need to do this."

"They've been identified. You can give me the info on what happens next. You don't have to come inside."

I closed my eyes for a moment, trying to let myself be talked out of it. Tom was right, I didn't need to see my boys. But the desire to do so was consuming.

Tom pulled open the drawers that held my family. The mechanical clatter from the drawer, combined with a short blast of cold air, jolted my eyes open. Tom met my eyes one last time before drawing back the white sheets that covered them.

I regretted my decision to see them immediately.

They'd been cleaned up, but like Tom said, they were still clearly broken beyond repair. I could see what had likely killed my husband, the side of his skull caved in. I swallowed back a wave of nausea and pulled back the hand that had instinctively moved to smooth his broken bones.

Matt's nose was broken, his face…different. I couldn't figure out exactly what was out of place, but clearly some of the underlying bones that built his beautiful face were also broken. They were both too still, too cold. I shouldn't have come here.

My hands closed around the edge of the cold steel table, and I hung my head. My knees bent, my body giving out.

I felt a hand on my arm. My eyes, blurry with tears, stayed trained on the floor as Tom led me from the room.

"What can I do for you?" Tom asked.

"Nothing. Give me a minute."

Outside of that cold, depressing room, I gulped in air, trying to fill my lungs. No matter how hard I tried, I couldn't get enough air. The room was spinning faster now, and I stumbled.

"Careful, Jo," Tom said softly. "Deep breaths. You're okay."

He helped me into a chair. I clung to his arms as I tried to calm myself, but my body refused to listen. I was hyperventilating, dizzy, my vision cutting out.

I shouldn't have seen them. I didn't want to remember them like this. I wasn't ready to make it real that they were gone.

"Do you need me to call upstairs and get you a doctor?" Tom asked.

I shook my head, determined to rein myself in. "I'm fine," I gasped.

It was a few more minutes until I was fine. First, I could breathe again, then the room stopped spinning. Tom brought me some water. I sat silently, draining the cup, glad that I at least had the sense not to bring the girls with me.

"You can come back to do the paperwork another time," Tom offered.

Oh, God, I still had to do that.

"No, no, I want to be done," I replied.

"I assume we should send them to the Wallis Funeral Home?"

"Yes."

They were the only funeral home in town. I couldn't imagine sending them to another town.

"I can put in my notes whether they should prepare them for burial or cremation, if that might spare you a visit to the funeral home."

God dammit.

"I have no idea."

"Take some time to think it over. Honestly, Jo, you don't have to decide now."

Burial would mean they were always here in Haven, a place I'd never leave. Cremation meant they could be taken anywhere. Steve's parents could have some of him to take back to Charlotte with them.

Oh, my God, I'd forgotten all about Steve's parents. What did they know? What if they'd heard from the news? How could I have forgotten them? Had I been that wrapped up in myself?

My breathing started to get out of control again. His mother had never forgiven me for Steve moving away from her. She always hated that her grandkids lived in another city, the three hours between us apparently insurmountable. She'd make this my fault, because there was nothing Bethany loved like taking out every possible aggression on me.

"We'll bury them here," I said. "I'll figure out the details later."

"Okay. Is there anything I can do for you?"

I shook my head. "What else do you need from me?"

Papers were thrust in front of me, words were spoken about what I was signing, but I didn't listen, instead scribbling an approximation of my name where I was told to.

"Can I go?" I handed the last piece of paper back to Tom.

"Of course. I'll call if we need anything."

I stumbled to the elevator, needing to get away from this place, needing a distraction. I couldn't think about the things I needed to do, the funeral I needed to plan, the horrible phone call I needed to make.

Instead, I could stay here and continue to ignore the responsibilities. I could spend time with the one person who wouldn't push me to deal with them.

I didn't even greet Reston before I collapsed across his bed, sobbing against his chest. Other than an initial groan of discomfort, he didn't say anything, letting me cry myself out. After a few minutes, I felt a light thud against the side of my head and jerked upright.

"Sorry," Reston mumbled, holding up his right hand. "I keep forgetting I have casts now."

"When did that happen?" It hadn't registered how different he looked—his face and hair cleaned up, stitches and bandages now where cuts had been the previous night, bruises more pronounced, but the swelling receding.

"I don't know," Reston replied. "I have no concept of time since the crash. You were here, like, yesterday, right?"

"Yes."

"That's when the crash happened."

"Yesterday afternoon."

It felt like a lifetime ago already, but it had barely been twenty-four hours since I last saw my husband and son alive.

"Did you come to the hospital to cry on me? Don't get me wrong, I am glad to be here for you to cry on."

Of course he was. He always had been. "No, I…" I trailed off, not wanting to put words to my time in the morgue. "I had to…downstairs. I saw them. And I had to make some decisions."

"About Steve and Matt?"

"Yeah."

"Burial?"

"That's what I think."

"I know it's what Steve would want. He loved it here."

I nodded, thankful for the validation. I was making impossible decisions, the kind of decisions everyone hoped they'd never have to make. Steve and I hadn't gotten around to planning our eventually deaths, and no parent ever imagines needing to bury their child. My heart hurt with the agony of it.

"This is so much bullshit," I whimpered. "It's bullshit that I have to think about any of this."

"Agreed."

"If I'd decided on cremation, would you have told me it's what Steve wanted?" I asked, knowing that of anyone, Reston would be the one to validate my choices right now.

"Of course I would have. If there was ever a time for soothing lies, this is it."

"Thank you."

Then I bit my lip, trying to stop the tears that seemed to never dry up. I was tired. I was tired of hurting, tired of crying. Tired of seeing everyone I loved also hurting.

Reston groped clumsily for a box of tissues that sat on the table beside his bed and pressed it into my hands.

"How are the girls?" he asked softly.

I sniffed back my tears, wiping my nose with a tissue, and my cheeks with another. "Not good. Let me know when they can come visit."

"Once I'm doing a bit better. Or can keep track of what day it is."

"I should probably get back to them. I'll come visit again when I can."

Reston looked into my eyes. "Don't come here if it's bad for you."

"Everything's bad for me right now," I replied.

"Tell me about it."

Even being here with him was bad, seeing someone who had always been in my life in pain. But this, at least, meant I was doing good. He didn't have to say anything for me to know it made him feel better to have me close by, the same way his presence kept me steady.

Reston hugged me, and I lay my head on his chest, noticing that today his breathing sounded better than it had the day before. One last squeeze, and he released me back into the real world.

I braced myself before braving the gauntlet of reporters outside again. I could do this. It was just noise, ignore it.

The reporters called after me again as I walked, and even though I ignored them, my eyes stung with tears. I wanted privacy right now, to be able to pretend that my world wasn't falling apart. People begging me to talk about losing my husband and my son spit in the face of my grief.

CHAPTER SIX

For the first time, I understood why Reston wanted to die along with his team. Being here, being left behind, was torture. I couldn't leave my girls, but the urge to abandon my responsibilities was strong. I paused on my front porch, my forehead against the door, willing myself inside. I closed my eyes, hoping to let go of the last few hours, but all I could see was Matt, and Steve, and how cold and broken they were.

Inside, I waved toward my mom and kept walking, not ready to talk about what I'd seen, and knowing she'd ask what my daughters wouldn't.

I wanted nothing more than to return to my bed, to continue ignoring my obligations. Instead, I focused on those responsibilities, hoping they would keep me on my feet. The girls needed me.

They were in my bed, cartoons blaring from the tablet in Addy's hands. I snuggled in next to them. We didn't talk, our eyes fixed on the screen, my arms around the girls. I pressed my lips against their heads, breathed in the scent of them, absorbed their energy. I could do this; I could be here for them. I could be the mother my daughters needed me to be.

I didn't have a choice.

I was quiet the rest of the day, unable to stop picturing the boys. Their disfigured faces, their mangled bodies. My stomach churned whenever my mind flashed to them, then guilt swirled. How could anything about my husband and my son make bile rise to my throat?

I declined dinner, sitting silently at the table while Addy and Olivia picked at the mac and cheese my mom put in front of them. I helped the girls shower and change into their PJs, and I tucked them into their own beds in their shared room. Then I returned to the living room to make sure my mom didn't need me. I'd passively allowed her to handle the house for the day, and I knew I couldn't ask that of her for much longer.

"I got the kitchen cleaned up while you were getting the girls in bed," she said. "Do you want to sit and talk?"

I shook my head, my hand on the banister, ready to confront the next task on my unbearable to do list. "Did you tell the Grants?"

"Yes, last night."

"Good. At least I won't have to tell them what happened." Two steps up, I stopped and turned around. "How did they take it?"

"Not well. I didn't get a lot of words out of Bethany, mostly sobs. Aaron was a bit more stoic."

"I have to call them."

"You don't. You have your own grief, and your daughters, and you don't have to take on theirs."

"I'm not going to hand Bethany something else to be angry at me about." I started back up the stairs. Even now, I couldn't put aside all the slights I'd suffered at the hands of Steve's mother, who had never forgiven me for taking her son away from her. "Thanks for your help. I'll see you in the morning."

My mom kept the fundamental parts of my household running, keeping the girls fed and making sure dirty dishes didn't stack up and trash didn't overflow. The tasks I would forget right now. I couldn't get through the day without her, but I barely spoke to her, unable to put into words the gratitude I owed her.

I did my best to delay the obligatory phone call. I stood in the shower, the rivulets running down my face, and allowed the tears to mix with the water. I sobbed, my hands planted on the wall below the showerhead, my head bent. All I could see was my boys, but they weren't my boys anymore. I wanted to fix them, but there was nothing I could do. I wanted them whole again, wanted them to be okay. I wanted the water to wash it away, to undo it.

The water grew cold as I continued to howl. I turned up my face, letting the tepid droplets wash away the evidence that I'd been crying. It was time to make this phone call.

Surely it would go smoothly. We were all hurting too much to want to hurt each other, right?

I wrapped myself in the comforter that still smelled like my husband and dialed his parents' number.

My father-in-law answered, not a surprise. Bethany tended to avoid answering my calls.

"Hello, Josephine."

"Hello, Aaron."

"Nice of you to call." His voice was robotic, the same way it often was when the Grants spoke to me. It would have been nice for this to heal whatever wound they'd decided I'd inflicted, but it seemed things would instead be carrying on as they had.

"I'm sorry I wasn't able to call sooner. Things have been...hectic," I replied after a moment.

"I'd imagine."

I drew my knees up to my chest, resting my head on them. My body was heavy, too tired to hold myself up. "My mom said she spoke with you last night, but I wanted to talk to you both myself. I'm...I'm not sure why, but it seemed like the right thing to do."

"How are you and the girls?"

"We're okay. Not great. It's been hard." I was clearly not at my most articulate. How had I never learned how to talk to these people?

"Hold on, Bethany wanted to talk to you," he said, almost as if he hadn't been listening, had only asked because he was supposed to.

And Bethany had never once wanted to talk to me.

"I don't know what decisions you've made." Bethany didn't bother with a greeting. "We'd like to bring Steve home to bury him."

At least she hadn't surprised me with that request.

"That sounds lovely, Bethany, but I want to keep him and Matt together."

"You could inter Matt here as well."

I pressed my lips closed against the laugh that threatened at that suggestion. Never.

"I want to keep him here with his teammates. I'm sure you understand. The team meant everything to my boys."

It was true, of course. I wanted the boys together. I wanted the team together.

I also, somewhat spitefully, wanted to make this point to my mother-in-law. They were my family, mine to make this decision for. She didn't have to like my choice or agree with it. It wasn't for her to approve.

"You're being selfish, Josephine."

I set my jaw. Damn right, I was being selfish. "I have the right to that, Bethany. I know you lost your son too, and I'm so sorry. Right now, I have to think about myself and the girls. The girls need to have them nearby. Again, I'm sure you understand."

"You should bring the girls here for a few days."

"That's a sweet offer, but I'm trying to keep their routine as normal as possible."

"They're still out of school, aren't they?"

"They are, yes. But we have busy schedules. Sadly, much of that is time with our friends in the hospital and attending funerals."

I could picture her pursing her lips, narrowing her eyes, livid that I had the temerity to do as I pleased.

"Will you at least allow us to attend the funeral?"

"Of course," I replied. "As soon as I have the details, you'll be the first to know."

"I'm sure." Bethany's tone matched my own, both of us clearly full of shit.

Of course, I would tell them about the funeral and gladly have them attend with us. But they were hardly my first concern, not in a world where they'd never truly been kind to me. Not in a world where I had two daughters who needed me.

"Can I speak with the girls?" Bethany asked.

"They're asleep," I replied. "We'll give you a call in the morning."

"I'm looking forward to it. Good night, Josephine."

"Good night."

CHAPTER SEVEN

Even with the bed covers pulled over my head and pillows jammed against my ears, I could hear my daughters. They craved my attention and energy right now, when all I wanted was time alone with my grief. Olivia was beside the bed, trying to burrow in to find me. Her icy fingers closed around my wrist.

"Come downstairs," she begged, tugging too hard.

I waved her off. Didn't they understand? I couldn't be their mom right now. I couldn't give them attention, cuddle them, and calm their fears. I couldn't even make them breakfast. I'd used up all my parenting energy the previous day.

"Mom," I called out. My voice was strangled, muffled by the blankets. I emerged from my cocoon and called again for my mother. I heard her footsteps nearby. "Please take care of the girls," I mumbled before withdrawing again under the covers.

"Absolutely. For now."

Her tone made it clear that the clock had already started. It hadn't even been forty-eight hours, and she wanted me to be better.

I was wallowing, but hadn't I earned the right? Hadn't I lost enough to merit hiding away and letting other people handle the business of the world for a few days?

I'd barely slept, plagued by nightmares fueled by the appearance of Matt and Steve's bodies. The first night I'd slept hard, exhausted by the initial grief. Last night had been different, too much, brought on by a day that had been too much.

Lesson learned. I'd hide here until everything was okay out there.

Now it was Addy's turn to invade my space, crawling between the sheets to settle against me. Her body was warm, her bare feet cold, and for a moment I was glad for her company.

"What did they look like?"

Her voice was barely above a whisper, but I recoiled from her question. The answer was that she didn't want to know and I didn't want to talk about it, but there was no way to tell her without it sounding like an admonition.

Instead I called again for my mother.

"I can't," I said, my voice strangled, as I threw back the covers.

I pulled on clothes that might have been dirty, doing my best to ignore my mother's disapproving glare.

Settled behind the steering wheel in my van, I paused, unsure of where exactly I thought I was going. Running away from my daughters wasn't doing any of us any good. My grief wasn't more important than theirs, and my mom could only support them so much. They needed their mother.

But I needed someone too.

I picked up my phone and pressed the icon to video call my best friend. I hadn't talked to Amanda since the day of the accident, two days ago and a million years ago simultaneously. I hadn't checked on Landon, who I assumed was still alive because I hadn't heard otherwise.

The screen filled with Amanda's face, too pale with dark undereye circles and hair that hung in greasy strands.

"Oh, my God, Jo."

Instantly we were both in tears, a replay of my time with Reston immediately after the accident. If we were in the same room, we'd be wrapped in each other's arms, I knew from all the other times we'd weathered heartbreak together.

I gulped in air and rubbed a hand over my face. "I needed to check on you guys."

"We're awful," she replied. "I have a son in a coma. He has a traumatic brain injury. Everything is so stunningly awful that I can't comprehend it."

"A coma?" I repeated, instinctively shaking my head, unable to believe this could be happening to a child I'd held as a five-pound baby.

"He's stable, breathing on his own and all, but they don't know if he's going to wake up, or what things will look like if he does, because his brain is a disaster. And I tried looking for information online about what recovery from a TBI looks like, and I have so many regrets, Jo."

"Do you know how Isaiah is doing? Do you know where he is?"

"He's here in Raleigh too. It's his spine. I mean, some broken bones and stuff too, but there's a spinal cord injury. No one knows yet how bad it is."

I shook my head. "I need to reach out to his mom."

"How are you functioning, Jo?" Amanda asked. "How are you capable of getting out of bed or worrying about the rest of us?"

I shrugged. I certainly didn't think I was doing a particularly good job of any of it. "I don't know. I'm in my car hiding from my children right now because I can't bear to continue to break their hearts talking about this. I escape to the hospital to sit with Reston so I don't have to look at my broken-hearted children."

Amanda looked away from the camera but not before I saw her scowl. What was that about? Judgement at my terrible mothering? Annoyance that I was checking on Reston and not on her?

"What was that face?" I asked.

"Nothing," she replied. "I don't want to talk about him."

"About Reston? Why not?"

Growing up, we—Amanda, her then-boyfriend-now-husband Justin, me, and Reston—had been an inseparable foursome. Sure, that friendship had changed in adulthood, especially once Reston left

Haven, but childhood friendships always change. Still, we were all close, and the idea that Amanda had somehow turned on Reston, especially now, baffled me.

"Things are weird now," Amanda said. "He was driving. He crashed. Now my son may never wake up. I'm not ready to care about Reston."

"Yeah, but it wasn't his fault."

I had no idea whose fault it was, but I could never believe that he would have done anything to put our sons in danger.

"He was responsible for them," Amanda said firmly. "And I said I don't want to talk about him right now. Maybe that will change, but for now, just don't, okay?"

"Sure," I said, confused and angry on Reston's behalf. "Is there anything you need? I can bring you clothes or food or something."

"No, we've got family running back and forth. Focus on taking care of yourself."

"I don't know what I need," I admitted. "It's always easier to see what other people need."

"Well at least don't push yourself. Put what you do have into taking care of the girls."

I wrapped my arms around myself, curling up as best as I could in the driver's seat of my car. "I'm flailing, Amanda. I don't want to answer any more of their questions, but if I don't, are they going to turn on the TV and get their answers there? There are reporters outside the hospital, Amanda."

"Of course there are."

"Not the response I was expecting."

"Come on, every time there's some sort of mass tragedy, the media revolves around it for a few days, and then something else terrible happens. It's our turn, Jo."

She wasn't wrong. It seemed every time I turned on the TV or glanced at the computer, a town was engulfed in heartbreak. A shooting. Natural disasters. The outbreak of some scary disease. It happened so often, and yet it seemed impossible that it would even happen here, to the people we loved.

"I don't want a turn at tragedy," I moaned, leaning my head back.

"Too late. We're all in this now."

"I want out."

"Don't we all. You know there's a hashtag, right?"

I jerked upright. "A hashtag?" As if I didn't find it weird enough that we were news. As if it weren't bad enough that the deaths of my husband and son were entertainment.

"Online. For the stories."

"How do you know?"

"There's nothing for me to do all day long. I spend a lot of time online."

"What's the hashtag?" I asked.

"#HavenStrong."

Of course it was. That was the format for the tragedy hashtags—the way strangers showed support without having to expend energy beyond a tweet.

I didn't feel strong. I felt like I'd lost everything that ever mattered, and I was supposed to pretend that life was worth living. The girls would look back on this time and wish I'd done everything differently.

The girls. I needed to do better by them. This wasn't about me. Sure, I could take some time to mourn and wallow in that pain. But I also needed to support my daughters. I had to do better there. Two days after I'd lost Steve and Matt, and I had to be, like the hashtag suggested, Haven strong.

I sighed. "I have to go be with my girls."

"Give them my love."

"Tell Landon we love him. Even if he can't hear you."

Disconnecting the call, I pulled myself out of the van. I stood in my entryway, my back against the front door, and closed my eyes, hoping to let go of the last few hours. For now, I had to be my daughters' mother. I had to pretend I wasn't a widow grieving her husband and her son. Maybe after I put the girls to bed, I could sneak into Matt's room and sleep in there. I could envelop myself in his comforter, the way I surrounded myself with Steve in our room. Until then, it was time to focus on two little girls who had also lost nearly everything.

CHAPTER EIGHT

The girls were once again in my bed, Uno cards in a haphazard pile between them. Addy laid down a blitz of cards, skips and reverses one after another, shouting "Uno" triumphantly before laying down her last card. Olivia groaned dramatically, flopping back against the pillows.

"Not fair," she whined.

"Can I play?" I asked, climbing into the bed with them.

Addy gathered the cards to her, shuffling clumsily. "Sure," she said. "But we're not keeping score."

"Fine by me."

Our game was punctuated by sighs and groans, cheers and laughter, and it felt so normal when life had become anything but.

"I'm sorry about before," I said, passing out cards for another hand.

"Sorry we keep bothering you," Olivia replied.

"You're not bothering me. I'm sad, and it's hard for me to be sad and be your mom right now. I'll try to be better."

"Where did you go?" Addy asked.

"I was just in the car talking to Aunt Amanda."

"Is Landon okay?"

"Not really," I said slowly, trying to figure out how to answer. "His brain got hurt."

I wasn't sure how to explain any of this to the girls. I wasn't sure how to explain it to myself half the time. What their injuries meant, how long the recovery would be. It seemed like Reston only had some broken bones, so that was easy enough, but spinal cord injuries and traumatic brain injuries...that was more complicated.

"Will he get better?"

"I don't know," I replied. "They still have a while until they know for sure what's wrong."

"What about Isaiah?" Olivia asked.

"His back is hurt," I replied. "They're not sure how bad yet."

"That's terrible," Addy said with a sniffle that might have been the start of tears, but she swiped across her face, so I couldn't know for sure.

I couldn't argue with that. All of this was terrible.

"When can we go see everyone?" Olivia asked.

"I don't know. While everyone is trying to get better, they need a lot of quiet and rest. As soon as it's okay to go, we'll go, I promise."

I knew that seeing Reston looking as normal as possible would reassure them, prove that he was going to be okay. But that's not how Reston looked right now. And if I didn't want them seeing Reston in casts, I couldn't imagine taking them to see Landon while he was in a coma he might never wake from.

"When will they stop being in the hospital?" Addy asked. "Landon and Uncle Reston and Isaiah, I mean."

"I don't know. Once they're better enough to go home. Probably not for a long time."

They couldn't keep Reston much longer, could they? A few broken bones don't usually mean weeks in the hospital. Of course, that was assuming there wasn't more wrong with him. I should have checked on him. It would reassure me, and then I'd be able to reassure the girls.

But then, maybe I was lying to myself. Maybe I'd never believe that we'd all come out of this okay, because how could we? We'd all lost so much, and going back to our lives as they'd been before the accident might just be impossible.

I did my best to seem normal at dinner. I helped my mom set the table and did the dishes myself after we'd eaten.

I didn't feel like myself, but I could fake it at least. I did the girls' regular bedtime routine with them, snuggling up with them in their beds, first Olivia, then Addy, while we read together. I promised them we'd have a better day tomorrow.

I said good night to my mother, and once again retreated to my bed, the only place I felt safe.

I booted up my laptop for the first time since the accident. My fingers hovered over the keyboard. I'd avoided the news coverage so far, already knowing everything I needed to know about that terrible day. Did I want to know more?

Slowly, agonizingly, I typed out the letters of the hashtag.

In classic form, the internet discourse was full of garbage. Vitriol directed at Reston and the woman who had been behind the wheel of the car that hit them. They were somehow equally and solely responsible for the accident. Both probably drunk, her too old to be driving, Reston distracted by the noise of the players on the bus. Anger toward the state, for supposedly shoddy road maintenance. Toward the school district, who must have put the kids' safety on the line in a defective bus.

But it was also full of kindness, sweet words directed toward our boys. Articles talked about how Steve and Reston had coached together and how dedicated they each were to the team. Stories about the players that had little to do with basketball: where the seniors were going for college, good grades, other extracurriculars, and hobbies. Making them all into people who were here, and who were amazing, and now they were gone.

Every post used the same photos, and I wondered who provided them. Matt's was his most recent school photo, taken a few weeks after the start of his sophomore year. His hair was precisely combed, and he wore a button-down shirt. He looked exceptionally handsome, the internet calling him a heartbreaker, which he would never have been, too nice to hurt anyone. He'd never had a serious girlfriend, no prom or homecoming dance. There would never be a wedding, or children, or a chance to break hearts.

The photo they used of Steve was one of him coaching, standing courtside, and looking cross. Reston was calm and measured on the sidelines, but Steve was animated, and I loved that this picture captured that. In the picture, he had his arms crossed in front of his chest, his forehead creased as he glared at someone. I assumed the someone was either a referee or Matt, because things were always tense between my boys when they were on the court. Reston had frequently served as a mediator between them, Matt too stubborn to listen to his dad and Steve too passionate to let that slide.

Her picture was there too, of course. The woman who hit the bus. She was old, the internet speculating that perhaps she was too old. The investigation into the accident was ongoing, no answer yet on how it happened. It was unfathomable to so many people that the bus had tipped over the way it had. And maybe it was, maybe something worse had happened than we knew so far. I wasn't sure answers would make me feel better.

I knew something that would make me feel better.

I texted Reston, knowing that even a few words from him would reassure me I could at least make it through the next few hours. My phone buzzed in my hand, him calling instead of texting me back.

"I have a broken arm," he said when I answered. "I can't text."

"Ugh, of course," I replied. "I'm sorry."

"No problem. Just call me instead. How are you doing?"

I shook my head, then rolled my eyes at myself. "Sometimes better, sometimes worse, I guess. It's been a rough day. You?"

"I'm not doing so hot. The pain's a problem. I've been in and out of sleep all day. You probably would have missed me even if you'd stopped by."

"Reston? Are you going to be okay?"

I'd meant for the question to be somewhat light, but my throat closed around my words. More than a question, I was begging him to be okay.

"I'm going to be fine," Reston assured me. "I assume. It's brutally unfair, and part of me wishes I weren't, but it's what the doctors tell me."

I shook with the effort to hold back my tears. I wanted to be done crying, but there was always a new assault on my frazzled emotions.

"I'm glad you're okay," I managed before the tears began to stream.

"You sound it."

I breathed out a laugh. "Thanks."

"But they're here to take my phone away from me so that I can sleep, so we'll have to talk tomorrow," Reston continued.

"I can't wait."

CHAPTER NINE

"There's a police officer here to see you," my mom said from the doorway.

I burrowed deeper into the blankets, trying to block out her voice and the daylight, both continually reappearing each day. "No, thank you. Take a message."

"Get out of bed, Josephine."

I threw back the covers and followed her down the stairs.

I'd hated every moment of the last three days. It was all garbage and bullshit, and I just wanted my boys.

"Hello, Mrs. Grant."

It was the same state trooper from the first night. I still didn't remember his name, but I knew his face. I assumed I'd never forget that.

"Hello."

He extended a large plastic bag, a trash bag from the look of it, toward me, and I took it reluctantly.

"What is all this?" I asked, peering into the bag.

"These are the personal effects of Matthew and Stephen Grant."

Personal effects. What a detached and unnatural term.

My hands shook against the urge to drop the bag. Their things, the stuff that had been with my boys when they'd died.

"Thanks," I mumbled.

"I'm sorry for your loss, Mrs. Grant."

I nudged the door closed with my elbow, examining the bag's contents closer now. Matt's backpack took up most of the space, and I recoiled at the sight of blood on one of the straps. His blood? Someone else's? He would have been sitting with Landon on the bus, but would he have had his bag in the seat with them, or tossed into an empty row? It was a small bus, not too much extra space with fourteen people on board. He'd probably shoved it at his feet.

Their phones must be in here, their wallets, pieces of the real-life stuff that I needed to face—accounts closed, contracts dealt with. I needed to put this away somewhere until I was ready to deal with the contents. Who knew when I'd be ready to manage that?

I started down the hall toward Matt's room. I'd keep their things safe in there, where no one was going just yet.

At least I thought we were all staying out of Matt's room, but things looked different as I shoved the bag inside. I froze in the doorway, studying the room.

It was too neat, his desktop clear, no clothes littering the floor. His bed was made too precisely, the corners neat where he usually casually tossed the comforter over top. A basket piled high with carefully folded clothes sat on the bed. It didn't smell like a fifteen-year-old boy's room.

I shook my head, my mouth falling open, afraid of losing this piece of my son. I rifled through the laundry basket, stack upon stack of my son's clothes, tears streaming. I buried my face in the clothes, trying to catch the scent of my only son, but it was gone, another piece of Matt I would never get back.

"What are you doing?"

I whirled on my mother, who stood in the doorway. "Did you wash Matt's clothes?"

"It all needs to be done, Jo," she replied, her voice steady, void of the emotion that filled my own voice. "I'd wash your sheets if I could get the three of you out of that bed long enough."

"None of it needs to be done. Not right now. Let me mourn."

"It's Christmas Eve. Do you even have gifts to put out for the girls?"

"Of course I do."

They were ready and waiting in my bedroom closet, the same way they were every year. We had milk in the fridge and cookies in the pantry that we could leave for Santa, if the girls wanted that. The stockings were hung, the same way they always were on Christmas Eve.

"Are you going to remember the presents?" she asked gently. "It doesn't feel like you're ready to handle real life yet, Jo."

I saw red, enraged at the implication of her words. Half of my family had died, and I was the one left to make sense of it, to fix the broken parts of us left behind. Of course it was going to take some time before I had everything perfectly in hand. But I had yet to stumble. I was managing better than she had any right to expect.

"I'm doing my best," I snapped. "I lost my husband and my son. I think I've earned some leeway."

"Addy and Olivia lost their brother and their father. They can't lose their mother too."

"No one's losing me. Matt's laundry could have waited until I was ready."

"You have to be ready now."

"Says who? What fucking rule is that, Mother?"

She winced at my words and my tone. "Your daughters need you, Josephine."

"I don't care!"

I cared, of course I did. I wanted to do whatever I had to do to get my girls through this. But I couldn't rush my own grief. I could ignore it when they needed to be my focus, but only for so long.

We stared at each other for a moment before my mother spoke again.

"I think it's time for me to go. Your dad is going to come over in the morning for presents, as planned, and after that we'll both go back to our house. We're five minutes away if you need anything."

I flushed, embarrassed by my behavior. "I appreciate your help, Mom, it's just—"

"I'm starting to get in your way."

"It's not like that. I need to be able to do things myself, and in my own way and my own time."

Having her here helped, of course, but it also gave me a crutch, an excuse not to take care of myself and the girls. I was thankful for my mom, for all that she'd done for us, but I was ready for her to go.

The same thing had happened when the kids were born. After each birth, she stayed with us for a few days, until the moment her presence shifted from assistance to annoyance. She'd been figuratively shoved out the door much like she was now all three times. She'd kept coming back, so I knew she understood why I eventually cracked. And I knew she understood now.

"You want to mourn how you want, without input," Mom said.

"I do."

"I'm sorry I pushed you. Still, Jo, it's better if I let you and the girls get into a routine. Having me here probably isn't the best for you. I'm a few minutes away if you need anything."

"Thank you."

She pulled me to her, wrapping her arms around me. It was too much. All of it was too much. She was right, though. The girls and I had to figure out how we were going to live this new life.

Even if we didn't want it, even if I'd give it back in a heartbeat, it was ours now.

CHAPTER TEN

Daylight or not, Christmas Eve or not, I was getting ready to return to bed when my cell phone rang. I was going to ignore it, but it was Reston, and I couldn't imagine why he'd be calling me.

"They've decided to hold a vigil tonight—"

I was already declining before Reston finished his sentence.

"—and I need you to take me."

"Absolutely not."

"They said they'd let me out in a wheelchair for two hours," he continued. "I have to be there, Jo."

I knew he needed this, and I wanted to help him. But I was spent. I didn't want to be surrounded by tragedy. I didn't want to hear their names spoken, didn't want to hear people talking about my boys. I wasn't capable of that today.

"I don't think I can do that. Ask someone else."

"Goddammit, Jo," Reston snarled. "Come get me. Bring the girls."

"No, thanks."

"It's Christmas Eve, and the whole town is getting together to light candles and remember eleven people who should still be here and pray for two boys who are fighting for their lives. None of this should be happening. I need to be there, Jo."

"Get someone else."

His voice softened, begging me now. "You're my next-of-kin. You're the one they'll give me to."

"I can't, Reston."

"Come get me."

I stood, staring at my phone for a moment. Of all the ridiculous things he'd asked of me over the years…

But it might be good for me and the girls too. Being surrounded by friends and neighbors, feeling the support from the community, certainly couldn't hurt.

He was waiting for us at the hospital, the bruises on his face faded to a mottled yellow-green, his right arm and leg in casts, bandages covering some of the cuts on his face. His beard was growing in, mottled brown and grey, a new look for him. He was still broken, but the sight of me and the girls brought a smile to his face.

"It's so good to have you all here," he said.

The girls could barely keep themselves from crawling onto Reston. Olivia stood beside him, running her fingers over his casts. Addy chattered away, a million questions—what was wrong with him, when would he be better, how soon would he be home. He seemed at ease with them, the way he always had.

"Girls, stop climbing on Uncle Reston," I admonished.

They were surely hurting him, but he didn't complain. I signed a form, promising to bring him back or assume responsibility for the repercussions, and then I loaded him into my van, with the help of two nurses. We placed him carefully in the backseat, in something of a prone position, which couldn't have been comfortable for him. I could see the pain on his face, but knew he'd never admit to it for fear that he'd be packed back into his hospital room.

The vigil was back at the gym, on the court where the boys spent so much time. For a decade, my life had revolved around basketball courts. Practices. Games. Watching my son learn how to play, getting better and better, his skills growing along with him. Watching Steve teach Matt and the rest of the boys everything he knew, and the approving look that would take over his face when the boys did well. He was so proud of those kids.

Again, it felt like the entire town had shown up. People were passing out battery-operated candles, and when I accepted one for myself and one for the girls, I was mobbed by people, familiar and unfamiliar, everyone somehow knowing who I was and what I'd lost. I couldn't move further into the room. It was all I could do not to be separated from the girls as I was passed from person to person, wrapped in arms before I understood who was embracing me. It was too much of a blur moving too fast for the hugs to bring any real comfort. Reston, too, was surrounded, and I hoped he was handling the attention okay. Through the crowd, I caught brief glimpses of other families being gathered into hugs, parents and siblings of boys I had watched grow up who were now gone, just like my boys.

Some of these people were strangers. People who came to Haven to mourn with us, people from other cities, other states, who had heard about our boys. How odd to have strangers taking part in this. How odd for our most private moments to become a public spectacle. Performative hugs so they could tell people later they were here, so they could make a social media post with our special hashtag.

Jim—Mayor Williams—came over the PA system, welcoming everyone. He said a prayer, and read the names of our boys, and I squeezed my eyes shut, trying to keep the scope of the loss away from me. But I couldn't ignore it. I couldn't stop the words from entering my mind, from picturing those boys, from seeing clearly, for the first time, what we'd lost.

Julian Acosta.

Nicholas Arnold.

Matthew Grant.

Stephen Grant.

Ashton Hunt.

Brian Ingram.

Aidan Lawrence.

Cameron Miller.

Gabriel Owens.

Zachary Patterson.

Jackson Reeves.

Tears began to flow, and I did my best to stop the flood before it started. I looked at my girls, the only light I had left. They were bickering over a candle, being children, and it struck me how unfair it was that they'd grow up without their dad. Who would walk them down the aisle at their weddings? I'd pictured those moments, and now they were gone.

The glance at my daughters was meant to stop the flow of tears, a finger in the leaky dam, but it had been more like dynamite, demolishing the walls of my defenses.

I still wasn't sure how we were going to move forward. All I knew was that we'd have to. Me and my girls. Three musketeers.

I handed Olivia my candle, stopping the bickering, and knelt beside Reston. It was strange to see him here in his native environment but utterly incapable of his usual movement. He'd played here long before he'd coached here. Today he looked lost.

"You okay?" I asked softly.

He nodded. "It's weird. Now."

"Are you sure you can keep doing this?"

"I'm fine."

The mayor wrapped up his speech, his words in memory of Steve and Matt and all those boys. Then he opened the floor for anyone else who wanted to speak. I saw most of the other team parents, though none of us moved to speak. I didn't know what I'd say.

But plenty of others did. Classmates shared stories of the boys: some funny, some heart-breaking, some mundane. I heard tales

58

about my oldest child that I'd never heard before. It felt good to hear about the boys, to feel them around me. It warmed my spirit to see people around me, supporting me, supporting each other. Finally I could contemplate a future that no longer looked the way I'd expected it to.

"Coach?" a voice boomed over the PA. "Coach Tucker, do you want to say anything?"

Reston paled beneath his bruises. There was a squeak as someone passed a megaphone toward us. Reston stared at the megaphone. He licked his lips, his eyes darting as he pondered what to say.

"I'm sorry," he finally croaked. He looked at me, his eyes wild, and I knew without him saying so that we needed to leave.

"He has to get back to the hospital," I whispered to the person beside me, not wanting to draw extra attention, but knowing that the information would make its way through the crowd.

It was harder to maneuver him back into the car, and every time I jolted him, he sucked in a breath. I apologized, but he shook me off. I longed to make this better for him, to reassure his guilt away.

I helped settle Reston back in his room, and the nurse went to retrieve the pain medication he surely needed. He didn't complain, but his jaw was tight, his eyes pained.

"I can stop by tomorrow after we do presents and stuff," I said, tucking him into the bed.

"If you think the girls want to be here."

"I think they will. Anything besides us sitting in our half-empty home on Christmas."

He nodded. "Makes sense. I'll see you tomorrow then."

I turned to go, but he called me back.

"I don't know what's going to happen when they release me."

"What do you mean?"

"Well, they can't possibly keep me until my bones heal. But I can't take care of myself. I can't walk. I can't cook. I can't go to the bathroom on my own."

"I hadn't thought of that."

The hazard of living alone. Even with a roommate or a loved one, taking care of him for the next few weeks or months could be a full-time job. Even if I opened our guest room to him, the work of his recovery would be too much for me right now.

"I assume they'll send me to a rehab facility, but there isn't one in Haven. I guess they'd send me to Raleigh. And how do I pay for that? How long am I going to be out of commission? Will I be able to go back onto the court without falling apart?" He paused. "Will they even take me back at Haven High?"

"They love you, Reston. Of course they'll take you back."

"The accident wasn't my fault, but I will always feel responsible, Jo. And some people will absolutely blame me."

It was chilling to think that people could be that angry at Reston. He'd been a staple in our town, his family here for generations, even if they were all gone now. I couldn't picture this town without him now, after too many years when that was the reality. I'd move heaven and Earth to ensure that he kept that job, if it came to it.

"When you're feeling well enough to get back to work, then we can worry about that. And you know I'll do anything I can to help you. Just like Steve would have."

"Thank you."

"We'll stop by tomorrow. Call if you need anything else."

I collected the girls from the waiting room, needing to get them home and into bed. It was almost time for Santa to come.

CHAPTER ELEVEN

Christmas morning was sedate, the quietest I could remember. Presents were opened mechanically, gifts barely remarked upon. The toys the girls had spent months begging for were now shoved aside in a pile. I'd hoped we'd have a respite in our grief, an hour or so remembering that we could still have moments of happiness. It was too fresh, too raw. Maybe next Christmas would be different. The night before, I'd shoved gifts bought weeks ago for Matt and Steve to the back of my closet, trying not to remember. I'd think about what to do with them later.

It was nice to see my dad. While my mom had been staying with us, he was a five-minute drive away, and we hadn't even spoken. I didn't mind, I understood. I barely knew what to say to the girls, and I hadn't yet spoken to the other moms who lost a son that horrible day. How could I judge my dad for being awkward in the same position?

After breakfast, I hugged my parents goodbye and sent them back to their house, the way we always did, the girls usually too wrapped up in their presents to notice that my parents were gone. We'd be running around town to visit our friends, dropping off gifts or food, or we'd have friends over, the house full of children and noise. Today though, we all felt their absence acutely, if only because it highlighted the fact that Matt and Steve were absent as well. The house was painfully silent, achingly empty, and I hated it the way I'd hated everything since we'd lost the boys. I tried to wipe my tears away before the girls could see them, trying to at least seem strong to them, knowing that at this point, they were well aware of how heartbroken I was. I didn't cry at the dinner table every night when the boys were here. I didn't spend most of the day in my pajamas, or leave the chores undone.

I half-heartedly attempted to clean up the living room, balling up discarded wrapping paper and tossing it distractedly toward the trash. The girls were sitting near the tree, surrounded by their new toys. They weren't playing with them, mostly shuffling boxes around. Addy sat hunched over an unopened book in her lap. Olivia lay on the floor, staring at the toy in front of her, as if willing the box to open itself. Suddenly she jumped up and ran to me, tears streaming down her face. The day had gotten to her.

"This is the worst Christmas ever," she sobbed.

I couldn't disagree with that.

"What can I do?" I asked. "Is there anything that will help?"

Olivia shook her head, burrowing closer to me.

"Can we go somewhere?" Addy asked. "I don't want to be here without them."

"I don't know where we'd go," I replied. "Nothing's open."

"Can we go to the hospital?"

I'd been right to tell Reston they'd want to visit.

He looked worse than he had the previous night, presumably because of how active he'd been. He finally listed his injuries for us: his right wrist was broken, as well as his right clavicle, and two broken bones in his right leg. His left shoulder had dislocated, the easiest fix of all. And apparently late the previous night, his spleen had been removed.

"Amy has regrets about letting me leave last night," he said. "I reminded her that I signed paperwork saying I wouldn't sue her. I'm pretty sure the spleen was probably already busted."

I was more diligent than usual when the girls tried to clamber over Reston, now that he'd added a fresh surgery to his list of injuries. He was paler than the previous day, and I briefly wished I'd been more forceful in my refusal to take him to the vigil. It had clearly been too much on his body.

"How are you other than all of that?" Addy asked.

"Oh, you know, fine." Reston paused. "My body hurts a lot. And I'm scared, because it's going to be a while before I'm feeling better."

"What's a spleen?" Olivia asked.

"I have no idea."

"Are you going to have to get a new one?"

"Nope. Apparently I'll mostly be just fine without it. I can get sick easier, so I guess I'll have to be more careful. But other than that, it's no worse than any of the rest of what I've got going on."

"Did you get any Christmas presents?"

I winced. Why hadn't I thought to bring his gifts?

"I'll have plenty waiting for me when I get home, I'm sure."

"I'm sorry," I said. "I'll bring them tomorrow or something."

"Jo, it's fine," he replied. "What am I going to do with presents right now? I wouldn't be able to unwrap anything."

It would be normal though. Opening presents together on Christmas morning was a completely ordinary occurrence. Sitting in a hospital room talking about spleens was the antithesis of that.

Reston frowned at me, then looked at the girls. "The nurses have a ton of cookies out there, and I bet they'd give you some."

They scrambled out of the room, and I collapsed into a chair, realizing how worn down I felt. It wasn't even lunchtime, and I was dreaming of going to sleep.

"Are you okay?" Reston said softly.

"Not really."

"Well, obviously," he said, and I shot him a peeved look. "I meant it more like are you completely falling apart, and if so, do I need to call your mom?"

"Absolutely don't do that," I replied.

I needed to stand on my own, prove I could do all of this. I couldn't lean on other people forever.

"It's only been four days," Reston said gently.

"And what number of days do I get before I have to be perfect?"

"Who says you have to be perfect?"

No one. And yet it was always there in the back of my mind. I had to heal because I had to be a good mom. I had to be myself again.

"The girls are depending on me," I said after a moment.

Reston nodded. "Sure, sure. But I can't imagine they expect perfection."

"They deserve it. And they just lost their dad and their brother, and they need me to fill that gap."

"You're asking a lot of yourself."

"That's a little rich coming from you," I said with a slight smile.

He smiled back. "Fair. I've seen you on Christmas morning plenty of times, and I know it already wears you out, even at the best of times. You do so much. Take it easy on yourself for once."

"The rest of the day will be calm, I promise."

"Not with the amount of cookies I'm sure the nurses are filling your daughters with."

"I hate that you're alone on Christmas."

"I'm not alone. You're here, and once you leave, the hospital staff will be all over me again."

"Are you actually feeling as well as you say?" I asked.

"Oh, God no, every muscle in my body hurts, and I feel like my stomach was just torn open."

I jumped up. "Why didn't you say something? I'll get you pain meds—"

"The staff will take care of it, and I'm fine. I'm their problem for now, and you can focus on yourself and the girls."

I closed my eyes and took a deep breath before opening them again.

"Are you okay if we go?"

"Of course! I'll just sleep."

Reston had spent every Christmas since his mom died with my family, the same way he was always with us for Thanksgiving. I refused to let him spend the day alone on a family holiday. It felt negligent. But he was right, he had plenty of people here to keep him company.

I opened the door. "Come say bye to Uncle Reston," I said to the girls.

"I'll see you all soon," Reston said. "Have the merriest Christmas you can for me, okay?"

The girls promised they would, and I rounded them up to head home.

CHAPTER TWELVE

Back home after our hospital visit, it finally felt like Christmas morning. We distanced ourselves from the pain of holiday grief. The girls were more interested in their new toys. They played together, bickering occasionally, and I could breathe in the relative normalcy.

With cries of "That's mine!" and "You said you were done with it!" echoing from the other room, I sat down at the kitchen table, ready to tackle the terrible job ahead of me: funeral planning. I wanted to get it over with before the end of the year. And tragically, I had other funerals to work around to pick a date. Our lives were an endless parade of funerals.

The funeral home had a similar issue. We settled on the day before New Year's Eve, sandwiching us between Nick's funeral and Zach's. It was surreal and horrifying. How could life go on with all of these people gone?

And how was I supposed to tell people about the funeral? Did you send invitations? Their obituaries had already run, though unnecessary, given the numerous articles the paper was publishing on a daily basis, still, about the accident. I could text people the funeral details, but what if I missed someone?

I started making lists, people to call, food to prepare, things to buy. The girls needed formal clothes for this. Should I order flowers? Would other people send them?

I set down my pen with a sigh. What was I even doing? I was planning a funeral for my husband and my son, an impossible task. I would have given anything to not have to do this.

"Mom?"

I looked up from my lists. Addy stood in the doorway to the kitchen, nibbling on her bottom lip, looking as if she regretted breaking my concentration. I ran my hands over my face, erasing the trails of unconsciously shed tears.

"What's up, Addy?" I asked, my voice cracking.

"Is it almost time for dinner, or could I have a snack?"

I glanced at the clock. Time flies when your world has come apart. "Oh, yeah, it's getting close to dinnertime."

"What are we having?"

I blinked at Addy as if she'd spoken a foreign language. The last few days, my mom had handled all of that. Did we have leftovers? Maybe a frozen pizza? I could always order pizza. Oh, right, we'd had that the first night. Well, there had to be something.

The doorbell rang. I stepped away from the dinner concern for a moment. I made dinner all the time. I could figure this out.

"Oh, Connie, hi."

Connie lived two doors down, a gray-haired woman a little older than my mom. She was carrying a paper grocery bag and a casserole dish.

"Hey, Jo. Honey, I'm so sorry."

"Thank you."

"I brought a lasagna. I know your mom's gone back home, and I wanted to make sure you were fed."

Hallelujah.

"Thank you," I said, taking the dish from her hands. The aroma of sauce and cheese slammed into me, my stomach grumbling immediately. "I can't tell you how much I appreciate this."

"Glad to help. We're trying to coordinate taking care of all y'all. It's a lot, but we're working on it. Hopefully at least once a week someone will drop off something."

"That's so thoughtful, Connie, thank you."

"If you think of anything you need, text me, and I'll add it to the spreadsheet we're keeping."

A spreadsheet. Incredible.

"You guys are beautifully organized."

"We're trying. We have to be." She left the because there are so many who need help right now unsaid, but I heard it anyway. "Can you think of anything you need?"

"Oh! Yes. The funeral will be December Thirtieth at Eleven. Could you pass that along?"

"Of course. All of Haven will know by the end of the day."

"You're a savior, thank you."

I hugged her clumsily around the dish, thankful to be part of this community. I knew I wasn't going to have to navigate this alone, but sometimes I needed the proof in my face to remembered that.

The grocery bag held a salad and some garlic bread, which I popped into the oven. The lasagna was still hot. I set it on the stove while the bread baked. I should inventory the groceries, figure out what we needed. I could do this. I pulled myself up straighter. Maybe the illusion of confidence would help me act like I had more faith in myself than I did at the moment.

The girls and I ate at a table that was now too big, missing two people who commanded much of the space. Dinner was quieter. I didn't know what to say to the girls, didn't know how to comfort them, didn't know how to pretend that life was normal. I couldn't lie to them. I couldn't reassure them. I was floundering.

So dinner was largely silent, eating the food someone else had prepared for us. The sound of forks scraping against plates was our soundtrack, drowning out the echoes of the chattering of three kids with busy lives.

"I don't want to go back to school," Olivia said, breaking the silence.

She'd been poking at her dinner, not actually eating any of it, a shame, because it was delicious. She didn't look up when she spoke.

My girls were talking to me now without looking at me. As if they couldn't bear to see my reaction. As if they thought I'd be hurt or mad or...what? I couldn't hold any of it against them. They were still doing better than I was.

"I know it's scary," I said after a moment. "I think it'll feel good to go back to school and be with your friends."

"Everyone is going to know."

"They know now," Addy said.

"But they're going to talk about me. They're going to think something's wrong with me. And then I'll start crying, and they'll make fun of me for that."

As if this was her fault? As if losing the boys tainted her? I knew what she meant, because I'd felt it too, the eyes on me, the hushed voices, "That's her, the one who lost her family in that crash." The idea that someone might say something like that to a child irked me.

"Is something wrong with you?" I tried to eat my dinner as if I wasn't panicking inside, fearful of bungling this conversation.

"Daddy and Matt are gone."

"They are."

"I don't want people to talk about it."

"I'm sure if you tell people that, they'll stop."

Oh, God, was I putting too much faith in children?

"It's not like we're the only ones," Addy said, and I wasn't sure if she was helping.

"What about those friends?" Olivia asked. "What if they're sad?"

"Of course they'll be sad," I replied. "You should talk to them. Ask them what they need from you. Tell them what you need."

Yeah, putting too much faith in children.

Still, I stuck with my overconfidence. "Your friends love you, and they want you to be okay, Olivia. Friends will always be there for you." She looked up at me, biting her lip, her eyes watery. "And we have days until you have to go back to school."

I was emotionally spent by the time I got the girls in bed. I could barely muster the energy to text Steve's parents with the funeral details. I couldn't let someone else tell them.

And then, so that I couldn't obsess over what I'd said to Bethany or what she might say back to me, I phoned Reston at the hospital.

"Do you think they'll let you come?" I asked after I'd given him the details of the funeral.

"They won't be able to keep me from being there, Jo."

"You're not terribly mobile. All they'd have to do is take your wheelchair."

"I'll army crawl with my busted arm all the way to the funeral home."

As always, tears stung my eyes, but I smiled through them, picturing what he'd described. Sometimes Reston was the only thing keeping me afloat. I'd never be able to repay him.

"Thank you."

"I wish there were more I could do."

"Get better."

"I'm certainly trying."

"Aren't we all?"

The other end of the phone became muffled, Reston arguing with someone with the receiver covered up.

"They're telling me I'm not allowed to be on the phone this late," he said.

"Terrible."

"Come visit soon."

"They won't be able to keep me out."

CHAPTER THIRTEEN

"I got a lawyer. We're going to sue the bitch."

It was an incongruous text in the ongoing group thread with the other team moms. Normally we were discussing canceled practice or carpools to the games. Now, a week after the crash, we were talking about suing bitches.

I didn't know if she was a bitch. I knew her name was Evelyn Jean McCourt, and she'd been eighty-four when she lost control of her car and slammed into the side of a bus. Our bus. The medical examiner wasn't sure if she'd suffered her heart attack before or after hitting the bus, but it didn't matter. She was gone too.

Suing her, or her estate, or her family, or whatever, had never occurred to me. Why would we?, I marveled as the other moms chimed in with enthusiastic texts about the lawsuit.

"Do we know what to expect from insurance payouts?" Keely asked.

"I haven't heard anything," Amanda said. "But I've started getting bills."

"Are we really discussing money right now?" Emily asked.

"Shouldn't we be?" Amanda replied. "What are the funerals costing you guys? Jo, how are you going to support your family?"

Just like I'd been surprised that Reston was unable to work for a while, I hadn't contemplated that Steve was our family's breadwinner. I'd taught at the high school until Matt was born, and then being his mom became my fulltime job. I was class mom, bringing all the best themed snacks to class parties. I wore my

"Matt's Mom" shirt and stood in the bleachers screaming my heart out. I was "Addy's Mom" at dance recitals and competitions. "Olivia's Mom" running from one end of the soccer field to the other. All my time and energy went into being Mom.

"I'll go back to work," I wrote. "I'll be fine without suing a dead old lady's family."

"And what about Reston?" Natalie wrote. She'd been the one to enlist the lawyer. And she'd said the one thing that would get me into this idea.

Regardless of whether Haven High would keep him on as coach—and I was sure they would—when would he be physically capable of coaching again? Would he want to return to coaching with a new team? He'd always bristled at the scrutiny here, and this felt like the kind of thing that would push him away.

"It strengthens the suit if we're all in," Natalie added.

"I don't want to do this," Heather replied.

"Me neither."

I typed it with conviction, no matter how torn I felt. I couldn't punish another family.

"As long as the insurance payout covers costs, I'm out," Keely added.

"How are you putting such a small price on the lives of your sons?" Amanda wrote.

"No price brings them back," I typed, slow and deliberate. "No price fixes this. No amount of money will make me happy again."

And Evelyn Jean McCourt had already paid with her life. Her family was as mired in grief as we were with the added guilt of knowing what she'd done. They didn't need us demanding money, our grief greater than theirs.

"I can ask Reston if he wants to join you," I added. "He's worried about the finance stuff too."

"This isn't just about money," Amanda wrote.

"It feels like it is," Keely replied.

"Some of us are going to need a lot of money," Vonda said. "That's just the way it is. Do you have any idea what it costs for someone to receive round-the-clock care? For the rest of their lives?"

"I can't imagine," Natalie replied. "This is why we're doing this. We have to help the survivors."

"Shouldn't the rest of us stay out of it if it's about the survivors?" I asked.

"They'll take the whole thing more seriously if it's all thirteen families."

"What's the harm in joining?" Amanda asked. "You'd be helping us."

"And then we'd be going to court and listening to someone describe what happened to our boys," Heather replied. "I don't ever want to relive this time or be forced to contemplate their last moments."

"I already know that Brian suffered," Linda wrote. "I can't listen to someone enumerate his suffering."

"Honestly, it feels like you're being a little selfish," Amanda said. "Whatever, we'll figure out how to take care of our kids without you."

I didn't know what to do with that statement. I would have done almost anything to help her, to help Landon, to help Isaiah. I wasn't telling her not to sue, if that's what she wanted to do. I was asking to be left out of it. I wanted the grief to stop, and it never would if we turned on each other, if our friendships became another casualty of this horrifying mess.

"I want out of this conversation," Heather wrote.

I instinctually began to compose a text begging everyone to stay calm, to stay together. But I didn't want to be part of this anymore either. I wanted to be allowed to grieve however I felt was right. In this moment, that meant walking away from this lawsuit conversation.

I tapped the button in the corner of the screen, then "leave conversation." I needed to take care of myself right now, and this wasn't helping me.

That night, the girls tucked into their own beds, I wrapped myself in the comforter that still smelled the faintest bit like my husband and sent a text to Amanda. I wasn't going to let this accident take my best friend from me too.

"Tell me what else I can do for you," I wrote. "Anything. Do you need food? Can I watch Elliot for you? Clean your house?"

"All of that," she replied. "I'm sorry I'm so angry. It's not you. It's everything. I feel like I've lost my son, but I didn't. You're not the only one telling me that I'm lucky, but I don't feel that way in the least."

To me, she still looked lucky. As long as Landon was still alive with a chance he'd recover, she would be luckier than I was. She had what I wanted, even if Landon was going to struggle with daily life, once he woke up.

"I get it," I replied, instead of telling her how fortunate she was. "I'm feeling it too."

"I know. It's hard, because I expect all of us to be feeling this the same way, and we aren't. I don't know how to understand how everyone else is feeling."

I exhaled hard. She was saying all the things I'd been thinking. "Oh, girl, same. All of it. Same. I don't know what to do. But I'll do what I can."

"Honestly, what are you going to do about money?"

I still wasn't entirely sure, but I answered with false confidence. I'd been making a plan, figuring out my next steps, and was somewhat sure I wouldn't lose everything.

"I'll get my teaching credentials in order and go back to the school, subbing at least. I'll be okay, Amanda. And if I'm not, don't you think the town will rally around me? Don't you think everyone here will do whatever it takes to help me? That's why I love Haven."

I knew it happened in other places too, that it wasn't unusual that people were dropping off food or offering to help with whatever we needed. Somehow it was different here, where people I'd known for decades were helping us.

"What can we do to help you right now?" Amanda asked.

I paused. I had no idea. It had only been a week since the world fell apart. It would be a new year soon. The accident felt so far away, and yet as if they were dying over and over again every moment. I wanted my family back, and no one could give me that.

"I want things as normal as possible," I replied. "Not pretending that they're still here. But being ourselves again."

"Do you have everything settled for the funeral?"

"I think so."

I'd crossed nearly everything off my to do list, friends and neighbors volunteering to handle the details as I dragged myself toward the imaginary finish line that was this funeral. Nick had already been buried, my boys were next, and then Zach and Gabe would have their funerals over the weekend. The wound reopened every time. Seven more funerals were going to happen before it was over, and I wasn't sure how I'd manage that.

"Let me know if I can help with that," Amanda wrote. "The food or planning or whatever needs to be done."

"Thanks."

I wished I could hug my best friend and fix everything, but there was nothing left to fix.

Chapter Fourteen

There was always someone coming to the door. Food being dropped off. Friends offering to help with chores. Today it was the school secretary on my porch. I suppose I'd been expecting her, or at least someone from the school, since the day of the accident. My boys still had possessions in that building. And when everyone in town was stopping by, it was bound to happen.

"Hi, Jo."

"Hi, Chelsea."

She held a box in her hands, with another at her feet. "S. Grant" was scrawled across one box, "M. Grant" on the other. I knew what I'd find in those boxes.

I licked my lips, my mouth parched, reaching for the box with shaking hands.

"We cleaned out Steve's classroom," Chelsea said. "And Matt's locker. I'm so sorry."

"Thanks."

I still fumbled with what to say to that, but thanks always seemed to work.

The boxes were heavier than I expected. Surely the school had reclaimed their computers and books, right?

"Someone from HR should be in touch with you soon," Chelsea said. "To hash out payouts and things."

"Thanks."

Another thing done. Another ending. Steve wouldn't be going back to work. Matt wouldn't finish school. Everything they'd both worked so hard for, and none of it mattered. It was over.

Chelsea hugged me awkwardly, then turned to go, leaving me alone with the boxes.

I expected them to be full of memories. But these weren't my things. They weren't our things. They were pieces of the boys' lives that didn't include me. Matt's binders, homework, notes from friends. I flipped through the pages of his notebooks, the meticulously organized papers full of nearly illegible writing. It should be so easy to get rid of most of this. I didn't need his Algebra II notes.

But that beautifully sloppy handwriting…

Nearly all of it went back into the box to deal with later.

Steve's box should have been simple as well. I could hand his lesson plan over to the sub, along with the homework that clearly needed grading. I wasn't sure who would handle his class when Christmas break ended, or when or how they'd replace Steve. Surely someone would be standing where Steve had stood all these years, only now with the added pressure of guiding those kids through this tragedy. I didn't know how they would do it, how any teacher at Haven High could walk into the building and teach their class when winter break ended. In a few days, the high school would be buzzing again, but clouded with loss. And I didn't know how anyone could act as if it was business as usual there.

I rifled further into Steve's box, past the papers and notebooks to the personal items. The family photos he kept at his desk shouldn't have knocked me back. I'd seen those photos dozens of times. Copies of some were hanging in our house right now. But these photos had looked back at Steve from his desk for years, and now, they're stuck in a box. I swallowed hard as the image of Steve in his own box now, bile threatening the back of my throat. Not today.

Jammed in the frame that held our family photo was a snapshot of me. I wasn't looking at the camera. I may not have known he was taking the photo. The beach was behind me, my hair whipping around my face. It could have been taken last summer, or twenty-plus years ago when we had our first trip to the shore. I flipped it over, looking for a clue about when it had been taken. The back of the photo simply said, "Jo," in Steve's meticulous writing.

This photo was never going to leave my possession.

Steve was our family photographer. Sure, I had a handful of photos on my cell phone, but Steve had a real camera. He dragged it out on vacations, holidays, special occasions. For the first time, I thought about the pictures that must be sitting on that camera, waiting for me to find them.

The camera was right where Steve kept it between uses, on a shelf in our closet. Why hadn't I been more diligent about taking pictures? With Steve was always behind the camera, I probably wouldn't find many new pictures of him. I wouldn't get to see his grin, breaking my heart with the knowledge that he'd never smile again.

But I loved the photos he'd captured, seeing our family through his eyes. The kids' last birthdays, I compared their expressions as we all sang to them over cake. The girls and I would never be that happy or innocent again.

More than that, I loved the ones taken when the subject didn't notice Steve was watching. Photos of Matt and Olivia in the backyard, him running soccer drills with her. Addy warming up before dance recitals.

And me. Sleeping. Wrangling the kids. Cooking. Wading into the ocean. He had always been watching me, lovingly recording even the most mundane moments.

I only wished we had more of them.

How was it over? We had worked so hard to create this beautiful life, and it was gone before we'd had the chance to enjoy it. Now I'd have to create a new life, one that I could only hope would be close to as beautiful as the one we'd had before.

I shut the boxes up in Matt's bedroom to deal with later. This was enough grief for one day.

*   *   *

The next day, I sat in the school district offices meeting with HR, getting my business life in order.

"That's it?" I looked at my notes in disbelief.

Jeremy, the HR Director for the school district, chuckled. "Yep. Do those online tests, your license will be valid, and we'll get you back in the classroom."

"Thanks. I don't suppose there's an open classroom." I hoped I didn't sound like I was begging.

"Not at the moment, but you never know. We'll put you at the top of the sub list, if that would help."

"Anything would help, honestly."

"I can do that now. Hopefully, we'll get you subbing some this semester, and as soon as a classroom opens up, you'll be at the top of the list."

I had to restrain myself from throwing my arms around him. I blinked back the tears that seemed my constant companion. "I can't thank you enough," I said, my voice choked.

"Jo, it does no one any good to compound this tragedy by seeing you guys lose your house or something."

"We're not going to lose the house. The life insurance, you know."

"I know. The point stands. In Haven, we take care of our own."

"That we do. Thank you again, Jeremy. For the info on my certification update, and with Steve's leave and pay and the health insurance stuff and everything. I appreciate you reaching out."

"Of course. And thank you for bringing Steve's lesson plans." Jeremy placed his hand on the stack I'd brought in with me. "I'm sure his sub could have managed without it, but this will make lives easier all around."

I spread my palms out on my thighs, resisting the urge to snatch back the papers with my husband's beautiful writing on them. "It's always hard to let go of something that was part of them. I know you need this though, and I don't. I have plenty of other mementos."

Indeed, the house was becoming a museum dedicated to the memory of what had been. I didn't see how that would change. How could I get rid of the only pieces I had left of them?

But these things—Steve's lesson plans, kids' homework, tests, his gradebook—these weren't mine to keep. I was putting these things back where they belonged.

And working toward building a new life.

CHAPTER FIFTEEN

The day before I was hosting a funeral for my husband and son, I was on my way home from Nick's funeral. I'd left the girls with my parents and stopped by the hospital to check in with Reston before I retrieved them. He was miserable he couldn't attend the funerals, and I told myself he'd appreciate my visit.

I puttered around his hospital room, opening the curtains to let in the waning light as the sun set. We had a half hour or so until his dinner, a perfect amount of time to hang out.

"I appreciate you checking in," Reston said. "But you don't have to. You can focus on yourself, I mean it."

"This is how I'm taking care of myself right now," I replied.

"If you insist."

"I do."

The flower arrangements on the window ledge were drooping. I pulled desiccated stems from their bouquet fellows, sweeping fallen leaves and petals into the trash. The vases appeared a couple each day, from where I didn't know, and the colors at least seemed to keep the grayness of the winter at bay.

"What else can I do for you?" I asked. "Do you need me to bring you anything?"

"What I need," Reston replied, and his tone was harsh enough to command my attention, "is for you to stop."

"Stop what?"

"Taking care of me."

I laughed. "I'm not sure that's possible."

"Please, Jo."

"Are you turning against me too?"

Reston frowned. "No, of course not. Who's turned against you?"

"Everyone." I sighed. "Amanda and I are…things are weird."

"Sounds like high school."

"This is far worse than two teenage girls finding petty reasons to bicker."

"What happened?"

"You ask me to stop taking care of you, but you can't stop yourself from taking care of me?" I shook my head, hoping to stave off the tears that were brimming.

"I get why you're doing this, and I appreciate it. But the doctors are shipping me off soon. We need to have a serious conversation about how maybe I don't come back."

I'd barely made it through the time we'd had this conversation in high school. His insistence that leaving was the best thing for him, and that I'd be okay without him, and the world would go on.

"If that's what you think is best," I replied, my voice flat, doing my best to keep from showing how much he'd hurt me.

"It has to be. I don't think I want to be here without Steve and the boys."

"That's how a lot of us feel, Reston."

"Then I'm the lucky one who gets to act on it."

I understood why he was saying it, but still my jaw clenched. How little did any of this matter to him? How could it be that easy for him to leave us?

"Lucky," I spat. "To put all of us behind you. To forget the last ten years of your life here."

"Right now, forgetting feels like a blessing."

"I can't argue with that."

"I know you don't have that luxury, Jo. You still have Addy and Olivia to worry about."

"Not to mention, oh, everyone I know and love."

"I get all of that. I've always understood that. I'm not suggesting you leave. I'm asking you to let me go. Don't guilt me. Don't pressure me. Don't ask me to come back."

"Don't ever contact you again?" I rolled my eyes. "We've done this before. I get it, Reston."

"Not if you're angry, you don't."

How did he expect me to react to this? Anger felt spot on. He'd run away before. When he'd come back, it had been good for everyone—him, me, the entire town. In the midst of everything else, facing the rest of my life without my husband and my son, losing someone this important to me may be the final straw. It didn't matter if I understood why he might want to leave. The urge to scream at him, huff out of the room, and slam the door behind me coiled inside me, and I pushed past it, hoping he'd listen to reason.

"With all this town has lost," I started, "all that I've lost, one more loss is too much. Especially when it's your choice."

"I'll still be around. And maybe I'll come back, when I'm ready."

"I do always enjoy waiting around for you."

"I'm not asking that, Jo. I never did."

He had, in fact, never given me the option. This time, I wasn't going to let him leave without a fight.

"The girls and I will visit you in Raleigh. Check in on you. Keep you sane."

He sighed. "I don't suppose I can talk you out of that. You have plenty of other things to worry about that aren't me."

"You absolutely cannot. We need you here."

"That remains to be seen."

"There's a lawsuit, apparently." I remembered I'd promised to mention it to him. "Against the woman who hit you. Or her estate, I guess."

"You don't sound thrilled about it."

"I'm not going to be part of it. I don't want to put that family through anything else. But I don't need the money the way Amanda's family does. The way you might."

"Even though Steve supported your family? Are you making money?"

"They've put me on the sub list, and I'm getting my teaching license back in good standing. I'll be able to get a job, no problem."

"There could be a problem. Getting a job isn't ever a given."

His lack of confidence in me stung—I thought he knew me better than that.

"It's Haven. I'll land on my feet."

"That's why you love it here."

It was. No one would let us go hungry, or lose the house, or worry for a second about how we were going to pay our bills. That was the beauty of our small town. They'd have a fundraiser in place if I gave them a hint that I needed for anything.

"This town would help me."

"Okay, yes, you're right about that."

"Anyway. Amanda wants you in on the lawsuit. The more people, the better it is for them."

"It's going to take a lot of money to take care of Landon and Isaiah."

"I've never said otherwise," I replied.

"Don't be angry at her for doing what she feels she needs to do to take care of her family, Jo."

"I'm trying my best."

He bit his lip, looking up at me with eyes that were still swollen and bruised from the crash. Clearly, he disagreed.

"What?" I asked with a raised brow.

"Nothing. You're an adult, and you make your own choices."

"Like the rest of you are doing? Suing the family of a dead old woman? Moving away and threatening to never speak to your friends again?"

"It seems we all need to cut each other some slack."

"It's hard to do that when I feel like I've lost everything that matters and the people around me are ready to walk away from anything that's left."

"You haven't lost everything. We're still here, putting ourselves back together in the way that makes sense to us."

"How do I convince you to come back home when you're well again?" I asked.

"You can cut me slack and recognize that I probably know what's best for myself."

"It wasn't best for you when you left last time, or you wouldn't have come back."

He shook his head. "It was at the time. Leaving taught me about myself."

"It taught you that you belong here."

"Not exactly. Do you and the girls need anything? I know you're helping everyone else, and it's okay for you to ask us to help you."

"I can't ask that of you. You need to concentrate on getting better. And it's not going to take a lot to keep my family solvent."

"Then maybe you're the lucky one."

I snorted. "Oh, yeah. The luckiest."

CHAPTER SIXTEEN

Reston's dinner arrived. I stood to leave—I had to get the girls and head to the restaurant to meet Steve's parents. He was right that I needed to focus on myself sometimes. Today that means eating a real dinner.

I navigated the halls to the hospital exit, passing through an area that was busier than it had been the last week while I'd been in and out for my visits. I prayed there hadn't been another emergency.

But I recognized the blond woman leaning against the counter talking to the nurses. Amanda looked better than she had when we'd spoken via video chat, but not much. She'd taken a shower at least, for sure.

"Amanda?"

She looked up. "Oh, my God, Jo, what are you doing here?"

"I was checking on Reston," I replied. "Why are you here?"

I pulled Amanda into my arms, squeezing her hard to make up for all the hugs we hadn't given each other during the past week.

"They got Landon moved over here, finally." She drew back to arm's length. "Today's been nuts."

"Why didn't you tell me? I would have helped."

"We weren't sure when it would happen. Waiting on a room, then on transport, and he had to be completely stable."

"So he is? Stable?"

"Stable meaning he hasn't gotten any worse, but he's also not improving."

"Can we sit and catch up for a minute?"

She glanced at her watch. "Yeah, not long though. I promised I'd be home in time to see Elliot before bedtime."

We found some empty chairs in the waiting area. I didn't know what to say after all this time apart, time when everything was the worst it had ever been.

"You were with Reston?" Amanda asked.

"Are you okay with him again?"

She shrugged. "I don't know about that, but he's here. Me saying it would be better if he'd died was shitty of me."

Her words were a punch in the gut. "Yeah, that's pretty awful."

"What does Reston think about the lawsuit?" Amanda asked.

"He seemed to be okay that it was happening, but non-committal about joining."

"I'll try to find some time to press him about it."

I pursed my lips, wanting to chide her for pressing him to do anything, but I let it go. Reston was an adult. If he wanted in on this lawsuit, that was his business.

"How is Landon? What exactly does stable mean?" I asked.

"The same. He's not awake, but they're seeing brain activity, so he's still there."

"That's always good."

She shrugged. "I still don't know if it's better for him to wake up or not. I don't want to lose him, Jo."

"Of course you don't."

I hadn't wanted to lose my son either. I would have fought every doctor in the world to force them to make him better if the option had existed.

Amanda continued. "But I don't...I don't want him to exist in a broken body that can't do even the most basic things. I don't want to watch him fight to learn to feed himself or walk again. It sounds nightmarish to think of this kid who has always been so active and done so much not being able to do anything. This is so complicated. And I'm sorry that I'm not being better for you right now. I can't imagine what you're going through."

"Don't imagine it. It's awful."

I wrapped my arms around myself, trying to ward off the thoughts. The logistics were hard enough—arranging the funeral, finding a job, packing up or getting rid of their things. Harder still was how I needed to keep going without my husband. How our family functioned with two people missing. How we got out of bed every day with this hole in our hearts and our home.

"I don't think about it," I said finally. "I distract myself with the girls, and things I can do for other people. I have to get certified for a job, but I don't want to think about that. I want my husband back. I want my son. And I'm never going to get that."

I ached for them, especially at night, when the house was silent and I was alone. Despite that initial push from my mother, I had yet to go through their things. I couldn't bear to part with any of it, but seeing their things sent me spiraling. When I was with my daughters, I had to be strong, to pretend that I was okay, because they needed to see me being okay.

They were generally doing well themselves and rarely collapsed on me at the same time. But they missed their dad, they missed their brother. They mostly understood what death meant, but Olivia especially would try to bargain them back. "If I'm good enough, if I work hard enough at school, can I have Daddy and Matt back?" And it was heartbreaking to say no to that.

"How is Elliot dealing?" I asked.

Amanda pushed her hair back from her face. "Oh, God. I don't even know what to say to him, Jo. There's so much unknown right now, and I don't want to tell him Landon will wake up but he's going to have problems, because we don't know if he will, or what they will be. We know that he had a traumatic brain injury. His chances for ever being normal again are slim. I don't want Elliot to have to contemplate being the one to care for his brother someday."

"Can I see him? Landon?"

Amanda's eyes lit up. "Of course! No one ever asks to see him."

What if I saw him and started crying? What if I screamed? What if seeing him was so hard that I collapsed and couldn't get back up?

"Will I be shocked?"

"He's had some facial and cranial reconstruction, so, yeah, it's rough to look at him. But he's Landon."

Matt and Landon had been best friends from birth, obliging their mothers, who had been inseparable since childhood as well. Amanda and I had been friends from the first day of kindergarten, rooming together in college, standing up in each other's weddings. I'd been thrilled that we'd been pregnant with the boys at the same time, and that her second pregnancy fell so neatly between my second and third. Matt and Landon had always played together, teammates since age five. I'd pictured them playing together through high school and college. I'd pictured their friendship being like mine with Amanda, their kids becoming friends, perpetuating the cycle.

I couldn't picture Landon without Matt.

And no matter what Amanda told me, it was hard to see Landon inside the body that lay in the hospital bed.

There were cuts and stitches crisscrossing his face. A tube down his throat and another in his nose. His head looked lopsided, misshapen, the cranial surgery she'd mentioned probably responsible for that. I couldn't stop myself from gasping when I saw him. I covered my mouth, ashamed of myself.

"It's okay," Amanda said. "You're doing better than I did the first time."

"Oh, Amanda." I grabbed her arm.

"I know."

Suddenly, it made sense that she might want him to let go. I took in the machines, the beeping, wondering if all of this was keeping him alive, or if it was supplemental. Something must be feeding him. Was it the nasal tube? Was the tube in his throat breathing for him?.

"It's supplemental," Amanda replied when I asked. "Backing up his body when it fails. He can't be trusted to keep breathing."

I ran my hand lightly over his cheek, bumping over a jagged mess of stitches. I remembered the day he was born, too early, but seemingly undaunted. He'd needed help with his breathing then too.

He'd managed to come back from that spectacularly. How had this happened to him? How was he ever going to be whole again?

"Can he hear me?" I asked.

"We're not sure."

I nodded. "Hey, Landon. It's Auntie Jo, kiddo. We're all pulling for you."

My throat closed, the tears I held back choking me. I wanted to squeeze his hand, but the hand I could reach had a cast on it. For the first time, I realized it wasn't just his head.

"What else happened to him?" I asked.

"Broken arm. Broken ribs. His left tibia or fibula or whatever. A lot of the same stuff Reston has going on. But also a crushed skull."

"Jesus."

"All of the bones will heal, so we don't worry about them. His brain...that's probably irreversible."

"I'm so sorry, Amanda."

"Thanks. And you're right, in a way we're lucky we still have him. I'm grateful. It's hard to see my baby so broken though. To know he'll probably never be whole."

"I don't judge you for any of it," I said, reflexively moving to brush Landon's hair off his forehead as I'd done so many times while he was growing up. But they'd shaved his head, and the rumpled locks were gone, replaced with a patchy stubble. "I don't judge you for the lawsuit. For acknowledging the difficult road you're walking with Landon."

"I think you do judge me, but it's okay. I'm doing it too, because I don't understand what you're dealing with. The grief is so much, Jo, and we're all being too hard on each other. I'm sure that will fade."

"Or we'll continue to think that we're doing it right and everyone else is wrong."

"Or that," Amanda replied with a shrug. "Hopefully we'll be better friends to each other."

"If we're even friends anymore. There are two group texts now," I said. "Us and them. Us and you, I guess."

"Who started that?"

"Does it matter?"

"We were a team," Amanda said wistfully. "Just like the boys were."

"There isn't a team left."

"Do you think that's fixable? Do you want to fix it?"

"I can't lose anything else. I'm tired of loss."

I told myself this would blow over. That emotions were high, that we were all raw, and every tiny slight was magnified. Most of these women had been my friends since childhood. Surely we'd remember that, remember all the times we'd supported each other, and that past would override this horrible present.

"We didn't start the lawsuit to hurt anyone," Amanda said.

"It's going to hurt her family though, Amanda. I understand why you're doing it, but you can't act like they aren't hurting too. I know we don't know them, so it's easy to forget that they're real people too."

"It feels like she wasn't punished. Like she got off easy."

"She's dead," I replied, stunned. She'd paid with her life, and how Amanda thought losing money was a just punishment was beyond me.

She crossed her arms over her chest. "And she has no idea what she did."

"Doesn't that depend on your view of the afterlife? Maybe she's being punished with eternal damnation."

"Sure, I suppose."

"I don't feel like it's up to me to punish her. You do what you feel is right."

"And you'll still be my friend?"

"Always. It's not as if this is the first time I've disagreed with you about something."

Reston was right—this felt like high school, when Amanda and I had fought about any number of slights, real and imagined. We'd come back together just fine, the way we always had.

"Everything feels bigger," I said. "I guess because we're all feeling so much. Nothing's the small stuff anymore."

"But that won't last forever. The grief isn't going to go away, but it won't always be this sharp."

"And then we'll remember that we were always on the same side."

"God, I hope so."

CHAPTER SEVENTEEN

"I should go soon," I said, turning to leave Landon's room. "Steve's parents get into town tonight for the funeral."

Amanda cringed. "Not Bethany! I'm sorry. I wish I could be there to act as a buffer for you."

"Thanks. I keep telling myself they'll be different, that they understand I'm grieving. But it's possible I'm giving them too much credit."

"From what I've seen from her? Yep. Far too much credit."

"She's not a bad person," I replied, reminding myself.

"No, of course not. She's an overprotective mom who goes too far."

"When she accused me of trapping her son, she was watching out for him and keep him safe," I said dryly.

"Good luck with dinner. And I hope tomorrow runs smoothly for you. I wish I could be there."

"Me too. I'm trying not to think about it."

I had no choice; I had to get through the funeral. My girls depended upon me to be strong and help them cope with their fears. Still, I couldn't imagine it. I couldn't see a world where my boys were in the ground and I was carrying on with life as if everything was normal. I clung to my best friend, not ready to move into that next step of this horrible process. I took a deep breath, steadying myself, and pulled away.

I collected my daughters from my parents' house, knowing the girls would have a better time at dinner than I would. They'd be excited to see their grandparents. We hadn't seen them since the summer, when we'd spent a week at the beach with them like we always did. They were good grandparents; Aaron and Bethany liked everyone in my family except me. Even with Steve interceding on my behalf, they never warmed up to me, and this certainly wasn't going to fix that.

I had one more errand before dinner.

On the way to the restaurant, I stopped briefly at the funeral home. I'd promised to drop off the boys' clothes for the next day. I left the girls in the still-running car and dashed inside, not bothering with a coat.

"Thanks, Jo." Luke Wallis took the garment bag from my hand.

"Thank you. I'll see you in the morning."

"Before you go, would you like Steve's wedding band, or is it okay to bury him with it?"

My eyes lit up. "I want it," I replied in a rush.

"Let me grab it while you're here."

I hadn't examined Steve's ring before. I expected it to be tarnished or dinged up, but it was still perfect, no evidence of twenty years of wear. I slid the ring onto my thumb, the only finger it had a chance of fitting. It was loose, but not loose enough to fall off. The cool metal weight of it served to remind me that it hadn't been a dream. I'd had an amazing husband. Tomorrow I'd bury him, but for the moment I could focus on the good.

The ring distracted me for the remainder of the drive. I couldn't stop rubbing my index finger against the gold band, the novelty driving my action.

I'd only agreed to meet with my in-laws for dinner to be the bigger person for my daughters. My in-laws weren't great in-laws, but they were exceptional grandparents. No matter how I felt about Bethany and Aaron, I'd never deny the girls a relationship with them.

And I reminded myself they were here to bury their son. I knew firsthand how agonizing that was.

When Bethany and Aaron stepped out of their car at the restaurant, the girls ran to them, throwing their arms around their grandparents. Olivia was in tears, and I swallowed hard, trying to keep my own at bay. I wanted to move forward with a clean slate, but I would never have the capacity to pretend that the last twenty-plus years of Bethany's behavior hadn't happened.

We barely had drinks on the table when Bethany said, "We'd love to take the girls for a week this summer."

I instinctively began to decline but stopped myself.

"That would be helpful, thanks," I replied.

With the girls still out of school for winter break, I was exhausted at the end of every day, barely able to clean up after dinner, or find the energy to change into pajamas before crawling into bed. I blamed it on the grief most of the time, but I also didn't have time off from mothering now. Maybe I'd get used to it, but knowing I'd have some time when I wouldn't have to worry about the girls was a lifesaver.

However, Bethany couldn't keep from saying something that would enrage me.

"Are you okay for money?" she asked, leaning over the table and dropping her voice.

"We are. I'm getting my license together to get back to teaching, and I'll be substituting in the meantime, and we have the life insurance. But I'd rather not talk about this further, especially not in public."

She straightened back up, moving to a topic she considered more appropriate for public consumption, I guessed. "If you need to, you could move in with us."

This was the woman who sobbed, broken-hearted, through my entire wedding. The woman who wouldn't stop asking me when we were going to have kids already, even after we begged her to stop asking. The woman who then complained about the names we gave those babies, none of our choices meeting her stringent requirements. The woman who thought I could do nothing right.

My fingers went to Steve's ring on my thumb. I turned the band as I responded, drawing strength from the man who had always stood up for me.

"Thanks," I replied. "I've got this. It's scary, but I'm going to figure it out. I appreciate the gesture."

"We're glad to help," Aaron added.

"Having the girls out this summer will be a great help."

"You're sure there isn't more we can do?"

"Not at the moment."

"I'm sure your family is helping."

"Gran was staying with us," Olivia said. "But she went home."

"Gran and Mom got in a fight," Addy added.

Dammit. Classic Addy.

"Grief makes things complicated," I said after a moment.

I didn't need to apologize to anyone, and yet I felt compelled. My mom and I were fine. She understood why I'd reacted the way I had. No one should be judging me for how I behaved during the first week after my husband and son died. Still, I couldn't stand anyone thinking I had somehow failed during those days.

I had failed, sure, in plenty of small ways. And I was failing now in a lot of those same ways. But I was also succeeding in plenty of ways too, and that mattered more.

The waitress returned to our table.

"Your bill has been taken care of, Mrs. Grant," she said. "We're so sorry for your loss."

"Thank you," I replied, by habit now.

"Please let us know if there's anything we can do for you."

"Of course."

Everyone was so kind, and it all meant so much to me.

And I didn't want any of it.

"I should get the girls home and into bed." I rose from the table, already exhausted at the thought of the next day.

"We'll see you in the morning."

CHAPTER EIGHTEEN

The morning of the funeral, I woke up to six inches of snow on the ground, with more falling. Some unfortunate soul was going to have to dig through that and six feet of frozen dirt so we could bury the boys. And my boys would be in that frozen ground, their bodies no longer able to register the cold.

I still didn't want to do this, and would have put it off indefinitely if I thought I could get away with it. The funeral home had been understanding, I assume in part because they knew us. Like everyone else in town. They knew what had happened, the magnitude of the grief.

I needed to do this, though. I needed to say goodbye so that I could at least appear to be doing better. It hadn't escaped my notice that people were watching, judging, whispering, every move I made examined under a microscope.

I pulled my dark hair into a low bun, rather than my customary ponytail, and tugged on my most sensible black dress, the same one I'd worn to the other funerals, that I planned to keep wearing. I'd thought about getting something special for this funeral, but I'd never wear it again. I couldn't wait to throw this dress in the trash.

At the service, the girls sat beside me wearing matching black dresses purchased specifically for this, and also likely never to be worn again. Addy rarely wore anything that wasn't pink, and Olivia almost always wore pants. They never matched.

The boys matched too. They wore identical suits with identical ties, even though no one could see them because their extensive

97

injuries didn't allow for public viewing. So instead, everyone saw their identical caskets topped with identical flowers.

I hated everything about this day. I hated that we were saying goodbye to Matt and Steve. I hated that so many people that we loved couldn't be here, mostly because they were gone too. I hated that Reston, Steve's closest friend, couldn't sit with us, still stuck in the hospital. I hated how many funerals our town had seen since that horrible day, how many more were to come.

I nuzzled the girls, trying to keep my tears at bay, and failing at every attempt. My preference was no funeral, preferring to grieve in private, but it didn't feel right with the whole town's involvement in the crash. Other people wanted to have this chance to mourn, and to offer us comfort. And the girls needed this. They needed the closure that only a funeral would give them. I wouldn't deny them anything.

Several of Matt's friends from school spoke. I'd asked Reston to say something, but he declined. The doctors refused to let him out after his last time out of bed had possibly ruptured his spleen. I was jealous he had an excuse to miss this, as if he was opting out of being part of this stuff. I didn't have that luxury.

He also got out of watching the caskets lower into the ground. That made it real. Watching those boxes that held my boys disappear. I would never see them again. The new snowfall made the already somber moment that much worse—it was colder, quieter, emptier than if it were a bright, sunny day.

After the service and the interment, we proceeded to our house. People had brought food over, enough to feed the town, and it was nice to be taken care of. For years, I'd occasionally dropped off casseroles or sandwich platters or dessert trays when neighbors had funerals. Matt and Steve had been gone for a week and a half, but suddenly it felt final. Everything was over. There was nothing I could do for them anymore. The funeral was my last task.

It was wonderful to see so many people loving and remembering my boys, and heartbreaking that it was happening. It shouldn't be happening. It should be a normal day, Matt and any number of his teammates taking over my living room, video games blaring, or in my driveway, playing a quick pickup game, if the weather cooperated. Steve and Reston would be at the kitchen table, diagramming plays or discussing practice strategies. I wanted that, not comfort.

Especially because it always went away. At the end of the day, our friends and family went home. People returned to their lives, and their jobs, and all the things that occupied them while I stayed home, wishing everything was different. Once the girls were tucked into bed, the house was silent, a new phenomenon.

Matt had always been a night owl, from the moment he was born. It came in handy once he started high school, when he'd put in a full day at school, followed by practice, followed by the homework that comes from taking all AP classes. He was usually the last one standing at night, Steve and I having turned in hours ago. Sure, it was sometimes hard to pry him out of bed in the morning, but he was never late for school. He was smart, and dedicated, and he'd set his sights on a basketball heavy college in the Midwest or Great Plains, ready to get away from the small town and everyone's expectations.

None of it had mattered. He could have skipped every class, spent every moment goofing off, slept through math, passed notes through English. He'd had dreams, and it didn't matter.

Steve had dreams too. Watching his kids grow up. Winning another state championship with the team. We had just celebrated our twentieth anniversary and had a trip to Europe on the books for the summer. I'd need to remember to cancel that.

I'd pictured the future differently. I'd imagined spending a hundred years with Steve, and seeing Matt meet the person he wanted to spend a hundred years with. I'd imagined grandkids and travel with my husband. I'd imagined a future, and now they wouldn't have that.

I tried to keep these thoughts at bay by staying busy. The bathrooms shone, the kitchen had never been cleaner. It was going to take a bit of work to get my teacher's license up to date, so I studied every night. I still hadn't gone through the boys' things, and still couldn't bear the idea of it. What would I even do with that stuff? Could I give away their belongings, admit that they were gone, and no longer needed them? Who would want their things?

No, all of that was something to worry about on some mystical day in the future when I could face the idea that they were truly gone.

I wished I could talk through this with a friend, but all of my friends were in the thick of it too. None of us seemed to be on the same page. I talked to Amanda, but there was a disconnect, her need to focus on her son rightly more important than listening to my gripes and moans. I hoped our friendship would survive this. Half of the team moms weren't sold on the idea of the lawsuit, but most of them were vilifying the other moms. I couldn't deal with that right now either.

I couldn't waste my time playing around on the internet, because it was wall-to-wall stories about the crash. Still. I pretend I didn't see cameras near the funeral home and the cemetery, but they were there. There were probably stories being written about the day, the only double funeral among our depressing lot. I understood why it was news in Haven, where everyone knew the boys we'd lost. But why was the world watching us?

It increased the pressure. The news cycle would turn over eventually, and people would forget about us. But what about when it was a year out, and the stories began anew? "Haven, North Carolina: One Year Later." No, thank you.

Part of me wanted to forget that this all had happened. Not forget Steve, and Matt, and all the boys who perished with them. But forget that they had died, and in such a public way. Forget that there were people who didn't know them, but knew the details of their deaths. People who knew there had once been a fifteen-year-old boy named Matthew Ryan Grant, but knew nothing of his crooked smile and his stellar basketball sense and his ease with math. They knew Stephen Adam Grant had been the team's assistant coach, but they didn't know about his sense of humor or how proud he was of his players. They were unaware of how he'd been an accountant for years but had fallen in love with coaching and had started teaching at the high school so that he and Reston could keep coaching together. They invaded the privacy of our grief without understanding what we'd lost.

They didn't know what the boys meant to us, their families and friends. They didn't know how much we missed them.

And how much we'd give to have them back.

CHAPTER NINETEEN

I didn't want to make a thing of the girls' first day back at school, but it felt momentous. When school had let out for winter break, life had been normal. Now it was anything but. I tried to pretend, to do exactly what I'd done every other school day. I dropped them in front of the school like I always did, waving goodbye, promising I'd be back at the end of the day. And I would. And then we'd go home to our too empty, too silent house, and we wouldn't be able to pretend that it was a regular day.

As long as I was already out of the house, I ran as many errands as I could. I filled the car with gas. I dropped off a book I'd checked out of the library, the psychological thriller far too serious to contemplate finishing now. And I stopped by the grocery store, needing milk and bread.

One thing I'd always loved about Haven was the way we all knew each other. Everyone said hello when we ran into each other around town. Everyone asked how you were, and listened to your answer. Everyone asked what they could do to help.

But now people saw me coming and averted their eyes. They turned abruptly, suddenly remembering they'd forgotten something in the produce aisle that couldn't wait. Obviously some people were taking care of me, food still arriving every few days, people offering to watch the girls for me, or help with small repairs around the house. But there were people who couldn't deal with the fact that I was now, apparently, death personified.

It hurt, and it hurt worse when it was the people who had been my people. I rolled my cart up to the dairy case and heard Natalie and Sarah behind me. I hadn't seen them since the funeral, when they came but pointedly didn't speak to me, that stupid lawsuit still a wedge between us. I wanted my friends back, but when I turned to talk to them, they froze.

"I forgot those, uh," Natalie sputtered.

"The Pop-Tarts?" Sarah suggested.

"Yes. Let's go back."

I stared after them, their names dying on my lips. Why, in the face of all of this awfulness, were we doing this? How was anything worth our years-long friendships falling apart?

I grabbed the rest of what I needed and headed for the check out. I had other things to do today.

"Hi, Mrs. Grant," the cashier said as she started ringing up my groceries.

"Hey, Antonia."

"How are you?"

"Terrible, thanks."

She mewled at me, and I cringed. I wanted sympathy, but I didn't want...pity. I shouldn't have been honest. I should have said I was fine now.

No, then I'd be chastised for moving on, for forgetting about two people I'd loved more than anything in the world. I had to be appropriately sad, but not so sad as to seem pathetic.

I hated that I was concerned with how people perceived my grief. I hated that I couldn't feel however I was feeling, without worrying that someone was going to have a problem with it.

I loaded the last of the bagged groceries into my cart and turned to go as Natalie and Sarah pulled into the line I was vacating.

There were no Pop-Tarts in their carts.

"I hate this town," I grumbled to Reston over the phone while I put the groceries away.

Once the new year had rolled around, he'd been shipped to a rehab facility in Raleigh, the staff better able to assist his recouperation. While I was glad he was getting the best possible care, I hated that he was further away. Our chats could only happen by phone unless I had the time to trek up to him.

"You don't hate this town. You hate the tragedy that ruined this town."

"Fine. Whatever. You didn't have to see someone who used to be your friend turn away from you."

"Natalie doesn't take my phone calls anymore, Jo," Reston replied. "I coached her son for six years, and I'm fairly certain she'd spit on me if she saw me in the street. She blames me for Ashton's death. She won't say so, but she does."

At least I wasn't the only pariah in Haven. And how obnoxious was I, complaining as if he wasn't also suffering?

"I'm an asshole," I said softly.

"No, she is," Reston replied. "She's hurt right now, and sometimes hurt people lash out."

"How are you so analytical about this?"

He paused, and when he spoke again, his words were halting, carefully chosen. "I've got, like, a counselor type person here. She tells me stuff like that."

"That you can't take it personally when your friends hate you now?"

"Yeah. Because they don't hate me, no one does. But it feels like it."

Living in a small town created the illusion that we were all the same, that our backgrounds were the same, our futures the same. That nothing bad would ever happen, and if it did, we'd rally around each other, because our reactions would all be the same. This unexpected and unwanted lesson was revealing how different we all truly were.

"I wish I knew how to fix this," I said.

"Me too. The counselor-type person says to give it time."

"Time heals all wounds?"

"Something like that. Or at least we'll see whose wounds heal and whose don't."

"How are your wounds?" I asked.

"Healing."

"Good to hear."

"For the first time in a long time," Reston said, "I actually miss Haven."

I laughed. "Haven misses you."

"I don't think it does. The school board doesn't return my calls either. I have no idea whether I have a job to come back to. It'll be the fall before I'm back. If I'm out of work, someone needs to tell me."

"I'm hoping they'll take me on."

"You're going to come back to teach?"

He sounded more surprised than he should have, but I reminded myself that Reston hadn't been around when I was teaching. He knew it as one of those things that occupied the gap in our history, not as a thing that had been a central piece of my life for years.

"I have to work somewhere."

"Right. And of course that's what you'd do."

"I've thought of trying another school instead of Haven. Another district even. But how would I get the girls to and from school if I have to be at school somewhere else?"

"Good thing you have time to figure out the logistics."

"Yeah."

The stupid logistics, always making things more difficult.

"Eventually I'll be able to drive again," Reston said. "I'll help out."

"Thanks. Of course, everyone will, one way or another."

"And here a minute ago you hated Haven."

I had to laugh at that. "Okay, you're right, I take it back."

"Are you and Amanda okay again?"

"Hard to tell. The lawsuit stuff has been...rough."

"You know they dropped that."

I juggled my phone, nearly dropping it in my shock. "What?"

He sighed, his breath rasping across the phone. "They dropped the lawsuit. It was going to be messier than they thought."

"How so?"

"For instance, it turns out I couldn't join in on their side, because I would be, in fact, on the other side."

Something about that broke my heart. Reston as the enemy. Reston as other. Reston as anything other than part of this community.

"Why?"

"Because I was driving the bus."

"But the accident wasn't your fault."

"No. But there's some...uh, you know, a car hits a bus, even a small bus like the one we were on, how does that much bigger bus end up laying upside down in a ditch?"

"I have no idea."

Since the beginning, I'd refused to read the articles about the accident, the reports, the myriad information that would have answered that question for me. Someday, perhaps. If things ever stopped hurting.

"In this case," Reston said, "they tell me it's because we were pushed onto the shoulder, and there was some ice there, and we skidded a bit and we tipped and so forth. I cling to that official explanation, and the official report from the investigation, because it can't be my fault. I can't live with that."

"And it wasn't your fault," I reassured him.

"It wasn't."

He didn't sound as sure as I did.

"They dropped the lawsuit and no one told me?" I was annoyed. They knew how angry the whole thing made me, and how much of a wedge it had put in our friend group.

"I only know because I had to get a lawyer, and they had to notify him. It's not like I'm exactly in the loop, Jo."

"I should call Amanda."

"You should, regardless. I can't picture one of you without the other."

"Things used to be simple."

"They'll be...easier again."

I nodded, glancing at the clock. "I have to go. See you this weekend?"

"Can't wait."

CHAPTER TWENTY

I dropped the girls at school and drove to the hospital. The reporters were gone now, on to the next tragedy, ready to gawk at another town's grief. At least something was returning to normal.

Amanda wasn't in the waiting area, where I usually found her. When I got close to Landon's room, a nurse nearly threw herself between me and the door.

"Sorry," she said. "You can't go in."

"What's wrong?" I asked, still trying to move around her.

"Ma'am. Mrs. Grant. I'm sorry, the family has asked for privacy today."

Oh, shit. What if…

"I am family," I replied. "If you'll excuse me."

Before I could open the door, Justin burst into the hallway. Like Amanda, he looked greasy and unwashed, his clothes wrinkled beyond repair.

"Jo!" he said, pulling up a few inches away from me. "Hey. Are we expecting you?"

"No, I'm just…always here, it seems. What's going on?"

"Landon's, uh…" He gestured to the door with both hands, then held his hands up in a gesture of defeat. "Landon's up, and it's a mess. Let me…" He turned back to the door, which he'd shut behind himself. "Let me grab Amanda. Mand! Come out here. Jo's here."

They traded places, her in the hall with me now and Justin shut up in the room with their son.

"He's awake?" I stepped toward the door before Amanda grabbed my arm.

"More or less. It's not good."

"I'm sorry," I said, trying to understand what not good could possibly mean.

"What's up?" Amanda asked.

"I came to check on you guys. See if you needed anything."

"I'm kind of busy at the moment."

She kept glancing back at the door to Landon's room. I was in the way, but I needed reassurance, needed to know they were okay, and that they knew I was here if they weren't.

"Of course you are. I'll come back."

"Just text me. I'll get to you when I can."

"Amanda. What can I do?"

"You can leave me alone for now, Jo. I have to worry about Landon right now."

"I can pick up Elliot from school."

"Someone already has that, Jo, thanks. Do you mind?" she said, nodding toward the room.

I stood in the hall, staring at the closed door, stunned into silence. I'd always been her first call. When Landon was born, I was here before his grandparents. I was his godmother; we were his second family. Getting shut out now was a punch to the gut. Amanda would have been my first call if our places were swapped, and instead she sent me home.

"Mrs. Grant?" The nurse who had tried to stop me waved me away from the room. "Come have a seat for a bit."

I sat, blinking, staring at nothing. Landon was awake. It wasn't good. How was that possible?

*   *   *

I had no idea how much time had passed before Amanda came back out of that room, the lack of windows making it impossible to gauge the time of day, but I hadn't moved. I couldn't contemplate moving. It was the night Landon was born all over again, me sitting alone in a waiting room, while they were behind closed doors.

"You stayed." Amanda dropped into the chair beside me.

"I couldn't have left if I wanted to," I replied.

"Sorry I was a bitch."

"You weren't. You had more important things to deal with than my emotions."

I knew I had been intruding, too insistent of her attention. I needed Landon to be okay, because I couldn't take another dose of tragedy. But it wasn't Amanda's job to reassure me.

"It's exactly what I was afraid of," she said softly.

"He's awake. It's not good." I'd repeated it to myself over and over from the moment she'd closed the door on me.

"Yeah."

"Is it ever going to be good?" I asked.

"Too early to tell."

"What can I do?"

She leaned her head on my shoulder, her body shaking as she sobbed. It was what she'd been so afraid of all this time.

She'd lost her son.

"I don't know that person in there," she said.

Landon was sedated now, sleeping, Justin watching over him, while Amanda and I ran out to grab lunch. Of course, neither of us were eating the lunch we'd ordered.

"I was afraid of what he'd do. I was afraid of my son, Jo. My baby."

"That's natural. And he'll change. He'll get better."

I couldn't stop myself, couldn't stop from trying to see the bright side, but how was there a bright side in any of this? I needed to believe that this horrible accident wouldn't take everything from us, because it had already been enough. It was unfair of me. Amanda needed me to empathize with her. I wanted to, wanted to hold her while she mourned the loss of the life she'd imagined for her son.

My own grief was too much, and I couldn't push it aside to focus on hers.

"He might get better. And what if he doesn't? He hurt someone in there. He hurt himself."

"He's scared too, Amanda."

"What if he can never see Elliot again?"

"That would be awful," I replied. "For both of them. All of you."

"I told you this would happen." She stabbed a bit of salad onto her fork with every word. She brought the laden fork to her lips, then set it down on her plate without eating the bite. "I'm sorry. I'm scared and I don't know what to do. What to say."

"Say whatever you want. I'm immune to terrible things now."

I wanted that to be true and hoped it would be someday.

"He's strong still," Amanda continued. "Surprisingly. Laying in bed for two weeks has taken some of his muscle, but when his adrenaline starts going, I'm not going to be able to fight him off."

"Fight? What did he do?"

"He ripped his IV out. Ripped out the oxygen tubes. Bit the nurse. Broke the monitor. Punched his father."

I stared at her, incredulous. Not Landon, happy-go-lucky, teddy bear of a kid Landon.

"Everyone else will be fine," she said. "Landon won't."

I bit back the desire to argue. That wasn't going to help. "You said his memory was spotty. Maybe he won't remember doing this. And you guys know he's not himself right now. It'll be okay."

"If he never gets his short-term memory back, he won't be able to live on his own."

"Not being able to remember the accident sounds almost like a blessing right now."

Amanda barked out a laugh. "Right? I'd give anything not to remember."

"He used to be a tiny, helpless preemie," I said.

"For about five minutes, and then his stubbornness took over," she said with a slight smile, tears gathered at the rim of her eyes.

"I've got to believe that he can get better, Amanda."

"I know. Me too. But I don't want to be disappointed."

"As long as he's alive, he will never disappoint me," I said. "He can bite me if he needs to."

Amanda pressed her lips together against a threatening smile. "I need to know that everything will be okay, and no one can promise me that."

I hated to admit losing Matt and Steve outright put me at an advantage, but having them gone, having it over, certainly meant I wasn't still worrying about when the next shoe would drop. Medical and life insurance had paid out. The funeral was paid for. I still had their belongings to deal with, but I had the rest of my life to do that without worrying about their next problems.

"You'll get answers," I said finally.

They might not be the ones she wanted, but eventually, they'd know more.

At least there was that.

CHAPTER TWENTY-ONE

The girls were boisterous on the short drive to Raleigh, asking a million questions in between repeating their endless stories about how their first week back at school had been. I'd promised Reston we'd visit as much as possible, and I intended to keep that up. Besides, it helped fill the endless weekend days. The girls were occupied during the week with school, and me with getting my teaching license back in order, but this first weekend after school started again was agonizing, trying to manage two energetic children along with all my chores and errands. It would be summer before I knew it. How would I cope with having the girls home with me all day long? I was used to having Matt and Steve to divert their attention sometimes.

Reston answered the door to his room, still in a wheelchair, but his arm cast-free. The sleeves of his sweater bloused a bit over his upper arms, used to more musculature to fill them out, but it was a relief to see him looking more like himself, with fewer obvious injuries.

"Look at you." I grinned as Reston wrapped me in a hug. "Full use of your arms!"

He laughed. "It's amazing. And physical contact with someone who isn't my caretaker. This is great."

"And I see you decided not to keep the beard."

He ran his hands over cheeks that looked freshly shaved. "It was time for that to go."

"For the best. It aged you. You could still use a haircut though."

He flashed faux-angry eyes at me. "I appreciate the critique."

"Can I sign your cast?" Addy asked.

"Which one?" Reston replied.

"All of them!" Olivia cried.

I left the girls with Reston and went in search of a marker. The nurses obliged me, handing over a stack of colored Sharpies. The girls were going to love this.

I turned them loose on Reston, giggling along with them as they went to work. They spread out on the floor in front of him, the better to reach his legs. I lay on my stomach across Reston's bed, my feet kicked up behind me, watching him entertain my girls, hoping they weren't hurting him as they scribbled on his cast, chattering as they passed markers back and forth, consulting each other on planned decorations.

"How are things at home?" Reston asked.

"Landon's awake."

He nodded in acknowledgement, not with joy or excitement that progress was being made. "How's that going?"

"Not great," I replied with a shrug. "He doesn't remember the accident, and his memory isn't working right. If we tell him what happened, before long he's forgotten, and we have to start over again. He's angry because he doesn't understand what's wrong with his brain and his body. Multiple times every day, he re-learns all of his best friends are dead. Amanda wants to lie to him. But what happens when his memory is working correctly, and he finds out that we've been lying to him? I can't be part of that."

"It feels impossible. I don't know what I'd do if I were Justin and Amanda."

"How diplomatic of you," I said.

"And honest. I don't know how any of you are doing what you're doing."

"How are you?"

He shrugged his shoulders, rotating his arms so that his palms faced up. "Healed enough to lose some of my casts. I'm doing physical therapy to build my strength back up."

"And your legs?"

"One's doing better than the other," he replied. "Obviously, since one was broken and one was just…in a car crash. They're probably going to do some work on my right leg. Maybe re-break it and reset it. We'll see."

"That sounds awful, Reston, I'm sorry."

"Thanks. It's…all of this is awful." He looked at my daughters sketching on his casts. "I appreciate you guys coming to see me. Not everyone does. I know everyone is busy, but it helps to see a familiar face."

"It helps us too."

"Girls! Tell me about school," Reston demanded.

Addy shrugged. "They're treating me different, and I hate it."

She didn't look up from her artwork. It was the first time she'd complained about the way anyone was treating her, but I'd assumed it was happening. I experienced it too. The pitying looks. The extra care. The unnecessary apologies.

"I like it," Olivia replied. "I like being special."

"We're not special," Addy spat. "Everyone's brother died."

"Addison," I admonished.

"What? That's what happened, and it's what happened to everyone. I guess not to Elliot, but Landon's messed up, so it might as well have happened."

I wanted to fight her, to argue, but she was right, in a way. There were six kids at the elementary school who had lost a sibling in the crash, plus three middle schoolers and two high schoolers. Still, I didn't want to hear about that, about the sheer number of people in our town who were directly affected by that horrible day.

"I wish I were getting special treatment," Reston said.

I gawked at him.

"What?" he said. "They're making me do uncomfortable PT, I keep having to eat terrible hospital food. It's super unfair. I deserve, like, milkshakes and TV all day."

"I don't want special treatment," Addy snapped. "I want my dad back."

"Addy, your dad was my favorite person in the entire world. Your dad and your brother and the rest of those boys were my only family, and I miss them so much. And you can be as angry or as sad as you want. I will never tell you that you can't be, because I am so angry and sad too."

"She shouldn't have been driving," Addy said. "That lady. She shouldn't have been driving because she was old and sick."

I hadn't really talked to her about the woman who had caused the accident. I didn't want my girls to find a villain in this situation. I still didn't believe that Evelyn McCourt was truly responsible. I wanted to, would have loved something to latch onto, to blame for all of this. By all accounts, she was usually alert, active, spritely. She was in excellent health, prior to the accident. She was certainly old, but plenty of older people drive safely, and she had for some time.

I didn't know what else to tell Addy. I had found that I had answers for almost anything, but not for the things my daughters said.

Perhaps I was too close, with all the same questions. Why did our family have to lose so much more than everyone else? If they'd been able to save Landon, Isaiah, and Reston, why couldn't they save Matt and Steve? I had their medical records, but I wasn't sure I could bear to read them. I thought I wanted answers, but what if the answers weren't what I wanted to hear?

"If there's one thing I've learned over these weeks," Reston said, "it's that nothing will make you feel better. There is never going to be a time when I decide that it was okay to lose all these people that I love so much. I'm never going to be okay with what happened to me, even if I make a full recovery, and it doesn't sound like I'm going to. Be angry, Addy. Be angry at her. Be angry at me. Be angry at the world."

"And what about when I don't want to be angry?"

"Then just be Addy. We all love her, and we'll be thrilled to have her around."

"When are you coming home, Uncle Reston?"

"I need to get my casts off. I need to be able to walk by myself, so that I can be alone in my house."

"You could come stay with us."

I laughed at that.

Reston smiled. "That sounds nice. Jo, I'm going to crash in the guest room."

"We'd be delighted to have you."

"I won't pay rent or help around the house at all."

"Well, that doesn't sound entirely fair."

"My legs are broken!"

"That excuse is only going to fly for so long, Reston."

"Then I'm going to have to milk it for as long as I can."

I was willing to endure just about anything, thankful to have him here. I would have gladly taken him into our guest room, even without help with the chores. I would do just about anything to hold onto any piece of what I'd lost.

CHAPTER TWENTY-TWO

When I got my first call with a sub assignment, I felt woefully unprepared. I hadn't been in a classroom full-time in nearly sixteen years. Sure, I'd subbed here and there, once Olivia was in school, if we had a surprise car repair or wanted to go on a nice vacation or something. This was different. Our finances depended on me being able to do this again.

It was strange to be in Steve's world. There was a new math teacher in his classroom, some short, bald guy with glasses who I couldn't bring myself to greet. I knew he was the replacement teacher because I'd never seen him before. No one in Haven wanted to be the new Steve. No one wanted to step into his shoes as if he could be replaced.

I wasn't ready to be here. When I'd gotten the life insurance check, I'd debated keeping things the status quo: staying at home, being the hands-on mom. The money would have lasted a year or two at best, and I would have been right back here, needing this job but without a financial cushion.

Maybe in a year or two, I wouldn't catch myself watching for the husband I'd lost who would never reappear. By then I wouldn't avoid the trophy cases in the main hallway, where framed photos of my husband and son hung with the trophies that they'd brought the school – not state champions, but the runner up still gets some nice hardware. Maybe in a year or two I wouldn't expect Matt to be sitting in the classroom, like he was supposed to be, shooting me his lopsided grin whenever I caught him talking to the kid in the next desk.

If I couldn't handle subbing, I wouldn't be able to teach full time this fall. I needed to be able to do that. What else could I do after so long out of the workforce? I hadn't signed up for surprise single parenting and I wasn't sure I could cut it.

"You're going to be fine," Reston said when I called him later that night, after the girls had gone to bed.

"I've been away from the classroom for too long," I lamented, emptying the dishwasher while I talked. There wasn't time to have a conversation and not be doing something else too. I still needed to make the girls' lunches for the next day, and I had laundry to fold.

"Your life is basically a classroom," Reston argued. "It's not like you haven't spent that time raising children and dealing with homework and all of that. And it's like riding a bike, Jo. Trust me."

"When will you be back at school?"

I needed Reston there, needed backup every time grief caused me to stumble.

"I'd be there now if they'd let me. Something about how I'm a huge liability for the school as long as I'm wearing a cast."

"I can't believe they won't let you wheel yourself into a classroom."

"Eh. I can believe it. I don't mind it, honestly. I don't enjoy people seeing me like this. I don't want people to know that there was ever a time I couldn't do everything I've always been able to do."

"You'll be your usual self soon enough," I replied.

"God, I hope so. Someday these bones will be healed and I'll be able to come back."

"I'll be good to have someone at the school who—"

I stopped myself from finishing my sentence, from saying "who knows what I'm feeling when I'm there." I honestly couldn't imagine what Reston would feel being back where he'd spent so many hours with his team. That team was his life. Those boys meant the world to him. How could he possibly walk the halls of the school again, knowing that they wouldn't?

"I'm eager to return to school," Reston said slowly, "even if it's haunted now."

"It certainly feels like it is."

"I want my routine. I want my normal life."

Didn't we all, I thought. "You'll get it back."

"Who do they have teaching my classes anyway?"

"Casey Shields."

"Oh, okay, she always does a good job. One less thing to worry about."

I loved that he was worried about his classroom. It had always felt like a back burner thought, his team occupying most of his time and attention. But he took this part of his job seriously as well.

"I still marvel at how you ended up teaching history in the first place," I teased.

"Even I was smart enough to know I'd need a career to fall back on in case basketball didn't work out. Given that it, uh, kind of didn't."

"Whenever I try to picture you studying, I fail."

"Yeah, yeah," Reston replied with a chuckle. "In high school, I was a bit of a goof off. I get it."

"What do I do when one of my students turns out to be like that?"

"You'll figure it out. Maybe you push them. Maybe you trust them to push themselves."

"Maybe I ruin some poor high school kid who was this close to graduating but then they got me for junior year English."

"If your class is the only thing standing between a kid and graduation, there's something bigger happening. You've done all this before, Jo. You'll be fine."

"Thanks."

"How hard is it? Being there, I mean, not the teaching part."

I paused in my chores, regarding the ceiling as I fumbled for the words to adequately express how it was.

"Part of me hates every second that I'm there," I finally answered. "I assume it would be worse for you."

"Oh, hooray, a spectral workplace, just what I always wanted."

"I heard some of the teachers talking about it," I said, trying to keep the bitterness out of my voice. People I'd known for decades, but they wouldn't look me in the eye. People who whispered about me, and around me, who may have thought they were protecting me, but they were only singling me out, making me feel worse. "You know, in passing, because no one would dare talk about it in front of me. I've heard there's a shrine in the gym."

"A shrine?"

"You know, pictures of the boys and flowers and battery-operated candles and things. I don't know, I can't bring myself to go in there."

"How lucky that the option exists for you."

"It will be a while before you're ready to be on the court though, right?"

"Physically, yeah. I'd be out there right now if anyone would let me. I think it would help my mental state, but no one cares about that."

I had no doubt that being on the court would be good for him. Maybe being able to see how far he was from the skills he'd once had would be hard for him, but he'd also be able to work on those skills.

"Get those casts off," I said, slamming the dishwasher shut, ready to get onto the next task. "And then get home."

"As soon as possible."

CHAPTER TWENTY-THREE

School hadn't been back in session long before the girls brought home a flyer, letting parents know that the school had brought in a crisis counselor. The counselor was available for any student who wanted to speak to her, whether about the accident or about something else. It felt like a godsend. I'd thought about having the girls see a therapist, but I wasn't sure how to find the time for that. Adding one more thing to my schedule right now felt impossible. This would be perfect. Assuming they were interested.

"I'm fine," Addy insisted.

"You could talk to her once and then never again," I replied. "I won't force you. But I think it would probably be useful for you to have someone you could talk to when you need to."

"You're not talking to someone."

She had me there. Again, the scheduling was an issue. And I wasn't ready to talk to a stranger about losing the boys. I talked to my friends about it plenty. Maybe someday I'd be ready to let a stranger in on what this was like for me. If that was possible.

"How about the three of us go for a meeting with her?" I asked. "You guys can decide for yourselves if you want to talk to her about anything, but this way we'll at least meet her."

Addy rolled her eyes, but she didn't say no, so I counted that as a victory.

"Olivia?"

She looked up at me with her father's eyes, a baby who should have had no bigger experience with death than that of a carnival-won goldfish. Having another person to talk to her about this horrible change had to be a solution. It had to make things better. If this didn't, I didn't know what could.

"Yeah, I'd talk to her," Olivia mumbled. "I guess. Sometimes."

"Okay. I'll make an appointment for all of us."

The crisis counselor's name was Larkin Banks. She didn't look old enough to understand what a crisis was. But then again, none of the kids she was here to help was old enough for that either.

She wore jeans and flats, not beholden to the teachers' dress code, her white blond hair flowing in waves past her shoulders. She shook my hand when we introduced ourselves, her fingers long but her nails bit short.

"I'm sorry my hand is so cold," she said. "I'd blame the winter, but that's just how my hands are."

"Winter certainly doesn't help."

"It's nice to meet all of you. Who's Addison and who's Olivia?"

The girls were slumped on either side of me on the small couch that occupied most of the space in what was clearly a closet hastily reassigned as office space. Dr. Banks sat in an armchair, her elbows on her knees, leaning toward me and the girls.

I paused, waiting for the girls to answer for themselves. Addy was usually quick to correct people when they used her full name, but today she was silent, her eyes fixed on a landscape painting on the wall. Olivia stared at the floor, gnawing on a fingernail. I hadn't expected them to come into this meeting with enthusiasm, but I was expecting more than this.

"Addy," I said, placing a hand on her head. My other hand went to Olivia's head. "Olivia."

"I'm glad you came to meet me. I know the last couple months have been just awful."

Addy flopped back on the couch and rolled her eyes. Here we go.

"You don't know anything," she spat.

123

"Oh? Tell me more."

"It's not going to work that easily."

Dr. Banks smiled. "Okay then. Olivia?"

"It has been really awful, yeah."

"Do you want to talk about what's been awful? What you might want to talk to me about later, if you see me again without your mom?"

"You know that already," Addy said, cutting off her sister. "You're not here because nothing happened."

"True enough," Dr. Banks replied.

"And talking about it doesn't fix any of it."

"Don't you think it would be nice to have a space where you can talk about it? I'm sure you're careful not to talk about it too much with your mom, or your sister, because you know they're hurting too. I'm sad for all of you that you are going through this terrible thing, but it won't hurt me to talk to you about it."

"It'll hurt me," Addy replied, staring down the counselor. "I don't talk about it because I don't want to think about it. I don't want to hear about it. I don't want to think about how, even if they lost their brothers, all of my friends still get to have their dads. And I read the news, and they only ever talk about the kids, like it's so sad they died, but somehow it's less sad that my dad died."

"I'd imagine that's pretty aggravating."

"So how am I supposed to say anything to anyone? It's going to hurt my mom if I say anything, it's going to hurt my friends."

"Like I said, you can talk to me," Dr. Banks said. "As long as I don't think you're in danger, I'm not going to tell your mom what we're talking about."

"How am I supposed to believe that? I don't know you."

"Do you think the school brought me in here just to mess with you guys? To stockpile stories to chat about behind your backs?"

"Well, no, I assume they brought you in so that it would look like they're doing something."

I'd never heard such an astute observation from my middle child before. I didn't agree with her, but I saw how easy it was to think that way.

Addy continued, "And I assume you'll be here long enough to look like they care about us, and then you'll disappear."

Dr. Banks shifted in her seat, leaning closer. "That would be incredibly unprofessional and dangerous of me. I promise you I won't do that."

"And how do I trust you?"

The counselor shrugged. "I don't know. How do you trust anyone?"

The simple answer, at least where Addy was concerned, was that she didn't. Not anymore. Addy trusted Steve with everything. I knew he kept her secrets from me, and I had no problem with that. He was a safe adult for her. He would have fixed anything she was up against.

The more I thought about that, the more amazed I was with how Addy had conducted herself since the accident. She'd lost her safe space, and she was still getting up every day and going out in the world, and she was still so little. I was never going to replace her father in her life, the same way a stepfather would never be enough.

"I tell you what." Dr. Banks slapped her thighs with her hands. "I'm here every day now. If you want to talk, or if you're having a bad day, or if you need somewhere quiet to hang out for a little while, stop by. We can talk, or we can hang out. Whatever you need. You too, Olivia."

"And if you're busy?" Addy asked.

"We'll figure something out. I will be busy; I have a lot of kids who want to talk to me. I'm finding time for everyone."

"And what about the kids who don't want to talk to you?"

"I'm finding time for them too."

Well, I liked this woman, even if Addy didn't.

CHAPTER TWENTY-FOUR

It was strange to find myself in a routine, flexible as it was. I'd gotten used to how things were: getting Steve and the kids up and out the door every day, keeping up with my cleaning schedule and my meal plans. I was still up early—too early—checking my messages for a sub assignment, making sure the girls had what they needed for the day, packing lunches, making breakfasts. There was more pressure to get things right, internal pressure, mostly, because surely the people watching understood. Or at least I told myself they did.

I kept my blinders on at school. I didn't go near the gym, unsure whether I'd ever be able to go in there again. If I was offered a sub assignment teaching math at the high school, I turned it down, needing to stay as far away from Steve's area as possible.

I slept on his side of the bed every night now. I couldn't bear to sleep on my side, staring at the emptiness left behind. This way I filled the space Steve had vacated. On that far off future day when someone else joined me in my bed, I wouldn't want them taking my husband's physical space.

As if I could contemplate having someone else in my bed at all.

Imagine how the people of this nosy little town would react to me dating again—not favorably.

Bile rose in my throat as I thought about dating again. Steve was the love of my life, the man of my dreams. There was no replacing him.

Still, I was lonely. Reston was in Raleigh, so I couldn't see him like when he was local. The rehab facility was also stricter about his phone time, meaning I was limited on how late I could call. Amanda was at the hospital twenty-four seven, but Landon's behavior was erratic, and triggered by changes to his routine, so I couldn't stop by there as often as I'd like either. Once the girls were in bed for the night, the oppressive silence of the house was overwhelming. I'd catch up on the housework that was sliding now that it wasn't my primary objective, or sit in front of the television while something blared unwatched.

Doing the mundane activities of life was strange—Steve and Matt were gone, but life continued. I'd done what I needed to do for them. I'd taken care of all the trivialities: I'd turned in their cell phones and changed our—my—contract; I'd sold Steve's car, my minivan more practical than his sedan. As insurance money came in, I paid off the mortgage, the funeral costs, and started college funds for the girls. I was busy and responsible, as hard as it was. I'd even written and sent thank you cards to people who'd brought us food or helped with the funeral or with the girls.

I was also dealing with the everyday bits of life for Reston. With him out of town indefinitely, I was collecting his mail, making sure bills were paid, depositing checks. We did that for him when he traveled, so I already had a key to his place. I was used to intruding on Reston's space, and he was used to our intrusion.

I even found time here and there to help out the other families—taking meals to their houses, handling school drop off and pick up for friends, keeping an eye on kids. It wasn't much, but I wasn't sure it needed to be much. I was slowly filling Reston's freezer with food, trying to take something off his shoulders when he was well enough to return home.

Keeping myself busy felt like the only way to get through the days. I ran myself ragged, until I dropped into bed, too exhausted to do anything but sleep. I couldn't lay awake, thinking about what I'd lost. I couldn't think about the man who was supposed to be in bed beside me. I couldn't think about the son who would probably have still been up, doing homework or texting his friends.

When I had nightmares—and boy, did I have those now—there was no one to comfort me, to hold me until my tears and shaking stopped. Those were the worst times.

The dead of winter had never felt so appropriately named.

CHAPTER TWENTY-FIVE

I dropped the girls at school and headed to Amanda's house to grab a few things she'd requested. Justin was at work, and they couldn't leave Landon alone at the hospital. His outbursts had gotten worse, louder and more violent, and they were worried he'd be forced to leave. Having parental supervision almost kept him in check, to an extent.

Their house was a disaster. Their mailbox was overflowing and there was a stack of newspapers on the porch. I was supposed to bring Amanda clean clothes, but I couldn't find any. I threw in a load of laundry while I straightened up, dealing with the sink full of dirty dishes and dragging the trash cans out for the next collection day. As far as I knew, someone was staying here every night with Elliot, trying to keep his schedule as normal as possible. But I wasn't sure who, and they clearly weren't keeping house. If Amanda needed me to bring her clothes, she wasn't planning to be home any time soon.

Maybe I should offer to have Elliot over for a day or two. It might be good for the girls. Addy had been doing better after venting a bit with Reston. The three kids might benefit from having one another to complain to.

At the hospital, I found Amanda in Landon's room. He was asleep, possibly sedated, as he often was lately. He wasn't himself anymore, as he battled through his brain injury to understand what had happened to him. Some days they kept him in restraints, though today didn't seem to be one of those days.

I wrapped my arms around my best friend, trying not to wince at the wave of body odor that radiated from her. I never missed a shower these days, sometimes taking two or three in a day. The time alone when I could cry or yell, the water covering my tears and drowning my voice, was sometimes the only thing that made it possible to get through another day without my boys. I could pound on the walls, or lie on the floor and let the water wash over me.

I wished there was anything I could do to genuinely make this better for her. To return Amanda to how she was before the accident. To make Landon himself. I couldn't even do that for myself.

"I brought your change of clothes." I gestured toward the overnight bag at my feet. "And some food, whenever you feel up to eating."

She looked more worn down every time I saw her, the deep bags under her eyes, the wrinkles around her mouth, hair, once bouncy and shiny now greasy and dull. How long had it been since she'd showered? Hopefully the toiletries I'd brought would be put to good use.

"Isaiah's being moved to Raleigh." She rifled through the bag. She glanced around the room, empty but for us and her sleeping son, then stripped off her shirt, exchanging it for a fresh one. She found the deodorant I'd packed and swiped it quickly under each arm before tossing it back into the bag.

"We're still looking for a place that will take Landon," she continued. "Nothing close will. Not after he got violent with that nurse."

"I'm sure once his memory is working correctly, his temper will calm down."

"If," Amanda clarified. "If his memory is ever back to normal. If he can use his body the way he always has. If he's ever remotely himself again."

"Or if he accepts that he won't be himself again."

It felt like a terrible thing to say, even if true. It seemed to be why Reston was handling things as well as he was. I'm sure it wasn't always that way, but he seemed resigned that things were going to be different now. If they expected Landon to be exactly how he had been before the accident, they were probably going to be disappointed.

"His friends are gone. All of them," Amanda said, her voice thick with tears. "I'm not sure I can ask any more of him right now."

"What can I do to help you guys? What do you need? I'd be glad to keep Elliot sometimes. It would be fun for the girls to have him with us for a couple days."

"I can't think beyond getting Landon help. Do you have an in with a rehab facility?"

"Not unless Reston has a ton of pull at the one he's in. Although I wouldn't put it past him to have already charmed everyone there. When he's not being a cantankerous ass."

Amanda flopped back in her chair, her arms crossed in front of her chest. "I can't believe that place won't take Landon. I told them that it would help to have his coach and teammate in the same facility. I want him to spend some time with Reston, It might bring him around, but we can't go to him and he can't come here."

"It would be good for Reston too," I replied. "He seems better when he's in coach mode."

"How is he? It sounds like he's recovering okay."

"Physically, yeah," I replied.

"That's good."

"He's not going to be a hundred percent again, but he's going to be well enough to return to his normal."

"I'm glad someone will."

"But he feels responsible, Amanda. Mostly because he was driving, but also because his job was keeping the team safe."

"I wish he'd seen her and, I don't know, steered around her."

I bristled under her accusatory words. I wasn't going to stand here and let her think for a moment that Reston was anything but another victim of this terrible accident.

"It's not as if the bus is particularly maneuverable." I tried to keep my voice light.

"Fair enough. Still."

"Do you blame him for what happened?"

I told myself that of course she didn't, but what if she did? What if her need to place blame extended to someone we'd been friends with since we were kids? How much had grief changed her?

"God, Jo, of course not," she replied. "Wishing he'd been able to avoid the accident doesn't mean I blame him."

I released a breath. "He blames himself. Obviously. I don't know if anything can change his mind about that."

"Well, the captain is supposed to go down with his ship."

I winced at her comment. She said she didn't blame him, but it certainly sounded like she did. "That's a healthy thing for Reston to think about right now."

"It feels as if you don't understand, Jo. Like you lost so much and you can't wrap your brain around the idea that we all suffered losses."

"Of course everyone did." I bit my lip against the rest of my sentence—"But I lost more." It wasn't fair, but it was true. Grief was quantifiable: one husband lost plus one son lost is greater than one son with horrible injuries. I was a terrible person for thinking it, but that didn't make it false.

"You act like you've cornered the market on tragedy," Amanda continued.

"God, that's a depressing thought."

"So maybe you could ease up on the rest of us?" Amanda suggested. "I get it, we all get it. But stop acting like we aren't in the trenches with you."

"I wasn't aware that I was."

She rolled her eyes. "Come on. It's like the stuff with the lawsuit, like if you don't want to be involved, and you lost so much more than the rest of us, why do we want it?"

"That wasn't my opposition to the lawsuit, and it's not what I think, Amanda."

It was easy for me to slip into, though—I had lost more. I had more pieces to pick up, more to lose if I couldn't. I didn't have the support of a partner who was experiencing this with me. At least her son had a chance to recover, to be himself again. How dare she lecture me?

"Thanks for bringing me my stuff." She jabbed at the overnight bag with her toes. "If you want to do something for us, Natalie is scheduling meals and helping with Elliot and stuff, if you can stand to talk to her."

"I don't know that I'm the problem there," I replied. "And you're all still my friends, whether I agree with you on everything or not."

"I know. It doesn't feel like it. Like with the group texts. There's the one I'm in and the one you're in. I don't want to ask you for help, because it's like crossing the picket lines."

"You have been my best friend for nearly forty years. We're on the same side."

"Except when we aren't."

This wasn't the time our prom dresses were the same color. Then, instead of embracing the joy of matching, she'd stopped speaking to me for a week. This was our lives falling apart and needing each other more than we ever had.

"Amanda."

"Thanks for the stuff," she repeated. "Text Natalie if you want to help. Thanks, Jo."

It stung to be dismissed. I glanced at her son, still asleep, and thought about everything that was going to be in his way moving forward. I was on their side. I wanted Landon to get the help he needed to try to heal. I wanted the same thing for Isaiah, and for Reston, and for the other families who had lost so much.

I wanted all of us to be better, to be healed.

As if we could be.

CHAPTER TWENTY-SIX

"Hey, Mrs. Clark." I dropped a box full of Valentine's Day treats on Addy's teacher's desk. "Hey, Heather."

My co-classroom mom waved at me distractedly as she hung a heart-covered banner across the windows. The kids were outside for recess. We had less than fifteen minutes to get this place looking as festive as possible before they came racing back in, smiling and red faced from their time on the monkey bars and swings. I hoped the tablecloths and confetti would help. I knew the candy would.

"It's so good of you both to do this," Mrs. Clark said.

"Distraction helps," Heather replied.

"If you need anything, I'll be out on the playground," Mrs. Clark said.

"Thanks, we'll grab you if we do."

I'd already dropped off my supplies to Olivia's classroom, where the other class mom was handling set up solo. I'd spend most of the party time over there. I alternated class parties; Addy had gotten the bulk of my Christmas party appearance. That day felt a million years ago, held a week before the accident that changed everything. It was a different time, in a different town.

"How's Chloe doing?" I asked Heather.

She shrugged, pulling a stack of paper plates from a tote bag. "Good and bad. I don't even know sometimes, Jo. Your girls okay?"

"Sometimes. We met with the new crisis counselor. I think they see her sometimes, but I'm not sure. Addy isn't remotely interested in talking to anyone about what happened, so we'll see."

Heather clucked her tongue. "And how are you doing? I feel like every time I see you, you're in the middle of something."

It was the only way to keep the grief at bay.

"I am indeed keeping busy," I replied. "It's like you said, the distraction helps. Next week I'm taking treats to Raleigh for Reston and Isaiah, and I'm meeting with the director of the rehab facility to try to talk them into letting Landon come up there, at least on a trial basis. He needs to be with the other survivors."

"Last I heard, he wasn't retaining what happened."

"It sounds like he doesn't remember the accident still, but he has held onto the memory of being told what happened."

"Oh, bless his heart."

The first time I saw him after his memory started to hold, he clung to me, sobbing, telling me he was sorry. Sorry for what, he never said. His speech had been slurred, his movements shaky, and his grip weaker than when he was a child. It had been one of the worst moments of this nightmare, watching this child I had known for an eternity grasp the fact that eleven people he had spent all his time with for years were gone, people he loved, people he'd never considered losing.

I sympathized.

"I wish there was more I could do for Landon," I said.

"I think you're doing everything that can be done, Jo. You can't do it all. You'll collapse. You have to take care of yourself."

"This is how I take care of myself," I replied. "Do you guys need anything? What can I do?"

Heather laughed. "We're okay. We're trying to figure out what to do with Aidan's things. Like...do we donate them somewhere? Where do we donate them? Who needs everything a teenage boy ever owned?"

"You're further along than I am on that."

Matt and Steve's things were still shoved into Matt's room, the door firmly shut. Someday I'd do something about them. I debated packing everything up and hoping that one of my daughters had a son. Then I could simply pass everything to them, keeping their things around forever.

"We'll figure it out," Heather said. "Each in our own time and our own way."

"If only there was a manual. How long to wait before getting rid of their things. How to keep your kids from losing their minds."

"How long you have to wait before dating again."

"The furthest thing from my mind," I said. "Can you even imagine me walking around this town with someone else?"

"Oh, you'll never hear the end of it," Heather said. "But what about the boys' girlfriends? They didn't have the time investment that you did with Steve, though I'm sure they loved the boys in their own ways. But they know people are watching them. Are they waiting too long? Are they not waiting long enough? It's a delicate balance, and they're teenage girls."

"Teenagers are not known for their excellent balance skills."

"Exactly," Heather said.

"Just when I think I've got a handle on the magnitude of this whole terrible thing, something else pops up." I pressed a hand to my chest. "Those poor girls. I know it's, you know, the guy they've dated for a few months when they were fourteen or fifteen or sixteen or whatever, but in Haven, that means a lot."

"Yeah, in my graduating class, at least fifty percent of us married the guy we were dating at graduation."

"And those of us who didn't get whispered about, like, what went wrong there. How did they screw up something so easy?"

It felt ridiculous, that expectation. Trusting teenagers to know what they wanted for the rest of their lives, and yet it was the norm here.

"You met Steve at college, right?" Heather asked.

"Yep. My high school boyfriend couldn't wait to get out of Haven, and I could never truly leave."

"That was Reston, right? I feel like that was the gossip."

I laughed. "This town does love its gossip."

"And he and Steve ended up being friends?"

"Best friends. Inseparable."

"But not competitive?"

I smiled, just a little, at the memory of Steve and Reston and their non-stop competition. "They both thrived on competition. Not competitive about me, but about everything else always."

I couldn't count how many hours they'd spent playing "one quick game" of one-on-one in our driveway. I'd come out to call them for dinner, only to be told that they were now playing to twenty-one or thirty-five or fifty-seven. They were like children.

I missed that. I missed it for me, and I missed it for Reston, who was never more in his element than he was on the court. I could only pray that he'd be able to play again, even if not at the level he used to. He'd lost the person who pushed him when he played, who forced him to try to be better.

"Do you want us to keep Addy some time?" Heather asked. "She and Chloe could have a sleepover, and your girls could get a break from each other. Growing up, I lived for getting a break from my sister."

"That's so sweet, Heather. I bet they'd love that. They never get one-on-one time with me anymore, and that would be perfect."

"Is next weekend okay?"

"Next weekend is great."

The bell rang, and the children flooded back into the classroom. I loved watching Addy with her friends when she forgot I was there. She seemed at ease, the way she'd been before the accident, the way I rarely saw her at home.

I passed out treats before handing over party management to Heather. Then I headed down the hall to Olivia's classroom.

Olivia seemed less herself at school, quiet and withdrawn. Even as we started playing games with the kids, she stayed at her desk, eating her treats, but staying out of the merriment. I didn't say anything to her, for fear of drawing attention. It could wait until we were at home.

Her classmates didn't try to approach her either. I hoped that wasn't a regular occurrence. Olivia had always been the sociable one, with tons of friends. I'd expected the girls to be different now, but I didn't think it would be this drastic. My mom instinct was to run over and engage her myself, to pull other kids over to interact with her. It wouldn't help, singling her out, so I stayed in place, no matter how much that hurt.

I didn't want to press her about talking to the counselor, but it felt like a necessity. I hoped she was taking this opportunity to have someone to safely vent to.

At least I'd have some alone time with Olivia soon. Hopefully that would help.

CHAPTER TWENTY-SEVEN

"I appreciate you coming in, Mrs. Grant." The rehab facility director shook my hand. "I'll think it over."

"Thanks for taking the time to see me," I replied.

I hoped our meeting would help Landon's situation. He needed to be at a specialized rehab facility that wasn't our ill-equipped community hospital to help him recover. Landon needed to be in this rehab facility around people he knew. I would move mountains to make that happen.

I'd already checked in with Isaiah's mom. He was settling in well, which was good news. His spinal cord injury luckily seemed to be an incomplete injury. He had some sensation and voluntary movement still, though it was more muscle spasm-style moves than, say, taking steps. But it meant that steps might come someday. I had to believe that they would, that he would be, if not back to how he was, able to live without constant pain or assistance.

I couldn't head home without checking on Reston, regardless of how we'd left things before. He was in his bed, staring at the ceiling, looking tortured. If he was bedridden, that was essentially torture, so it made sense.

I tapped on the doorframe.

"Back in the bed?" I asked.

Reston rolled his eyes. "Yeah, they've reconstructed my leg again They want me taking it as easy as possible for a few days. They implied I had perhaps pushed myself too hard before and that's why it didn't heal properly in the first place."

That sounded accurate.

"How are you feeling?" I took a seat on the chair next to his bed. The chairs were more comfortable than the ones in the hospital at home. I planned to be here as often as possible, sure that my presence would make everything better. Having somewhere tolerable to sit would help.

"I'm fucking awful," Reston grumbled.

"I'm sorry."

His eyes flicked toward me, and he sighed. "I'll be all right. Eventually. What are you doing up here?"

"I had a meeting with the director about trying to get Landon in up here."

"How'd that go?"

I shrugged. "Okay enough? He's going down to Haven and meeting with Landon. We'll see how that goes."

"If he doesn't want to do the rehab, there's no point in bringing him here."

"I know. Like I said, we'll see."

"You don't have to visit me, Jo."

"I wasn't going to come and not stop in. And I brought you cookies!" I pulled a Ziploc bag from my tote. "They're leftover from the girls' Valentine's parties."

Reston stared at the heart-shaped iced sugar cookies, then chuckled. I loved when he laughed or smiled, the creases around his eyes and mouth that hadn't been there when we were teenagers deepening. He was a serious man who didn't smile often, making it that much more special.

"Thank you." He took the cookies from me. "Sorry I'm being grumpy with you."

"Of course you're being grumpy. I bet your leg hurts."

"Like hell, yeah. I may have yelled at them to cut the damned thing off."

I winced. I knew it hurt and frustrated him, but that was extreme. "That's not going to solve anything, Reston."

141

"I know. I'm ready to be done healing so that I can start rehabbing. I want to be better. I want to be normal."

"Soon enough."

"Assuming it heals correctly this time."

"And that's what I'm going to assume."

He shook his head, looking away from me. I didn't pretend to know what he was going through. He'd lost his independence, maybe his job, his beloved team. Now he was stuck in bed, with nothing to do but contemplate all of that.

"Did you see Isaiah?" he asked.

"I spoke to Vonda and left her some cookies for him. He was in a PT session."

"He's doing great. Well, you know, better than I would be if they told me I wouldn't walk again."

"Vonda said there's a chance he gets movement back in his legs."

"That's not walking, Jo."

"I know. But I have to hope for that."

"You don't. You can hope that he's happy and healthy without making a full recovery."

I hated doing this with him. I needed to believe that everything could be the way it was, and Reston needed to know that things could be okay even if they weren't. His realism was hard to stomach some days.

"Don't you want to make a full recovery?" I asked. A person who said cutting his leg off would make life easier didn't sound like someone who thought he'd get better.

"Sure I do. But I'm not going to, most likely. I'm going to do every exercise my physical therapist gives me. I'm going to rest this leg as commanded. And even then, they've told me to expect a drop in speed and agility."

Speed and agility were Reston's forte, and I couldn't picture a world where he lost that.

"But you can always work on getting that back," I said.

"I'm almost forty-five, Jo. I can work on my athleticism all I want. I'm not going to get back to where I was. I was nearly a professional athlete. I know what my body can do."

"I'd forgotten about the draft."

He cut his eyes at me, rolling them slightly. The pros were supposed to come calling for Reston Tucker. And they did, sort of, in that he had good reason to believe that he was going to get drafted into the NBA. Then he just…didn't. At the time, even though we weren't in touch, I'd watched the draft, surprised not to hear his name called. I'd wondered if that was part of why he stayed away as long as he did. Haven had expectations for him, and he didn't meet them.

"I get what you're doing, Jo," he said, "but I don't need it. You can be honest with me."

I pressed my lips together, fighting back the tears. "I need as much back to normal as possible."

"I know you do. But you're not going to get that."

"It's not fair."

He leaned forward as best he could. "You're telling me."

"This is so hard, and I have to be positive and keep it together."

"No, you don't."

"What happens if I fall apart, Reston? Who takes care of my girls?"

"Everyone in town will band together to take care of your girls, Jo."

I shook my head. "No. My mom told me, way back when, that I had to be strong for the girls. And she was right, I do, but it's hard."

"Your mom has always been too hard on you."

"I don't think that's true. She isn't wrong, I do need to take care of my daughters."

"You're doing a great job with the girls, and with me, and with everyone in town who could possibly need anything."

I laughed, brushing the tears from my cheeks. "Thank you, Reston."

"I'm going to be difficult because I hold myself to an impossible physical standard, Jo. No matter how much better I get, I'm not going to be back to normal, and that's…I want to say frustrating, but that's not the right word. Infuriating? I've put a lot of effort into getting where I am, and I might lose all of it." I opened my mouth to respond, but Reston cut me off with a raised hand. "Don't. I appreciate that you want to be positive. That you need to be. Not with me. Not today."

"What can I do to help you today?"

"Take a break from helping."

That was impossible. Helping everyone else was keeping me sane these days.

"Something's wrong with Olivia." Would giving him a chance to help improve his mood?

"Depression?"

"She's eight, Reston. I'm sure she's sad, but depression?"

"It's not unheard of, Jo. What's going on?"

"She's quieter. Not playing with her friends."

"Okay, yeah, that sounds normal."

"Does it? I have no idea what's normal in this situation. I don't know a lot of people who lost a parent and a sibling in one go."

"How's Addy?"

Oh, well, apparently I did know people in the same position as Olivia.

"She's fine. Better since you guys talked. And they have a counselor at the school now, and I think they're talking. But I can't use Addy as a model for what to do about Olivia. They aren't handling it the same."

"Did you expect them too?"

"I think I expected all of us to react the same way," I answered. "I don't know why. But, you know, they talk about things like the stages of grief, so it seems like everyone should go through the stages and then…it's the same."

"But we don't go through the stages in the same order or for the same length of time."

"Clearly."

"Do you want me to give Olivia a coach lecture too?"

"That's sweet. But let's leave the coach lecture as a last resort."

Reston laughed. "Okay."

"I have to get back. Is there anything I can bring you the next time I come up?"

"I'll make you a list."

"I assume it starts with your own clothes?"

"Oh, God, yeah, that would be nice."

The list was slapdash, things from home, food that wasn't normally allowed on his strict athlete's diet. I was thankful to have the excuse to come back to Raleigh to check in with everyone here. The more distant I was getting from my Haven friends, the more I needed the people here.

Chapter Twenty-Eight

For our one-on-one time, I took Olivia to lunch at her favorite pizza place, hoping that her favorite food would encourage her to open up a bit. It wasn't working. She was slumped in her seat, her eyes level with the table, staring down the slice of cheese pizza in front of her.

"How are you doing, Olivia?"

She shrugged. "Fine. I don't want to talk about it."

"You don't want to talk to me about it, or anyone?"

"I don't want to talk about it."

This was going great!

"I've been thinking," I began, an introduction to something that had, in fact, popped into my head in that exact moment, "do you think you'd like Matt's bedroom?"

Olivia narrowed her eyes at me. "What?"

"I…I have to clean out his room," I stammered. "And I know you and Addy like sharing a room, but you might not always enjoy that. And if one of you were to move into Matt's room, it feels like that should be you."

She looked down at her pizza while she turned over my words. I prayed I hadn't misstepped. Giving that room a new purpose would force me to deal with the contents and not leave a gaping, empty room where my son used to be. And it would be a comfort to my youngest child. Olivia needed a way to hold onto the brother she loved so much. His room couldn't sit empty, taunting us, reminding us of how things used to be. I couldn't move the girls out of the only home they'd ever known, no matter how painful the memories. Leaving them behind would be so much worse.

"What if Addy wants it?" Olivia finally replied.

"I could explain my reasoning to her. You were always closer to Matt than she was, and I thought it was more appropriate."

"I'd like it very much. To have Matt's room."

"Okay. I'll clean it up for you."

"I miss them."

"I do too."

"Will I stop missing them?"

"I don't think so, but I think eventually it won't hurt so much."

She nodded. "I'm ready for it not to hurt, Mommy."

"Me too, baby."

I had selfishly hoped that this would be the panacea that gave me back my usual Olivia. She finished her pizza but declined a trip to the playground after. Instead we went home, and she settled on the couch with a book. I'd figure out how to help her, I was sure, but this time spent watching my daughter become a shell of herself was impossible.

Speaking of impossible.

I paused, my hand on the doorknob. Deep breath. I could do this.

Matt's room smelled musty, having sat unused all this time. It was just barely warm enough now to open the windows, and I let in light and fresh air as I faced the piles of things my son and husband had accumulated in life. I needed to start with something easy, something that I knew exactly where to put.

Matt's uniform.

The school board had informed us that they would be replacing the basketball uniforms for the next team. They didn't come out and say why, but I assumed it was something like not wanting the new kids to wear a dead kid's clothes. They'd been wearing their away uniforms when they'd died, but the school gifted their home uniforms to the families, giving us a precious memento. I could put his uniform in the same bin where I kept all his old uniforms, a chronicle of a decade of Matt's time on the court. Perfect. One thing done.

I would donate the rest of their clothes. Maybe I'd ask the girls if they wanted a few things. Olivia had occasionally stolen Matt's sweaters, even when he was alive. She'd probably love a couple to keep. I'd set a few things aside for them to go through.

It was too much. I'd never get through all of this today, not without a complete breakdown. I should have been doing a little bit every day since the accident. I should have organized myself better. I should have...

No. I'd done the best I could. I was taking care of my daughters. I was finishing the work I needed so that I could go back to teaching. I'd held a funeral for two people I loved more than anything. I had done so much, and while it may not have gone perfectly to now, I'd done my best.

Categories. I should put things in categories. Clothes, games, paper, keepsakes. Then I'd be able to see what things I could part with easily and what I needed more time for.

Or at least things would be organized when I simply packed it all away and stored it in the attic because I couldn't fathom the idea of getting rid of things that reminded me of them. Okay, things I thought I could go a while without seeing could go in the attic. Things I knew I'd want to see every day would stay out.

At least now I had a plan.

After an hour, I was sweaty and dust-covered, my face smeared with tears. This was going to take days. I could enlist help, calling in my mom or Amanda, or even Addy and Olivia, but what if they put something in the wrong place? I'd panic if I couldn't find some of the most precious things. Of course, I'd already sorted those out, Matt's uniform was packed away, Steve's wedding ring was still on my thumb, the most important of the memorabilia they'd collected throughout their lives. Still, what if six months or a year from now I remembered something that I absolutely had to lay my hands on at that exact moment, and I couldn't because someone else had packed it away for me?

I crawled into Matt's bed, emotionally exhausted. I hadn't found anything that I could bear parting with. I should have tried tackling this before I told Olivia that I'd clear the room for her.

My eyes lit on the small pile of Christmas gifts that I had wrapped for Matt and for Steve. When they died, I knew I couldn't see a stack of unopened gifts under the tree on Christmas morning. I'd hidden these presents in here, not knowing what else to do with them. Those I could get rid of. I had no strong associations with them. And I knew people who could use them. Okay. I was making progress after all.

I gathered a few things that I knew Landon could use, clothes, video games, books, and headed over to Amanda's to drop them off. It was an excuse to take a break from cleaning out Matt's room while actually, you know, cleaning out Matt's room.

"You didn't have to do this," Amanda said when I presented her with the gifts.

"I'd just throw them out if you guys don't want to take them," I replied.

She let me into her house, and we settled on the floor of the living room. We unwrapped the gifts, putting paper and boxes into the garbage and recycling. Clothes went into a pile for laundry, the video games went in a pile to go with Landon to the rehab facility.

"I appreciate you talking to the director of the rehab facility on Landon's behalf," Amanda said, her eyes on her work.

"Did it help?"

"Well, they're going to admit him on a provisional basis. It will at least give us time to find somewhere else, so we have a backup plan."

"How is he doing?"

She shrugged. "He's endlessly agitated. We can't keep him calm enough for him to start rehabbing his injuries. Maybe he needs, like, a psych facility, somewhere equipped for violent patients, but they won't take him if his body isn't functional enough. He's barely walking, so how would they deal with that at a psychiatric facility? They don't know what to do about fixing his body."

I wanted to do more, wanted to make this better. Nothing I did seemed like enough. I couldn't possibly solve this.

"Maybe the place in Raleigh can get his body well enough to be somewhere where they'll concentrate on his mind."

"Maybe. And maybe it doesn't matter if we get his body working right, because his brain is too broken. I don't know, Jo. Maybe none of this matters."

How could none of it matter? If people were trying to make her son better, shouldn't it have been the most important thing in the world right now? When would Amanda realize how lucky she was to have him here, to see him improving from where he'd been weeks ago?

"Is there anything else I can do to help?"

"You've done plenty." She wouldn't look at me. I couldn't tell if she meant it, and if it was a compliment if she did. Her voice was hard and cold, and that didn't bode well. "Sometimes I think you're single handedly keeping this town running. And this will mean a lot to Landon, to have some of Matt's things."

"If he ever feels up to it, he's welcome to come to the house and look through everything. I'm trying to clear out Matt's room, but…I hate it. I can't imagine getting rid of any of it, but I can't keep all of it either."

She grabbed my hand, finally meeting my gaze. "Oh, God, Jo, I'm sorry. That sounds awful."

"It is. All of it is. And I want to bury my head in the sand, and I can't. I already told Olivia she could have Matt's room, so I have to get it ready for her."

"You could take back the offer."

I shrugged. It wouldn't do me any good. The accountability was a boon, honestly. "She needs that though. I'm...I'm struggling to do right by the girls, Amanda."

"I'm sure when they're older, they'll look back on this time and know that you did your best."

"I want them to think that now. It does me no good for them to forgive me later for messing things up with them now."

"Don't be so hard on yourself."

I couldn't possibly. I couldn't stop worrying that I was ruining my daughters, that this time of overwhelming grief would be with them for the rest of their lives. Without a crystal ball to tell me that the future was going to turn out okay, I felt like I was fumbling on a daily basis.

"It's such a fine line, Amanda. Everyone's watching everyone else, because it's Haven. Everyone's judging. Everyone has an opinion on how I handle losing half of my family. I have to be perfect."

"Tell me about it." She sighed. "It's so easy to absorb in the abstract. My son bit a nurse. Okay, he's got this brain injury, and he doesn't always know where he is or who the people around him are. But then I think about it in detail. Landon bit Stephanie who sat behind me in AP Bio freshman year."

I grimaced. "Ugh. How mad was she?"

"It's not the first time a patient has done something they shouldn't. But she wasn't happy about it. Obviously. Part of me wants him out of Haven so that the judgment feels less personal. But part of me worries that in a place where they don't know him, they won't be as understanding when he acts out there."

"Haven isn't equipped to take care of him."

"No," Amanda said, shaking her head. "We have to send him away. At least in Raleigh there will be familiar faces."

"You know Reston will go into coach mode with him. As always."

"It's good to hear he's basically normal."

"Have you not talked to him?"

"I've got so much going on with Landon." Again, she wouldn't look at me. Was she being entirely honest about her reasons. "Reston's fine without me checking in on him."

"He's struggling with whether he'll be able to do the same things he used to do. I can't imagine Reston Tucker not capable on the court, you know?"

"How bad would things have to be to keep him off the court?" Amanda asked. "Like, if he is physically able to stand on two feet, he'll be there."

"I think he'd be out there if he was a sentient head in a jar. Nothing will keep him away. Unless it's decided that he can't coach anymore."

"No one in Haven would do that to him."

"Winning's important here."

"And Reston wins," Amanda replied.

She had me there. Still, I'd seen Reston run away from Haven before. I knew it wouldn't take much to run him off again.

"He's anxious about it, so now I'm anxious about it for him," I said.

"Oh, honey, don't take on our drama. You have your own stuff to worry about without worrying that Reston will lose his job and that Landon won't have a place to go when they kick him out of the hospital."

"Worrying about other people is what I do."

"And we all appreciate it. But now you can take a couple days off."

I could certainly use it, especially after today.

CHAPTER TWENTY-NINE

Cleaning out Matt's room was an endless, agonizingly slow process. In a perfect world, I would have kept it exactly as it had been on the day we lost him, a shrine to my beautiful, perfect, firstborn son.

Since I'd already promised the room to Olivia, I debated renting a storage unit, an off-site shrine, but I knew that would be ridiculous and expensive, and not actually helpful. A storage unit wouldn't satisfy my desire to be able to put my hands on precious momentos at any moment.

A handful of things I couldn't leave my sight. Steve's wedding ring was the worst. He no longer wore his wedding ring, which meant our marriage was over. I couldn't handle that finality.

I'd let the girls loose in the things Matt and Steve had left behind, they'd gone nuts. Olivia always had one of Matt's sweaters on, all of them reaching past her knees, none of them appropriate for the heat of the approaching summer. Addy wore Steve's watch now, once we'd poked a new hole in the band to tighten it, giving her a constant reminder of her dad no matter where she was. It made it easier to clear out their belongings, seeing them in the boys' things. It was still hard, but no longer utterly heartbreaking.

Many nights, I fiddled with Steve's ring, moving it back and forth between my fingers, the light glinting off the gold. What was I supposed to do with this? Put it away somewhere? Keep wearing it? Hold onto it in case the girls wanted it? Pawn it?

I was still wearing my rings, unsure of what to do with them as well. Those seemed like better heirlooms for the girls. I wanted to keep Steve's ring for myself, but what could I do with it? It would be nice to wear it, but it was cumbersome on my thumb. It might eventually be loose enough to fall off, and I couldn't bear the idea of losing it.

And that's how I ended up in a jewelry store, still not entirely sure what I was doing there. Downtown Haven didn't have much, a strip mall of businesses and shops. Some of them had been around since before I was born, some were new, but the feel of downtown never seemed to change. The bells on the door to the jeweler jangled as I walked inside, and the proprietor emerged from behind the counter at the sight of me.

"Hey, Jo," Carl said.

He'd run the shop for years, taking over from his dad, who took over from his mom, and back for generations. He'd know what I should do.

"Hey, Carl." I set the ring on the counter, jumping at the clatter of gold on glass. "I need to have this made into something."

"Steve's wedding band."

"Yeah."

We'd bought our wedding bands here, together, about a week before the big day. Apparently we should have done so sooner, because on our wedding day, my ring was still being resized. Bittersweet tears stung my eyes remembering how we'd scrambled to have something Steve could put on my finger during the ceremony.

"We could resize it so that you can wear it," Carl said. "Or melt it down, maybe add some sort of stone. What are you thinking? Earrings? A pendant?"

"If you melt it down," I asked, "can it be shaped like anything?"

"Pretty much, within reason."

If I could have a talisman, something to represent Steve for me for the rest of my life, what would that be?

"I'd like a pendant," I said slowly, "shaped like the number twenty-seven."

Carl nodded. "That's doable. What's the significance, if you don't mind me asking?"

"It was Steve's number. When he played."

"A great memorial then."

"I can only hope."

"I can't promise that nothing will go wrong in the construction," Carl said. "I hope you know I'll do everything in my power to make it perfect."

"Thanks."

I stared at Steve's ring for a moment, willing myself to walk away. I'd only be away from it for a few days. I'd get it back.

And even if that wasn't true, this ring couldn't fix any of what I'd been through. Having it in my hand didn't bring Steve back. Sending it out in the world, however briefly, wasn't a betrayal and didn't mean I was letting go of Steve.

"I'll call you as soon as it's ready," Carl said softly.

"Looking forward to it," I replied.

Further down the line of shops was a boutique full of random treasures, and I stepped inside, looking for something special to keep my rings in, when I was ready to take them off. Somewhere they'd be safe, for however long I needed them kept safe.

I found a beautiful decorative bowl, exactly the right size to sit on my dresser and hold these small, utterly critical heirlooms. It would be perfect when I finally talked myself into taking them off. I figured it would be a gradual process: first growing accustomed to seeing the dish on my nightstand, then placing my rings inside it when I was sleeping, then forgetting to put them on again in the morning.

I also picked up a few more plastic bins. I was making slow progress on packing up their things, but it was progress. That was all I was asking of myself.

Every time I walked into Matt's room, I was stunned by the state of it. This time it was the shock of how empty it was. It always felt like there was more to do, that I'd never be done. But I was close to finishing. By the end of the summer, Olivia could move in, if she was ready.

I folded Matt's comforter and tucked it into a bin, marveling at the passage of time. How had it been four months since the accident? Back then, it had seemed like time should stop, like we should stay as we were. But we were all getting better, moving forward, as painful as it was.

They had died on the winter solstice, the day with the longest night, the darkest day of the year. It had literally been getting lighter every day since they'd died. It was horrible to think that we were healing from the loss, but that was destined to happen.

I was nearly done finishing my teacher certification, and already had a spot promised to me at Haven High for the fall, teaching junior year English. I was subbing as often as possible, at least once a week, jetting all over the school district. I wasn't sure how going back to work fulltime would go, but luckily I had my old lesson plans to fall back on. They'd need updating, but I was sure I'd be okay, even with sixteen years off to raise my kids.

And enough time had passed that we had only one group text again.

I'd been the one to cross the line, after I'd told the people in my group that I was planning to. When I told them I'd be sending a message to the other group, Keely had responded, "Of course it's you. It was always going to be you who brings us back together."

"We're all sorry," I'd written. "You're all sorry. Let's all be better, because that's what the boys would want."

It had taken some time, but Natalie replied eventually, echoing Keely's words. "Of course you're the one reaching out."

It wasn't easy, and there was still some tension in the group. At first, I wasn't sure we still needed a group text. We didn't have snacks for practices or games to carpool to. We didn't have a team to manage.

But we were the people who understood the most. These were the women who were feeling all the same things I was. The women who had buried their sons. It was a terrible tribe, and none of us wanted to be part of it, but here we were. When someone didn't know what to say to their living children, they came to the group. When someone couldn't stop crying long enough to fall asleep at night, the group was there to talk to them until they could. When birthdays passed, the group was there to remember.

We had each other again.

CHAPTER THIRTY

I gasped at the sight of Reston on my front porch. I was rougher than I should have been as I threw my arms around him, forgetting that his balance was probably not at its best. He'd been gone for three months, and it was starting to feel like he'd never be back.

"You're home."

He laughed. "I am."

"Come in!" I backed up to give him space. "Why didn't you call? Are you driving yourself?"

"I am. I'm mostly normal now."

Except that he used a cane as he hobbled to my living room, favoring his faulty left leg. I did my best not to let that be a gut punch, but it was hard to see Reston, a lifelong athlete, unable to do the things he's always done. He wasn't tall like Steve, but he'd always been fast, dodging and darting around the court, no one able to keep up, including his teammates. Now his movements were slow and careful, and he grimaced against what I hoped was mere discomfort and not pain.

He sat on the couch with a groan, fumbling with the cane, unsure of where to put it.

"It's fine wherever," I said.

"I know. I hate it, Jo."

"I'm sure. I can't imagine…will you be able to stop using it?"

"Maybe. We'll see how the physical therapy goes."

"You're seeing someone here for that?"

"Yeah, Jesse, he's taken care of me and my players before, so it'll be good to be in familiar hands."

"I know Jesse. Have you seen him yet?"

"Tomorrow. I've been doing some stuff back in Raleigh, obviously, so I'm better than I was."

Reston was home, one piece righting itself after so much had been shaken up. I could breathe that much easier.

"I'm glad you decided to come back," I said.

"When I first came back, way back when, you told me I belong here. And I do, Jo, no matter how much I fight it."

"They didn't name it Haven to be cute."

"I'm fairly certain they did," he replied, smiling softly.

"Then it's nice that it worked out for the founders."

"They said I can come back to teach, but I'm going to wait until the fall. Unclear about the coaching. They want me to get a medical clearance."

"Do you think you can get that?"

He shot his eyes at the cane. "Not yet. But I have time before the season starts."

"Don't they need to look for someone else in the meantime?"

"There isn't a team right now, and who knows when there will be one again."

"How could there not be a team?"

It felt like a betrayal of the boys in a way I couldn't put my finger on. It felt like giving up, admitting defeat, and I wasn't prepared to do that.

"Who's going to play, Jo? I had twelve guys, none of them are coming back. I'd have to build a team from scratch, and I can't even walk."

"You're walking great," I said, thankful to see him walking at all after all these months in casts.

"I'm not. I will, but I'm not."

"Do you want to go back to coaching?"

159

He shook his head slowly. "I don't know. I miss my boys, Jo. You understand, of course, because you do too."

"Every minute."

"They're irreplaceable."

"They are."

Reston shrugged. "So, no, I don't know how I go back on that court without them. But I'm also not sure how I live the rest of my life without coaching. Or how I let someone else step into my job."

"You'll figure it out."

"I know. We'll all figure all of it out, right?"

"God, I hope so."

I couldn't stop staring at him, marveling at how much better it made me feel to have him home, where he belonged. This was the first sign that everything would be okay.

"For now I want to take care of you," I said. "What help do you need? What can I do?"

"I don't need help."

"What word do you need me to substitute so that you'll let me help? Assist? Can I be your assistant coach?"

Reston laughed, looking at his feet for a moment before flicking his eyes back up at me. "Yeah, okay. Assistant Coach Grant. That feels familiar."

His laugh set off the butterflies in my stomach. I wanted to get him to make that sound again. I pushed aside the nagging voice that told me that Matt and Steve would never laugh again, because I couldn't hear that right now. Today, I would hold onto a moment of joy.

"Should I be involved in your physical therapy? Maybe come up with a conditioning plan?" I teased.

"Good Lord, no, Josephine," he replied, still grinning at me.

"Just tell me what you need from me, Coach Tucker."

Suddenly he was serious. "I need to hear you call me Coach Tucker every day for the rest of my life." He held my gaze.

The way he looked at me knocked the air out of my lungs. I remembered how smitten teenaged Jo had been with him, with good reason. He'd sucked me into his deep brown eyes, and I was trapped.

"You know you are, right?" I asked once I could speak again. "You will always be the coach. No matter what happens from here."

"I know that sounds nice, and I wish it were true."

"Do you want something to eat, Coach?"

He snorted out a breath of laughter. "Sure, Jo. Since you so desperately need to take care of me, you're welcome to feed me."

I headed for the kitchen before he could change his mind.

"Have you lost weight?" I called over my shoulder. "I can help you bulk back up."

"I've lost muscle mass. Atrophy is a bitch."

"I'll get you some lean protein, gotcha."

"I need a weightlifting regimen, but that's for Jesse to deal with."

"It'll help your leg, right? To build the muscle back up."

"That's what I'm hoping."

I returned with a turkey and avocado sandwich. It was what I always made for my boys after a workout, or whenever they needed a post-game snack. I liked being in my normal routine. Maybe that's why I'd latched onto helping Reston.

"You know I'm here for you, right?" I asked. "Anytime you need me."

"I've always known that."

I sat beside him on the couch, so that I could look him in the eye. I needed him to hear me, to truly listen to what I was telling him.

"Anytime. I mean that. You can call anytime. Stop by whenever. We're always glad to have you. You're our family, Reston."

"I don't know what I'm going to do if I can't go back to coaching."

"Maybe you could go back to coaching kids."

"If I can't keep up with high schoolers, I won't be able to keep up with kids who need me to illustrate every movement."

161

"Then get a good assistant?"
"I believe I already have one."
I smiled. We were going to be a hell of a team.

CHAPTER THIRTY-ONE

When the jeweler called to say that my pendant was ready, I struggled to keep the car at a reasonable speed as I rushed over to retrieve it.

"We've got it on an eighteen-inch chain." Carl stepped behind me to fasten the clasp. "We can switch it out for something longer or shorter, whatever you'd like."

The gold was chilly against my skin, but I'd get used to it, the same way I had with the rings I occasionally no longer wore, but which had been so foreign when Steve had first slipped them onto my finger. I couldn't stop my thumb from looking for the ridge of my wedding and engagement rings now on the days when I forgot to put them on.

I traced the pendant, my eyes drifting closed as I pictured that Steve, number twenty-seven, who would make a basket and then look for me in the stands. I loved the glint he'd get in his eyes in those moments. He was proud of himself and showing off just a bit for me.

"It's perfect, Carl, thank you," I said, once I'd taken a moment to pull myself together. I didn't want to cry. Not again. "What do I owe you?"

"It's our gift to you, Jo."

"You don't have to do that."

"It feels like the right thing to do. It's important to us."

"Thank you."

"I wish there were more we could do."

I wished no one had a reason to do things for me.

It was wonderful how this town came together, how everyone took care of us and all the other families. The alternative, though, was having the boys here, and I would always rather that.

I grasped Carl's hand. "I can't tell you what this means to me."

I couldn't keep my hands off the pendant. Every time my fingers scrolled along the numbers, I'd get a flash of Steve, of his voice, his laugh, his touch. I felt him with me in a way I hadn't since I'd lost him, even though I was standing on the sidewalk, blocking pedestrian traffic. A breeze whipped around me, and I closed my eyes, letting Steve's presence envelop me.

And then Reston's voice pulled me back.

"Jo."

My eyes snapped open. "Hey. Hi. Fancy running into you out and about."

He looked stronger, more like himself, only older, changed by the last few months. He had color in his skin again, his usual haircut. Normal Reston.

"Sorry I interrupted you," he said.

"You're fine."

"You looked so happy. Like I haven't seen you in a while."

"I was. I was having a moment." I tucked a wayward lock of hair behind my ear. It was a rare nice day—the spring had been unusually rainy—only a light breeze and a smattering of clouds. A perfect day to stand outside and chat with a friend.

"Is that new?" Reston asked.

I glanced down at the pendant, my fingers once again going to it. "Yes and no. It was Steve's wedding band. They changed it for me. So I can keep it with me."

"That's nice." Reston nodded slowly. "And then you were having a moment. I'm even sorrier that I interrupted."

"It's honestly okay. What has you out of the house?"

"Physical therapy." He nodded toward Jesse's office a couple doors down the block.

"How's that going?"

"I hate it so much," he said with a laugh. "I'm weak and sore, and I hate it."

"But you'll get better."

"Yeah, I know. It's good for me, and I won't stop going, I promise."

"I wasn't worried about that. I know you want to get better. How are you feeling?"

He shrugged. "Good days and bad, of course. You?"

"Same."

"Today you were having a good day."

"I still am," I replied.

"Glad to hear it."

The wind blew my hair across my face again, and this time Reston tucked the errant strands behind my ear, his fingers brushing whisper soft against my skin. My mouth went dry. Surely we'd had physical contact over the years, but somehow this was different.

I licked my lips, trying to think of something to say, anything that wouldn't give away what I was thinking.

"So were you heading to your appointment, or heading home?"

"I am," he flicked his wrist, checking his watch, "late for my appointment, actually."

"Can I walk with you?"

He glanced down at the cane he held in his fist. He held it parallel to the sidewalk, not at all useful.

"I don't need help," he finally replied. "But yeah, you can walk with me."

"I haven't seen Jesse in a while. It'll be nice to say hi."

Jesse was waiting for Reston in the lobby of his office. When we walked through the door, he glanced at his watch and raised a brow.

"You get later every session," he commented.

"Yeah, yeah."

Jesse rose from his chair before crossing the room and wrapping me in his arms.

"Jo, I'm so sorry. I haven't seen you in forever, and I'm not sure I ever got a chance to tell you how sorry I am."

"Thanks. I appreciate it. I'm, you know, better, usually."

"Glad to hear it. You should talk to Reston about being on time."

"I think we all know how well he listens to others."

"And you can imagine how well physical therapy is going," Jesse replied.

Reston rolled his eyes. "Thanks, everybody. 'Bye, Jo."

"Good luck with him."

Jesse laughed. "Oh, I'll need it."

CHAPTER THIRTY-TWO

Even though Reston was back, we kept up our regular phone calls, propping each other up the best we could. Big problems, little annoyances. It was good to have someone I knew would listen these days.

Or someone who could come to me for anything, for better or worse.

"I have to go to graduation," Reston grumbled over the line.

"You don't have to do anything."

"That's what my therapist says."

As usual during our calls, I was in the middle of cleaning the kitchen, the girls in bed for the night. I slid the phone between my ear and shoulder as I wiped down the counter, doing my best to focus.

"You're still seeing your counselor type person?" I asked, somewhat surprised given how much he pushed back against his physical therapy appointments.

"I'm still seeing my therapist, yeah. Aren't you seeing someone?"

"No." I didn't have the time, and I was getting through each day well enough at this point.

"No?" He nearly shouted it, and I fumbled the all-purpose spray I had in my hand. His indignation shocked me, but what was I supposed to do? Taking any amount of time to focus on myself wasn't in the cards at the moment. "What about the girls?"

"They see the crisis counselor at the school."

"How's that going?"

"It seems to be helping," I replied.

After the initial reluctance, they'd both admitted that they were talking to her pretty regularly. And they both seemed a bit more even keel these days. It didn't magically fix any of this, but they were better.

Reston continued, and I heard the admonition behind his words. "It's been good for me to have my therapist. And to have the meds she gives me."

"You're on meds?"

"Yeah, for the anxiety, mostly. Why do you sound so shocked?"

"I don't know," I replied honestly.

It certainly made sense. The accident had been hard on him—understandably. And while he was stubborn, he'd always done what doctors told him to do to keep himself in the best possible shape. Apparently what he needed now was medication to make himself well.

Still, his initial reluctance to talk about getting help clouded my acceptance of reality.

"You should think about therapy," Reston said.

"Yeah, I'll cram it in between single parenting and my full-time job and everything else I'm trying to make time for."

"You have to prioritize yourself."

"I honestly can't, Reston. How could I? My best friend is barely speaking to me. Most of my other close friends aren't speaking to me at all. My parents have their own lives. Not to mention the effort that goes into finding a doctor, making sure they take my insurance. Oh, and they can't be too far away, because the added commute time is only going to make it harder. But I don't want someone here, because I'll be too self-conscious to talk to a local about my innermost thoughts. And what if it's not a good fit, and I need to go through it all over again to find someone else?"

"Okay, that's all valid," Reston said. "But it's also important to take care of yourself."

"I am, it just looks different for me. It's not talking to a therapist. It's helping people around town, and keeping myself busy, and making sure you're doing okay."

He laughed. "I'm great. Except for this graduation thing."

"Right," I said, remembering why he'd called. "You don't have to go."

"I always go. Not just to say goodbye to my players, but all my students. I'd hate for any of them to think that...I don't know. That I'm not proud of them. That I'm not impressed by how hard they have worked this year, after everything that happened."

"They all know what you've gone through," I replied. "No one would blame you for staying away."

"I know. But I want to be better. I want to be there for my kids."

"What are you afraid of? Why are you worried about going?" I asked.

"I don't want everyone to see me breakdown. And I know I will."

I listened to what he was saying, and heard what he was leaving out.

"And you don't want to look vulnerable?"

"Of course I don't. When have I ever?"

"Fair enough."

"I don't know how I sit there and see the empty seats where my players are supposed to be, where Steve's supposed to be, and not fall apart."

"No one will judge you."

"I know. And I know everyone knows I've been falling apart behind closed doors for the past five months. This feels like too much."

We'd all been falling apart behind closed doors, and some of us had been falling apart in public. And I needed to believe that meant that no one's grief was being judged, even if I knew that wasn't always true.

"Then don't go. Take care of yourself first."

"Oh, I see, turning my advice on me."

"Yep."

"It doesn't really solve anything though," Reston said. "If I'm not there, they all know why."

"Of course they do. Reston, everyone knows everything. If you don't go, they know it's because of the crash. If you go, and you're broken up, they know it's because of the crash. You're not hiding anything."

"I want to believe that I am."

"That's not how it works," I said, trying not to sound angry. It's not as if anyone would be fooled even if he showed up and managed to make it through without shedding a tear.

"How terribly unfair," he replied dryly.

"We could come to graduation with you."

"No," he said.

"Wow, okay," I said with a laugh.

"I'm sorry. But, no, there's no way you guys are there and aren't also crying. I can't do that. To you or to myself."

He wasn't wrong. We attended graduation every year, because Steve wanted to be there to celebrate his students and players, and these days Matt wanted to support his friends. I tended to get emotional. Basketball boys were always in our house, and I got to know them all. Seeing them on the verge of adulthood, of moving away, choked me up.

Now I'd be wrestling with the same things Reston was: empty space. The space where all those boys were supposed to be. The empty seat beside me where my husband was supposed to be. The empty space in our row where Matt fit.

"You're right," I said. "It would be a terrible idea for us to come with you."

"I don't know that there's anyone who could serve as my support for this," Reston replied.

"Well, no one there has it out for you or anything," I said, knowing it wasn't true, but wishing that the people of this town who had known Reston for decades would forgive him for what little part he played in this tragedy.

"That might not be true."

"I have to believe it's true, Reston."

"Yeah, I know."

"Does your therapist tell you it's okay for everyone to see you cry?"

"Yes."

"She's not wrong."

"No, she's not," he replied. "I know it will be okay, no matter how emotional I get."

"It will."

"She's always telling me that no one is judging me. That these are my friends."

"Exactly."

"It's still scary. And it's still hard for me to believe it all the time."

"Sure."

"Thanks for listening. Talking through it helps, even if I haven't figured out what to do."

"Of course," I replied. "It's the least I can do."

I was always willing to be a sounding board for Reston, as he tried to figure out how to navigate his life now. If only because I needed the same from him.

Hell, we all needed that.

CHAPTER THIRTY-THREE

Before I knew it, school was out for summer. I'd made arrangements with several of the girls' friends' families for childcare exchanges, me keeping groups of kids during the day and the other families helping me out on evenings or weekends if I needed to run errands. Our house was noisy again, bustling with preteen girls. I chauffeured trips to the pool, the park, the library. I'd canceled the trip Steve and I had scheduled, and instead the girls and I spent a week at the beach. I did everything I could to keep us all busy enough to forget about our missing pieces.

Then suddenly all was silent, the girls in Charlotte for a week with their grandparents. I couldn't remember the last time I'd been on my own for this long. Definitely before I got married. If I were in high school, I would have had a party, acting as if my parents wouldn't find out later, but of course they would. I'd either fail to erase the evidence of the party, or the neighbors would snitch on me, or my friends' parents would tell. It never stopped me from doing the same thing again the next time my parents were gone, or my friends from doing the same. For the first couple days, the calm was nice. I used the time to work on my lesson plans for the upcoming school year. Eventually, though, the quiet built up until it was too much.

I invited Amanda over, assuming that she could probably use a break. I let her into the house just as a low rumble of thunder sounded in the distance. It had rained so much in the spring, the skies weeping along with the people of our town, and now the summer was proving to be stormier than usual. I guess the Haven weather had moved from depression to anger.

"I appreciate you coming over," I said as Amanda and I prepared drinks and snacks in my kitchen.

She handed me a glass of wine, and we moved to the living room and settled on the couch. "I'm thankful for an excuse to leave the house. We spent so much time in the hospital, and now I find my house weird, I guess. Quiet. Not full of strangers."

"How's Landon doing?"

"Better! He and Isaiah spend a lot of time together at the rehab center. Thankfully it turns out that's exactly what he needed. Landon's calmer there, he's making progress. I finally have the sense that he'll be able to come home."

I squeezed her hand. "I'm so glad, Amanda."

"How are you doing?"

I shrugged, taking a sip of my wine. "I'm okay? It's all easier, but...I miss them so much. Having the girls off with Steve's parents has been impossible, like, what am I even supposed to do with myself?"

"You're a person outside of being a wife and mother."

"Of course, but that's how I've identified myself. Being a mom is my job, you know?"

"Soon you'll have an outside-the-house job too. All day every day, I mean."

"Exactly, and how do I manage being a mom and working full time, which I've never done before, and I'm on my own. What do I do if the girls are sick? What do I do if I'm sick?"

"You know I'll always help."

"You have so much of your own stuff to worry about though."

Amanda shrugged. "For the time being, I don't so much. It does more harm than good for us to be around Landon, because it just gets him agitated and he acts out. Until that changes or until he comes home, he doesn't get a lot of my attention."

I cringed. "That sounds awful, for him and you."

"Oh, it is, truly. I feel guilty about not seeing Landon more. Before that, I was guilty about basically ignoring Elliot. It's a tradeoff. I have to tell myself that the place in Raleigh's taking great care of Landon, and we go see him plenty. In the meantime, I'm doing all the things that fell through the cracks while he was in the hospital. The house might actually be clean at some point."

"I'd be glad to—"

"No!" Amanda said, holding up a hand. "You don't need to help me anymore. You have your own stuff to worry about."

"You know me, Amanda. I need to be helping."

"Of course I know that. But I think it's time for me to stand on my own feet, you know? This is the calm for us, while Landon's in rehab. Once he's home, things will be hard. I don't know how we'll manage, because I don't know how severe his issues will be by then. I'm trying to enjoy the last weeks of normal life."

I laid my head on her shoulder. "It's hard to accept that this is normal life. The boys are gone. Landon's...changed. I hate all of it."

"Agreed. Eventually we won't hate it. I hope."

"I can't believe it's been six months. For so long it felt like a nightmare I'd wake up from but now..."

"It's normal life."

"Exactly. And how can it possibly be normal for Matt and Steve to be gone?"

"How can it possibly be normal that Landon has to be taught to feed himself?"

"How is this life?"

Amanda shook her head. "We had everything figured out. Now we're starting over from scratch."

Of course we weren't, not really. So much of our previous lives were still there. The missing pieces, though, were staggering.

"Thanks for coming over," I said. "I don't know how I'm going to manage having friends once I'm working and have the girls on my own. It's nice to have this last gasp of my old life."

"I'll do my best to keep our friendship going," Amanda replied.

"Text me all the time. I feel like it'll be my only means of communication with the outside world."

"And I'll see you at practice." We both froze, staring at each other with wide eyes. Hanging out together while our boys practiced was our habit, and it had been torn from us, the same way the boys had. "Oh, my God. No, I won't. How could I forget that?"

It had been one of the most consistent things in our lives for a decade, and now it was over without warning. When the fall came, and I wan't sitting in that gym every week, it would make this more real. What would I do then? How could things possibly feel normal again without getting together at the gym?

"Reston says they might not have a team this year," I said softly.

Amanda shook her head. "How weird would that be?"

"Right? But also how weird would it be to watch some other team play on that court?"

"And for Reston to have a new team."

I paused. "Assuming they let him coach."

"There's something I hadn't even considered."

"He'd been talking about leaving again."

"Okay, that I'd considered," Amanda said. "That's standard Reston. Things are hard here, I'd better leave."

"I understand all of that."

"I'd want to leave if I were him. No ties. Angry townspeople."

I hunched my shoulders, pulling into myself. "I'm never going to be on Team Reston Should Leave."

"Me neither, but he's an adult and he gets to make that choice. He knows what's best for himself, as hard as that is to believe."

She had me there. Still, I fought back.

"I want things to go back to normal. As impossible as that is. If Reston leaves, it's that much worse, one more thing that's changed since the accident."

"I can't argue with that. But I also don't know that it's good for anyone for him to stay. Not even for you." I opened my mouth to protest, and Amanda held up a hand to stop me. "You take on so much of everyone else's pain. You can't keep doing that. It's not good for you. It might be better for you to have one less grieving person in your life."

"It would be nice if it were that easy, Amanda. I can't just turn off caring about people."

"Don't I know it." She sighed. "I should get home to my family."

I bit my lip, wishing I had a family to be with right now. "Thanks for coming over," I finally said. "We'll do this again soon, I promise."

And I was left alone again in my too quiet house. The silence never got easier. I couldn't imagine it ever would.

CHAPTER THIRTY-FOUR

Summer gave way to fall almost instantly as the school year began. The intense heat and wrathful thunderstorms gave way to cooler temperatures and brilliant foliage. If only I could have been as calm as the weather.

Even though I'd spent the spring in and out of classrooms and the summer preparing for the first day of school, agonizing over my lesson plans, worrying that I wouldn't have anything to wear, the day snuck up on me.

I dropped Olivia at the elementary school, Addy at the middle school, and continued on to the high school to start my first day. At the start of the previous school year, Steve and I had talked about how rough it was going to be to have the kids at three different schools, and how urgent it was that we get Matt a car to ease that burden, taking at least one school off my drop off list. Instead, I managed on my own. I'd have to get all three of us out the door with everything we needed for the day, and I'd have to get us to three different locations, and then collect everyone at the end of the day. It might be impossible, but I was going to try my hardest.

I had a hard time believing they had let me back into a classroom. I had my license back in good standing, and I was teaching English again as if I'd never left. I knew these kids, friends of Matt's, kids I'd known forever. I knew the material, the usual Hamlet and Beowulf, the same things I'd taught all those years ago.

And day one was easy, all administrative tasks and handing out syllabi and textbooks. I wouldn't have to worry about grading essays for a month or so. I wasn't sure how I was going to find time for that, but I'd figure it out. I didn't have much choice.

Still, it was hard. Figuring out the teaching stuff, yeah, but also the way that, after all these months, I still expected to see my boys here.

Why didn't I ask for a spot at the middle school or elementary school instead? Okay, that wouldn't be what I was used to, and I'd have to start over with a new curriculum, but I'd have figured it out. Why did I say I could do this? What if I failed? I'd have no job, no income, and then how would I support our family? My chest tightened, my breath quickening. I didn't have a backup plan. This was Plan A through Z. It had to work.

It would work. I'd be fine.

I didn't have a ton of time at the end of the day to get my classroom ready for the next one before heading out to get the girls from their afterschool program. I scrambled to clean off my desk and erase that day's notes from the blackboard.

"Hey."

I turned, somehow surprised that Reston was here. As if his classroom weren't a hall away.

"Hey," I replied. "How was your first day back?"

He shrugged. "Fine, because I've been teaching for a while, and luckily the past rarely changes. Impossible, because...it will always be impossible."

"I hear you on that."

"How'd it go for you?"

"Much the same. I need to get back in the rhythm of having my own classroom but I'll get there. And it's still hard to be here when they aren't."

"Do you lie to yourself too and pretend that will change?"

I nodded. "Most days. How's your mental state?"

"It comes and goes."

"That's not good."

Though it was, of course, understandable, especially today.

Reston shrugged. "It's better than when I'm completely off the rails. Sometimes I don't think the accident was my fault, which is nice. It never lasts, but those brief guilt-free moments are the best."

"It wasn't your fault."

"I know. Even when things are dark, part of me knows that's true."

"Is therapy helping with that?"

"Mostly. Eleven people I loved died, Jo. And I…" he sighed and looked away from me. "I was there. I was in that bus with them, watching them die."

I froze, nearly dropping the eraser in my hand, stunned. I'd never considered that. I'd assumed that he'd been unconscious on the bus. But they'd told me he'd identified everyone, so he must have been alert. He'd been in the thick of the accident, and I'd never given that a thought. Maybe because he'd never said anything, or maybe because it was too horrible to comprehend.

"I'm so sorry, Reston," I sputtered.

He looked at the ground, tapping his cane against his right foot. "I hadn't brought it up before, because I can't stand to think about it. I can't think about that time. It seemed like days, but it was maybe half an hour before I was stashed in an ambulance and whisked away from them. There's a recording of my nine-one-one call. I've heard it, and I don't recognize my own voice."

I squeezed my eyes shut, trying to keep the images out, the sounds, the smells. I could hear their screams now, echoing in my head, and tears spilled from under my lids.

"I shouldn't have said anything," Reston said after a moment. "You're not okay."

"I'm fine." I tried to keep the tears out of my voice.

But then I sniffled, and the jig was up.

"I can't really hug you at work," Reston said. "I'm sorry."

I shook my head, shaking off the tears. "I'll be okay."

"I don't know how to tell you about that time in a way to make it hurt you less. I shouldn't have said anything in the first place."

I paused, knowing I shouldn't ask, but doing it anyway. "Did they suffer?"

"I don't want to do this. Not here, not like this."

"Lie to me, Reston. Make it okay."

"I can't," he replied, his voice anguished. "God, Jo, I'm sorry, I…I'm sorry. What can I do?"

"I don't know. You went through that. How are you still standing?"

"Just barely, and only with assistance," he replied, gesturing with the cane he carried grudgingly.

We both needed that break, a moment of levity, and suddenly there was oxygen in the room again. I gulped in great gasps of air, wishing he'd never said anything, wishing this had never become something I considered. The final moments of my son's life, my husband's life, needed to remain a mystery. He was right. There was no way for those moments to comfort me. Even if they'd died instantly, they were gone, and there was no fixing that.

"How are the girls?" he asked.

"Better," I replied. "I think it's good for them to be in school. They'll be busy. Their counselor is here, too."

"I'm glad to hear that. If they need anything, I'm here."

"Thank you, Reston."

"And if you need me to look over your quizzes or something, let me know. I was never any good with Shakespeare, but I'll try my hardest for you."

I laughed. "Thanks."

"Walk you to your car?"

"Please."

I was ready to get out of here.

CHAPTER THIRTY-FIVE

I certainly hadn't believed I was healed from losing Matt and Steve, but suddenly I was broken all over again. The idea that Reston had been there for their final moments, that he could tell me exactly what those moments had been like…it was torture. And if that's what it felt like for me, I couldn't imagine what he was feeling. And now I worried that would be too much, that the pain would keep him from ever being able to heal from his own trauma.

I tried to behave normally. I went to work. I took care of the girls. I kept the house together. But once again, I was simply going through the motions. It was hard to remember that things had value when half of my family was gone.

My phone chimed, a gentle text from Olivia's soccer coach.

"Hey, Jo," Brandon wrote. "Will Olivia be back this season? I didn't see her on the sign ups."

Oh, God. Something had slipped through the cracks.

It had always happened, from time to time, too many activities among too many children, but now it felt monumental. Grief-stricken, unable to cope with life. It felt like everyone was watching. Maybe not judging, exactly, but having opinions on how I was coping. This felt like a failure.

"Of course," I wrote back. "I'm sorry, did I miss the deadline, or will they let me sign her up?"

"No one's going to turn her away. Bring the enrollment fee to practice on Tuesday and we'll do the paperwork. No worries."

"Thanks for understanding."

"Of course!"

Oh, God, what else had I screwed up?

I texted Addy's dance instructor, convinced I'd missed tryouts.

"Next week!" she assured me. "I'll email you the details. I can text you a reminder that morning if it would help."

"Thank you, yes please!"

What if they were on the same night? What if we had to be in two places at one time? How was I supposed to manage that on my own?

Was I even sure I had the things they needed? What if Addy had outgrown her dance gear? What if Olivia had destroyed her only pair of shin guards? They almost certainly both needed new shoes.

It was too much again. It was more than I could handle. I didn't want to rally the good people of Haven because I needed to buy my daughters new shoes. And yet the idea of having someone help me right now felt so good. I was supposed to have that. I'd had a partner, someone who would always be there for me when life became overwhelming, who could take over when life was too much. How was I supposed to do this without him?

I stopped and took a breath. It was going to be okay.

I could do this. Everyone was watching, and I could show them that I could be a single mom, and keep up with everything the way I did when I had Steve to help me.

I hustled the girls into shoes and out the door. We were going to run all our errands, in record time, I was sure of it.

After a half hour drive, we learned the sporting goods store was out of cleats in Olivia's size, but I kept myself positive, telling the girls, "That's okay, Target will have them," and then, "Walmart will definitely have them," when Target didn't.

And then they didn't. Between the driving and the searching, it had been an hour and a half, and we'd accomplished nothing.

"It's going to be okay," I insisted. "We'll figure something out. Let's grab the groceries while we're here."

"I don't see why I had to come," Addy grumbled.

"I know, Addy, but I'd really appreciate you having a good attitude about it." I forced a smile on my face as I wheeled the cart toward the refrigerated section of the store. We needed milk, because we always needed milk.

Still, Addy continued to whine. "I'm old enough to stay home by myself."

"I know you are, Addy, but—"

I stopped, staring at the dairy case. How was this possible? How could a grocery store be out of milk?

"Chloe gets to stay home by herself."

I sank to my knees on the dirty floor. This was not a big deal, but I failed to logic my way out of falling apart. I started sobbing, illogically, because surely I'd find milk somewhere. But I was tired, and today had been long and difficult. If the boys were still alive, Matt would have stayed home with Addy, and Steve and I would have split the errands, and everything would have been easier. How was I supposed to do this by myself?

There was rustling beside me, and an arm smoothed across my back.

"I'm sorry," Addy said softly.

"It's not you," I replied, sitting up and rubbing tears from my cheeks.

"I'm not helping."

I shook my head. "No, but you don't have to. You're the kid and I'm the mom. It's my job to take care of you."

"We all take care of each other." Addy grabbed Olivia's hand to pull her down onto the floor with us. "Three Musketeers, right?"

I took a deep breath and pulled the girls against me. "Right. Okay. We'll figure this out."

"We for sure don't need milk," Olivia said. "It's not good for anything but cereal."

I struggled to my feet, then reached a hand out to each girl, pulling them up with me. "No milk. Now let's figure out the cleat situation."

It was time to enlist the other team moms, asking if anyone had size twelve cleats we could borrow until we found our own, or keep, or buy off them. It was worth a shot, and I kept my fingers crossed that someone would be a savior.

"Yep, I got you covered!" Heather replied. "I'll send them to school with Chloe on Monday."

"Oh, thank God," I replied. "Thank you! I'd forgotten all about soccer."

"Tell me about it. We were supposed to do baseball this summer. Oops."

"Us too," Jenna added. "And swim lessons. I'm surprised we made it through the rest of the last school year. If it weren't for school lunches, I don't think Jamie would have eaten lunch. I kept forgetting to pack it."

I heaved a sigh of relief reading their responses. It wasn't me. I wasn't failing. I was normal. Life after loss was hard, and I was doing my best, and it was going to be okay.

And Olivia was going to have soccer cleats. All I had to do now was remember to take her to practice.

Addy had begged to be excused from watching Olivia's practice, so I left her at Heather's house, where she could play with a friend and hopefully get her homework done. It freed me up to be in Mom Mode at practice. I concentrated on the paperwork for Olivia to rejoin her team. She'd need her pediatrician to sign off on a health form. She'd had a physical over the summer for school, and I could just get them a copy of that.

This year's uniforms were blue, which thrilled Olivia. It was a small victory, but clearly those were monumental these days.

It was comforting to see Olivia in her element. She wasn't great at soccer, but she was good enough, and loved it. She was barely nine years old, so she had time to get better if she wanted to. She looked happy on the field. I didn't get to see my kids looking happy lately.

It was the same thing at Addy's dance tryouts later that week. I couldn't be in the room with her, but we were allowed to watch through a two-way mirror. She lost herself in the music, in the repetition of the steps, and it filled my heart with joy to watch her. She was great at dance. She was precise with the steps, and passionate about performing them.

Watching her perform reminded me of how different my kids were. My wild youngest, fearless on the field. My artistic middle child. And my oldest, who had the vision for the game, who could see every possible outcome on the court. Who may not have been fastest, or tallest, or most skilled with the ball, but who knew instinctively exactly what to do.

I was thankful that we were returning to our routine, even as I nearly botched it. And when there were days when we needed to be in two places at one time, I knew I could find another family to help us. Everything was going to be okay.

Our routine felt off, of course. I was still washing athletic gear, but much less of it. A measurable absence of my son. I could measure it in the lack of size thirteen athletic shoes littering my entryway. In the lack of thuds as wayward basketballs crashed into the garage door. In the lack of noisy teenage boys coming and going from my house at all hours, as if they lived here.

I wondered if any of them would ever do that again. It wasn't just the team, although they were of course the most frequent visitors. Any number of the kids from the high school would stop in, the kids I saw now at work. I hoped Landon would recover to the point that he might stop by again, but who knew whether he'd be able to be on his own like that.

Reston at least would still stop by, the way he always had once he and Steve started coaching together. And my daughters would have their friends over, our house filled with the noise of girls instead.

Our new normal would, eventually, feel normal. It was taking longer than I'd hoped, longer than I thought I could handle.

And yet I was surviving.

CHAPTER THIRTY-SIX

I stripped the sheets of my bed and headed downstairs, needing to toss them into the washer. My mom had the girls for a couple hours so that I could get things done around the house. I had to get the girls' bedding washed too, the floors mopped or vacuumed, and I was hoping to clean out the girls' closets too. They were growing faster than I could keep up with, and the clothes jamming their drawers and spilling out of their closets didn't all fit.

Shoving the sheets into the washer, I was surprised by a familiar rhythmic thumping coming from outside. Who was playing ball in my driveway?

I started the wash cycle and stepped out the backdoor. Of course it was Reston. It was so normal to have him here, and yet it stung that Steve or Matt should have been here with him. His eyes were on the basket as he dribbled slowly before arcing the ball in a perfect shot. Swish. Nothing but net.

"Nice shot," I said.

He stumbled, missing the ball that he was trying to gather for another shot. "Hey. Sorry, did I disturb you?"

"Nope. This is a nice distraction from my chores."

"Want to play?"

"I'm not particularly good."

"I'll go easy on you. I kind of have to. Recovering from a broken leg, remember?"

He bounced the ball to me. I dribbled carefully, worried I'd lose control of the ball and embarrass myself. It had been a long while since the days of parents vs. kids games at practice.

"Come on, Grant," Reston said, a teasing note to his voice. "Show me what you've got."

"Not much," I muttered, tossing the ball toward the basket.

It hit the backboard, skittering wide. Reston chased the ball down, bouncing it back to me again.

"Bend your knees. Relax your arms."

"Whatever you say, Coach."

It took a couple more tries, and more of his teaching, for me to get the ball in the basket. Once I had a feel for it, though, I sank a succession of shots.

"All right, now I'm going to play defense," Reston said.

"No," I protested. "I thought we were having fun."

"It'll still be fun."

"Not once you start trying to score too."

He laughed. "I said I'd go easy on you."

And he did, for a while. He'd knock my shots away from the basket, but he didn't rush me. He didn't pressure me to make a move.

For a while.

The game got more physical, Reston between me and the basket. I couldn't push past him and still dribble, so I turned my back to him, trying to get an angle on him. My back was against his chest, heat radiating from his body. I closed my eyes, inhaling the scent of his sweat, feeling the pounding of his heart, the rise and fall of his breathing. My mouth went dry, and I did my best to swallow. I wanted to turn around, but I knew if I did, I would kiss him.

We were in my driveway. All of Haven could have seen us, and then what?

"Everything okay?" Reston murmured against my ear.

I'd stopped dribbling, holding the ball in my hands. This was no longer friends goofing off, having fun together. This was me realizing that I wanted—badly—to take Reston inside and make love to him on my unmade bed. The lust had bubbled inside of me unexpectedly, but my husband, I couldn't do that to him, even if he wasn't...

"I have to get back to my chores," I replied, taking half a step away from Reston.

He straightened away from me. "I should have asked before I came over."

I shook my head, still not turning to look at him. "It's fine. You're welcome anytime. Always. That doesn't have to change. I don't want anything to change."

"Jo."

His voice was rough, barely above a whisper. His fingers circled my wrist, pulling me back. He tilted his head, looking down at me. I knew that head tilt, instinctively, a move I'd seen from Reston more times than I could count. I tried to inhale, but couldn't. We couldn't do this. Not yet. Not in my driveway.

I wasn't allowed to want him to touch me. I wasn't allowed to be happy. I couldn't do this.

"You're welcome to stay," I said, my head down, my eyes trained on the ground. Reston being at my house was normal. It was normal for him to come and go as he pleased, and telling myself it was normal didn't make it feel that way. Still, I was rushing toward my house, refusing to look at him. "And if you need some water or whatever, the house is open to you. Anytime you need it."

"Can we talk?"

"I don't think I can right now."

"Can I help with the chores?"

"It's just laundry and stuff. I've got it."

"Then I'm going to reiterate my request that we talk."

I paused, halfway through the door. "Another time, Reston."

I shut the door between us, struggling to breathe as tears streamed from my eyes. How could this be happening? How could

I have feelings for him, after all this time? Had I felt this way all along? Had Steve noticed?

The washing machine chimed at me, reminding me that life still needed my attention. I couldn't fall apart. No matter how awful this all felt.

CHAPTER THIRTY-SEVEN

When I came back downstairs after making my bed, Reston was sitting on the couch. I yelped at the sight of him.

He held up his hands in front of him. "I'm sorry."

I put my hand on my chest, once again trying to gather myself. "It's fine. I said you could come and go."

"You know that's not why I was apologizing."

"I'd hoped."

"I thought I could keep going along without anything happening with you, and I'm sorry I…couldn't."

"What are you talking about?" I sat on the stairs, a safe distance from him.

"These past few months, I let myself believe that there was some way we could…" He regarded the ceiling for a moment before looking back at me. "That this could be something. I shouldn't have let myself think that."

I frowned. "When did you start thinking of me like that?"

He shrugged. "When I was twelve, I think."

Oh, for crying out loud. Not the man who had turned me down the first time I asked him out when we were fourteen, whose mother had to force him to agree to take me out, who was dragged reluctantly along on our dates for months before he finally engaged in our relationship.

"Alright, if you're not going to take this seriously—" I started.

He cut me off, raising his voice. "Excuse me? You think you know better than I do how I've felt about you all this time, and how hard I have worked to make sure you don't know?"

"Then why?" I asked. "Why did you fight against dating me? Why did you leave? Why have you never said anything?"

He threw up his hands in defeat. "What was I supposed to say? I have only ever been sure of two things: how much I loved you, and how much I hated this town. Those things aren't compatible, Jo."

He wasn't wrong. No matter how I felt about him, it had never been enough to make me willing to leave behind everything I had here.

"All this time?" I asked, my head in my hands. "You've felt this way this whole time?"

"Yes."

"Did Steve know?"

Reston laughed, and I looked back up at him.

"Yes," he said. "From the first time Steve saw us together, he was aware."

"How is that possible?"

"For you, it was business as usual, you and me going right back to how we've always been. For him, it was seeing some guy flirt with his wife. He didn't waste time before letting me know I needed to watch myself. And I have been watchful."

"Why now?"

"I don't know. Because it's easy to tell myself that Steve's gone and that means something. But it can't mean something. Not in this town."

Never in this town, where our business was everyone's business. Where the judgment would come from all sides.

"No."

"And that's ignoring...you just lost your husband."

I nodded. "That's right."

"And he was my best friend."

"Yep."

"And there's no way I can ask that."

"What *are* you asking, Reston?" I asked, my voice soft, my tone gentle. He couldn't be enjoying any of this. I certainly wasn't. The pain in his voice, the misery of how impossible this future was, the shock of his revelation.

He rubbed his face with his hands, then met my eyes. "I don't know. I don't know what I want, and I don't know if I can give you what you want."

"I know you can't." I wanted none of this. I wanted my husband to be alive. I wanted Steve, and no amount of whatever might happen with Reston would change that.

Reston was great, and I loved him in my own way, and apparently when left to its own devices, my body had some thoughts on what Reston could give me.

But.

But he wasn't Steve, and he could never be Steve. And even if I believed that he and I could be together without every single person in this town voicing an opinion, nothing could change that.

Of course, no one would be Steve. And maybe that meant never dating again. But maybe it meant dating this man who had loved me for over thirty years and had the sense not to say a word about it while I was married to someone else.

"I don't know how you managed," I said, "to convince me you never cared about me."

"I knew I had to leave, and that it was going to hurt you. I was dedicated to the lie," Reston replied with a laugh. "And then there was Steve, and he was too good, and I could never have done anything. Once he and I talked about it, I doubled down on my dedication. My relationship with you was something I was tricked into in high school, and I never wanted it. I left it behind and forgot about it the same way I did everything else."

"You know I truly believed that." My hurt from all those decades ago was suddenly fresh.

"I know, and I'm sorry for that too."

"You could have been honest with me."

"When? When I knew I was leaving and you weren't coming with me? When I came back, and you had a husband and a family?"

"I don't know." I shrugged. "And I don't know what you want from me."

"I don't know either. But we need to talk something out," Reston replied. "I know how things have been between us for a long time. What just happened in your driveway was different."

"It was," I admitted.

He paused, gazing at the floor. When he looked back up at me, my breath caught in my throat. There was no way around it. I wasn't sure I was ready to consider dating again, but I was going to have to get ready.

"I'm have to get the girls soon," I said softly.

"Conversation postponed?"

"I think that's the way of it, yes."

"Genuinely, Jo, I never meant to say any of this."

"That was optimistic of you."

He cocked his head. "It worked great for over thirty years."

"Shockingly."

"Will you call me?"

"Of course I will." I paused. "And what I said before stands. You are welcome here, Reston. You're part of our family, regardless of…anything else."

One corner of his mouth lifted in a smile. "Thanks."

The house felt different once he'd left. Emptier. But I could think more clearly.

I hadn't thought of Reston romantically since we finished high school. At first, it had been hard to stop thinking about him that way. For months, I thought about how badly I missed him, and what I could do to convince him to come home. We'd known each other for nearly our entire lives, of course I thought about him. I wanted him in my life. He was supposed to be in my life. The alternative was depressing.

But I'd stopped loving him years ago. He'd left town and would never have spoken to me again if he hadn't come back years later. He'd hurt me so much, and I'd found someone who would never hurt me the way Reston had.

Then today happened, and I realized that at least part of me still thought of him like that. Part of me wanted to see what a future with Reston Tucker would look like.

And the rest of me was scared. Scared of what it would look like to my daughters, to my parents, to the people of this town. Scared of what it meant about my marriage, which had ended so suddenly and so horribly nine months ago. Scared that somehow Steve would know and he would be hurt. How ridiculous, I was worried about that.

I took a deep breath. I had to get the girls. We had a packed weekend ahead of us, and I was wasting the little time I had.

CHAPTER THIRTY-EIGHT

The next afternoon, I knocked on Amanda's front door before letting myself in. I was expected, and even if I wasn't, it was normal for us to walk into each other's houses unannounced. Or at least it used to be.

"Amanda?" I called. "It's me. I brought the groceries you needed."

"Thanks, Jo!" she called back. "Drop them in the kitchen. I'll be down in a sec."

I could barely squeeze through the hall to the kitchen. There were moving boxes everywhere, Justin's handwriting denoting where each box should go. Oh, God, were they moving? What would I do with my best friend in another city?

And if she hadn't said anything, was she even my best friend anymore?

"What's with the boxes?" I asked when Amanda joined me in the kitchen.

"Justin's moving out," Amanda replied, her voice far more casual than it should have been. "We're splitting up."

For a moment, I couldn't breathe. Splitting up? How? Why? In the midst of all this heartbreak, how did they willingly invite more?

"What happened?" I sputtered.

She waved her hand, still far more casual than I was. "All we do is fight. What's best for Landon? How are we going to pay for all of this? What treatment should we try?"

"That's not going to stop if you're divorced."

My tone was sharper than it should have been. This was none of my business. Their marriage wasn't mine to make decisions about. Still, I couldn't stop myself from arguing.

"I can't stand being around him anymore, Jo. I see him, and I bristle, because I know we're going to fight about something. And I don't want that in my marriage. I don't want to hate my partner."

Tears stung my eyes. How could they do this? I would have put up with anything to have my marriage back. I would have fought every day. Anything to have Steve back. Anything to not have this empty space in my heart.

"You...you wished your son away," I spat. "You're throwing your husband away. You've taken it all for granted."

Amanda threw up her hands. "For fuck's sake, Jo, you have no idea. You've been through none of this, but you're so quick to judge."

"My husband died. My son died. That's why I've been through none of what you have."

"Well, you've certainly moved on fast enough."

My face went hot. "Excuse me?"

"Everyone in town knows what's going on with you and Reston."

This town, I swear to God.

"Nothing's going on with me and Reston," I replied with a shake of my head.

"Please. You're picking up where you left off as if Steve never existed. You've been widowed less than a year."

"That's right, I have. And I'm not doing anything with Reston."

"I'm sure," she replied, not looking at me, and clearly not meaning it. "It's a small town. Word gets around."

"I don't know what words are getting around to you, but I remember a time when you would have trusted me if I said they were false."

She waved her hand. "It's fine, Jo, grief bang whoever you want."

"What does that even mean?"

"You know, you and Reston comfort each other, bonding over the death of your husband, his closest friend."

"We don't need to bond over that, or over anything else. Reston and I were bonded fine before any of this happened. But we're not dating or sleeping together or whatever else you're implying." I sighed, fighting back tears. "You used to be my friend, Amanda."

She brushed her hair back from her face. "And you didn't used to hold everyone to impossible standards, Jo. You don't know my marriage. You don't know what Justin and I have been going through since last year, or frankly before the accident. You can't decide what's best for us."

"I'm sorry," I replied. "You're right. I don't know what your marriage has been like."

"And I'm sorry I'm being an asshole about Reston. I'd kind of expected you guys to get together, so when I started hearing that you were...it makes sense, Jo."

"I know it does. And...I like him, Amanda. But I don't want everyone in Haven gossiping about how it hasn't even been a year, and what if I was seeing him before the accident, and shouldn't I be worrying about taking care of my kids and not about dating."

"Are you dating him?"

"Not yet." It was an instinctive answer, one I didn't consider before blurting it out.

"Because of the gossip."

"Partly."

It certainly didn't help. As if it wasn't hard enough to figure out for myself whether I felt ready to date again, and to worry about how my daughters might react, I had to manage the feelings of every person in town who felt they had a right to weigh in.

"Ignore the gossip."

"That's kind of impossible here. You know that."

"Yeah." She sighed. "We'd talked about splitting up before the accident happened. Me and Justin. Things have been bad for a while, but, like, low-key bad. No one getting violent, no secret lovers, as if anything can be secret in this town."

"The fact that you guys were having trouble turned out to be a well-kept secret."

"Then the accident happened, and...at first it was almost as if we could fix our marriage if we focused on Landon instead of each other. If we prioritized our poor injured son, we'd stay together, and we'd eventually be happy again."

"But it doesn't work that way."

"No."

I hugged my best friend, wishing I could take back my earlier harsh words.

"I'm so sorry, Amanda. Are you guys okay?"

"We are, yeah," she replied, pulling away from me. "Like I said, we'd been talking about it for a while. It's for the best for both of us. Things weren't working anymore, and it'll be good for us to get fresh starts."

"How's Elliot?"

"Oh, God. Yeah. That's...not going well. How are your girls? Are they up and down and sometimes totally normal and the next day they blow up at you because you're acting like things are normal?"

"Yes."

"Then it's not just us," Amanda replied with a laugh. "I guess that's a relief."

"Where did you hear that Reston and I were seeing each other?"

She paused. "You can guess who talks behind your back a bit as if apologies weren't said."

"Natalie." She'd done nothing but stir up drama in our friend group, as if anyone needed extra drama these days. "Natalie's spreading rumors about me."

"I mean, I've heard it from other people too. But yeah, that's who said something to me about it first. She acted like it's a problem."

I rolled my eyes. "Nice. My friends are spreading lies about me, so that they can condemn my behavior."

"You hurt people's feelings when you said we were money grubbing or whatever with the lawsuit."

My jaw dropped. "I didn't use the term money grubbing."

"Well, you implied it at least. And people were hurt."

"And now they've started a smear campaign?"

"Sort of. Hey, you admitted that you're basically dating him."

"No, I admitted that I'm thinking about dating him at some point."

"When will that be?"

"I don't know, when I think it's been long enough to keep people from gossiping about it, I suppose."

Not for quite some time, clearly.

"It's never going to be long enough."

I sighed. "Yeah. I know."

"Have you been into Reston all this time?"

"No. I hadn't even thought about it. When he left, I wrote him off. And when he came back...The affection eighteen-year-old me had for eighteen-year-old Reston didn't compare to how I felt about Steve. Once I'd met Steve, it was almost as if Reston had never existed."

"And now Steve is gone and you remembered Reston?"

"And now Reston told me he never stopped loving me."

Amanda raised an eyebrow. "Oh, nice, Reston. Geez. That's...ballsy of him."

"I enjoy his company, and he's good looking, and," I sighed, "it feels like a betrayal, and yet I want it."

"Yeesh. Complicated."

"Very much so." I glanced around at the boxes. "Like what you have happening here."

"It will be okay. All of it. Eventually."

I nodded. I wished it wasn't taking so long.

CHAPTER THIRTY-NINE

I returned home from Amanda's to find Reston on his back on my living room floor, lifting Olivia into the air and bringing her back down, like she was a barbell and he was doing bench presses. She was giggling and I smiled at the sight. He had taken me at my word that he was still welcome.

"What are you guys doing?" I asked.

"I'm helping Uncle Reston with his exercises," Olivia replied.

"This is great therapy," he added.

"I bet."

I went to the kitchen to put away the groceries. My mom was already there, stirring a pot.

"Are you making dinner?" I asked. "You didn't have to do that."

"It's no bother."

"Thank you."

"How's Amanda?"

"She and Justin are splitting up."

Mom turned away from the stove. "Oh, Jo, you're not serious."

"I am." I shook my head. "I don't understand. I'd give anything to have Steve here, and she's walking away from Justin like it's nothing."

"I doubt that. I'm sure it's painful for her."

"Not painful enough if she's still doing it. She says things were bad even before the accident, but...it's hard to see someone letting go of something I would give anything for."

Perhaps I wouldn't give anything to have my husband back if we'd been having Amanda and Justin's problems. Steve wasn't perfect, our marriage wasn't perfect, because perfection was impossible, but I'd wanted all of it for the rest of my life. All the squabbles, all the nagging, all the little frustrations.

"I don't know that you should be judging her, Jo," Mom said.

"After what I've lost?"

"A little bird tells me that you're perhaps not as despondent as you imply."

The gossip had gotten to my mother. This town, I swear.

"What little bird?"

"A number of little birds all around Haven."

"And what are these little birds telling you?"

She glanced toward the living room, and I saw red. Not this again. "What, Reston? You heard a rumor about me and Reston?"

"No one's judging you."

"Everyone's judging me, and we're not doing anything!" I hissed.

"It makes sense, Jo. That you and Reston would get back together."

"We're not!" I lowered my voice. "I'm not seeing Reston. He is my friend. He's dealing with a massive trauma, just like I am. It's been good for both of us to have someone to turn to."

"I'm sure."

"Mother."

She put up her hands. "It's not my business. I would think you'd want to wait a bit longer, but if you're ready, who am I to stop you?"

"I'm not ready. Reston and I aren't dating. This is ridiculous."

"Well, an awful lot of people think you are."

"Apparently."

He was right about this town, and how everyone felt entitled to everyone else's business. It was the unpleasant flipside to the way everyone took care of everyone else.

"You should stay and eat with us, Mom," I said after a moment. "Since you cooked and all."

"Thanks. I have to feed your father at home though."

"He can't manage himself?" I teased.

"He is still very much a child."

"I know he gets home from work and basically shuts down, but he's always welcome here."

Mom sighed. "He doesn't know how to talk to you guys right now. And he doesn't want to get it wrong."

"After all these months?"

I'd hoped that would return to normal, at least.

"It's not as if you aren't grieving anymore."

"The girls miss their grandpa. And I don't want them to miss anyone right now."

"Is that why Reston's always here, even though you aren't dating?"

I rolled my eyes. "That's enough, Mom. He doesn't have anyone. You know that. And he's part of our family."

"Well, I assume you know what you're doing."

"I do, thanks."

We stared at each other from across the kitchen for a moment, and then I turned to go, ready to talk about something else, anything else.

"How's the exercise going in here?" I settled onto the floor next to where Reston was lying.

"I'm going to be hurting later," Reston replied with a laugh. "Jesse should hire some kids to come in and really work his clients."

"Why didn't you say something? Girls, leave Uncle Reston alone."

His gaze fixed on the ceiling, he began to massage his left shoulder, which had been dislocated in the accident. It was the fastest healing of his injuries, but apparently agitated now.

"He said we could," Olivia said.

"I'm sure he did."

"I'm fine," Reston argued. "Aching is good. Pain is bad."

"Whatever you say, Coach. Do you need help up?"

He shook his head. "Yes, but it'll hurt. Give me a minute and I'll get up on my own."

"I could roll you onto your side."

"Keep your hands off of me, Jo," he growled. "I got this."

"Go get washed up for dinner, girls." I shooed them from the room.

"I'm honestly fine." Reston rolled slowly to his left side, then pushed himself to his feet.

"I'm sure. I can give you an arm to grab, or find your cane, which I assume you placed in the garbage."

He laughed. "It's by the door."

"Then I can walk you to the door."

"Thanks."

I walked beside him, there if he needed something to grab onto. It was slow going, but we made it to the entryway without him taking my arm. He was usually better than this, but clearly the girls had worn him out.

"Thanks," he repeated, fumbling with his cane.

"It's always good to see you, Reston." After the conversation we'd had the day before, I was afraid he didn't know that.

"You too. You'll tell me if you want me to stop randomly stopping by."

"I will." I paused, leaning against the wall, attempting to feign casual behavior. "This is going to sound crazy, but people in town have started a rumor that you and I are seeing each other."

Reston rolled his eyes. "Exactly what I love so much about Haven."

"I was thinking, you know, since everyone thinks we're dating, would you like to buy me dinner?"

It was easier to blame the gossip than to admit that I wanted this. I wanted to go on a date with Reston. I wanted to have a life again. I wanted time alone with this man. I wanted to believe that I could be happy again. I was afraid to say it out loud. The gossip had come in handy.

"I would like that very much," he replied, his dark eyes wide. "Are you...did you just ask me on a date?"

"Kind of."

It was normal for us, me asking him out, him seeming surprised and confused. It was precisely how we'd ended up together in high school. Even though he'd been more interested than he'd let on, apparently.

"Let's have dinner," Reston said. "Um, when? When should we...I guess you need to get a sitter or something? I don't know what I'm doing, Jo."

I laughed, loving flustered Reston, who had nothing to be flustered about. "Tell me when you want to take me out, and I'll find someone to watch the girls."

"Now."

"Okay, now is a little soon, and my mom already prepared dinner."

"Oh."

"Do you want to stay for dinner? And we'll do the date another day?"

Reston nodded enthusiastically. "Yes, I'd like that."

I turned away from the door. "Uncle Reston's going to stay for dinner!" I announced to the girls.

"Hooray!"

My mom raised an eyebrow at me. I did my best to ignore her. I was never going to be able to stop the Haven rumor mill.

I might as well enjoy myself.

CHAPTER FORTY

The girls were settled in front of the TV with some breakfast, and I kissed the tops of their heads before tugging on my shoes. The longer I thought about how I'd left things with Amanda, the more it weighed on me. During the week, I had no time to deal with my personal life. As soon as the weekend rolled back around, I was out the door to make sure we were still okay.

"I'm going to run over to Aunt Amanda's," I said. "Behave. Don't touch the oven."

I'd accused Amanda of pushing Justin away, and then I pushed her away as if it were nothing. I wasn't being a good best friend. And she probably needed me.

She looked disheveled when she answered the door. It may have been earlier than I thought.

"I'm sorry for being so angry," I said.

She laughed, just a little. "Thanks."

"Are you okay?"

"Not really." she shook her head.

"Can we do coffee later?"

"You could have texted me."

"Oh, my God, I hadn't thought of that."

"Yeah, Jo, let's do coffee later. I'll text you once I'm dressed."

I wrapped my arms around my best friend, something I wouldn't have been able to do if I'd sent her a text instead of coming over. She clung to me for a moment, and when she pulled away, her eyes were glossy with tears.

"I'm fine," she insisted. "Thanks again. I'll text you."

"We tried to fight for the marriage, and then we...stopped," Amanda confessed.

We'd driven fifteen minutes outside of town, doing our best to avoid the Haven gossip mill. Everyone would know about her divorce soon enough, but we welcomed every chance to delay.

"It feels like everyone is watching," she continued. "And I know someone will tell Landon that this is his fault. He can't handle that right now. His mind, he won't know that it's bullshit that someone's saying to get a rise out of him."

"Everyone is watching," I replied. "Guess how I know."

She sighed, idly stirring a sprinkle of sugar into her latte. "And I still love Justin, Jo. I wish this wasn't happening. I love him and I love our family. But our marriage is broken."

"I'm sorry I didn't process it well."

She waved the apology away with her hand. "I don't blame you. Like I said, we'd been talking about it for so long that it didn't occur to me that anyone else would be surprised."

"I shouldn't have questioned whether you knew what was right for your family."

Small town life led to the misconception that you knew everything about everyone.

"I shouldn't have antagonized you about Reston," Amanda said. "That was a low blow."

"It was, but I also got that from my mom, so it's okay. Everyone has opinions."

Amanda leaned across the table, dropping her voice. "I shouldn't say this."

"Oh, please do."

"I'm jealous that you've already locked up Reston."

"What, you had your eye on him?" I asked with a laugh. "As if dating my ex wouldn't have broken the girl code?"

"How many eligible guys our age are there in Haven?"

"You were going to settle for the only single guy in town?"

She laughed. "I like Reston enough. And it was going to be a while before I dated anyone. But I'd expected him to be available, if I wanted to date someone, in part because he hasn't dated anyone since he moved back."

"Maybe he'll be available by the time you're ready to date someone."

"Not if he told you that he'd never stopped loving you."

"I still can't believe he said that." I laughed. "True or not. Reston's great, but…I just lost my husband."

"How do you even…I've known for, like, a year and a half that Justin and I were probably getting divorced, and still the idea of dating someone else feels strange."

"Oh, yeah, I feel guilty as hell for wanting this. And it's Reston, and I've dated him before, and it feels like it should be easy."

"But it's not."

I doubted it ever would be.

"He had this past with Steve, too, and he feels guilty. And honestly, the idea that he felt this way about me all this time, while he and Steve had the relationship they did, I'm shocked he made it this long without losing his mind or running away or having an incredibly awkward conversation with Steve." The realization hits me. "Oh, right, it turns out he had an incredibly awkward conversation with Steve."

Amanda laughed. "Steve knew about your history, right?"

"Well, sure. But there's a difference between me telling him, oh, yeah, Reston's the guy who took my virginity then I didn't see for a decade. I didn't know Steve asked Reston if he still had feelings for me, let alone Reston's answer."

"I can't imagine either situation going well."

"Steve seemed matter-of-fact about my relationship with Reston. He saw us together and didn't see anything that bothered him. And I wouldn't have had this life with Reston. He would never have settled here and raised a family."

"But he did end up coming back and settling here, Jo."

I frowned. "I don't think I trust that. I'm still waiting for him to leave again."

"He wouldn't do that. Not now."

Now felt like the perfect time for him to leave.

"When they first sent him to Raleigh, he talked about not coming back. It would have been easy, you know. But he came back and...I'm attached. The girls are getting attached. We're going to go on a date."

"Ooh, things got serious."

I laughed. "Sort of, yeah. I figured, as long as everyone in town assumes we're dating..."

"I'll need all the details."

"I'm sure a play-by-play will be cobbled together by the various town folk who see us out."

"But who's going to report back whether you guys sleep together?"

That felt impossible, the greatest betrayal of Steve, when I couldn't possibly do anything to betray him.

"Okay, that's going to be a long while."

"And you'll call me immediately."

I flushed. "Amanda!"

"You did the first time you slept with him."

"That was different."

"Only a little."

"We'll see if I ever get around to sleeping with Reston again. Okay?"

"I bet you do."

"I bet you like having something to think about that isn't your personal life."

It helped me to have something else to occupy my thoughts than the tragedy I was still struggling to come to terms with.

"He was in love with you all this time," Amanda said, "and you had no idea?"

Over the past week, I'd turned over plenty of moments between us in the decade since he'd come back. I tried to find times when hands or eyes had lingered a little too long, when hugs lasted longer than they should, when he'd said something that should have tipped me off, but I couldn't. He'd done a remarkable job.

"When Reston left," I finally replied, "I convinced myself that he'd never truly loved me. That if he had, he wouldn't have left me."

"And you did that to get over him."

"Sure. Do you remember how awful I was to him during those last few weeks before he left? I was determined to hurt him back."

"I remember being pretty awful myself," Amanda replied.

"And he was so even-keeled about it. How could he possibly have loved me and not been hurt by all of that?"

"Ugh, poor Reston. Those weeks must have been torture."

"As if they were easy for me," I replied with a laugh.

It had become real with incontrovertible proof that Reston was leaving Haven once we were done with high school. I'd started acting out, so hurt that I wasn't enough to make him want to stay. Looking back, his calm responses to every terrible thing I said to him were tremendously kind, both of us hurting, and only one of us acting like it. At the time, I'd interpreted his behavior as cold, proof that I didn't matter to him.

I guess I was wrong about that.

"Thanks for the coffee, Jo," Amanda said.

"Thanks for the talk. I've been overwhelmed. This was nice."

"Good luck. Have a good time on your date. Tell me everything."

CHAPTER FORTY-ONE

The doorbell chimed, and I scrambled to get ready. I'd spent too much time agonizing over what to wear, not sure what message I wanted to send. It was just Reston. It was just dinner, and I'd spent two hours debating my outfit. I'd settled on a basic printed dress, because I was wearing it when he rang the bell.

As I started down the stairs, I could hear him talking to my mom.

"You'll have her back at a decent hour."

"Yes, Mrs. Franklin," Reston replied. "Of course I will."

"We're just having dinner, Mom," I said.

"Are you going on a date?" Olivia asked.

"We're going to dinner," Reston replied.

"On a date?"

Oh, had the girls heard the gossip too?

"Are you gonna kiss our mom?"

"Addison," I admonished.

"That's what happens on dates," she replied.

"How would you..." I sighed. "Good night, girls. Be good for Gran."

"This is going to be more nerve-wracking than I was expecting," Reston said as he drove to the restaurant.

"Which part? The nosy mom? The overly enthusiastic kids?"

"All of it. Being around your mom turns me into a teenager."

"I had no idea you felt that way about my mom," I teased.

"Jo."

"Just wait until everyone in town sees us out to dinner. My mom reminding you that I have a curfew will be the furthest thing from your mind."

"She said a reasonable hour. I don't even know what that is anymore. Eight? Do I need to take you to, like, a drive-thru so that I have you home by eight?"

I laughed. "Don't worry about my mom."

"How does she feel about this?"

"I don't care. I'm ready to decide for myself what I want."

Reston nodded, smiling slightly. "Okay. Good to know."

There was only one nice restaurant in Haven, the same restaurant Reston had taken me to on our first date back in high school. Reston held the door for me, and I walked inside, and instantly it felt like everyone was watching us.

"Hey, Mrs. Grant. Hey, Coach Tucker," the hostess said. She was a classmate of Matt's, though I couldn't recall her name. "Two for dinner?"

"I have regrets," Reston whispered into my ear as we were led to our table. "I should have taken you to another city."

"It'll be fine," I replied.

Our waiter, too, was a kid from the high school who greeted us by name. Half the tables were occupied, all of them with people we knew.

He was right, we should have gone to another town.

"Jo! Reston!"

I looked up at the familiar voice, knowing it was Natalie, knowing that she clearly had an issue with the idea of me dating Reston. Perfect. This was going to go great.

"Hey, Nat." I tried to play casual.

"Sorry to interrupt your date, but it's been so long since I've seen you guys, and I had to say hi."

Oh, God, how I wanted to snap that it wasn't a date, to wipe that smirk off her face. That wasn't going to do any good, not when people began to see us out on what were clearly dates, denying that they were.

And what was the big deal? We were both single adults. If my husband hadn't been dead long enough to satisfy everyone, that wasn't my fault. I was ready, or at least ready enough, and Steve would have been…he loved Reston. He would be happy for me.

"That's all right," I finally said. "It's nice seeing you. It's been a while."

"I'm sure you've both been very busy. And, Jo, you've got your daughters to worry about."

"Yes. Olivia and Addy take up a lot of my time. And I've gone back to work, and that took a lot of my attention as well."

"How are you feeling, Coach?"

"Doing great, Natalie, thanks," Reston replied tightly. "How's your family? How are you all doing?"

"It's been rough, but things are better now. And it's great that you two can be out in the open now."

"I'm not sure what you mean by that," Reston said.

"It's been a few months now since the accident, and…" she shrugged. "You've waited long enough to avoid the gossip."

"It seems as if we didn't."

"Congratulations, in any case."

"Thanks."

She walked away from our table, and Reston and I stared at each other for a moment. I bit my lip, trying to keep in the mirth. Reston snorted, and I lost it, laughing until tears were streaming down my face. Reston laughed too, spurred on by my own amusement.

This whole thing was ridiculous. No one was ever going to accept that I was "allowed" to move on from my marriage. I could be widowed for decades, and it would never be enough.

But I was happy. I was having a good time with Reston. I felt supported, and loved, and comfortable, and I needed this.

"This is going great," I gasped out, wiping happy tears from my face for once.

"I'm glad you think so," Reston replied with a smile.

It felt like old times. I was shocked I could feel this happy.

We made it through dinner without any further drama. It was nice to connect with each other, not in a hospital, not in a rehab center, here in this restaurant, just the two of us, even though there were plenty of other people around.

After dinner, Reston walked me to my door, the same way he had all those times when we were teenagers. We stood on my porch for a moment, not quite looking at each other, both of us, I assume, pretty sure of what was going to happen next. Then he tilted his head the same way he had in my driveway a few days ago that felt like it was a million years ago.

His lips on mine felt familiar and different at the same time. Of course they did. Reston had kissed me dozens of times, twenty-five years ago. His skills had improved, I noted, and I hoped mine had as well.

My fingers slid into his hair, tugging lightly. He growled against my lips, sending a shock between my legs. I wondered if sex would feel familiar too.

Then I thought of Steve.

And then I broke the kiss.

"I'm sorry," Reston murmured, brushing my hair back from my face. "Sorry."

I shook my head. "Don't be. That was nice."

"I shouldn't—"

"You should," I replied. "As often as possible."

"Then why'd you stop me?"

"That's me, not you."

"Are you telling me to kiss other women as often as possible? Because I don't plan on doing that ever again."

I took a deep, shaky breath. "I was never supposed to love someone who wasn't you. And then I met Steve. And I want him back, more than anything."

Reston nodded, turning away from me. He looked ready to disappear down my driveway, never to return. I called out to him, and he turned back.

"Kiss me again, Coach Tucker."

He moved faster than I'd seen him since the accident. His hands went to my waist, and he barely kept from slamming me back against the door with his enthusiasm. I grinned as he kissed me, unable to remember the last time I'd had as much fun as I had at dinner. The accident had left me thinking I could never be happy again. It felt traitorous to smile like this, to be happy in the arms of another man. Yet I knew this would have made Steve happy for me. Not if he were still here, of course. But if we couldn't be together, this was the ideal situation.

"I like this," I whispered.

"I do too."

"Thanks for dinner."

"Anytime."

"Now I have to hope my mom didn't hear any of that."

Reston laughed. "Good luck with that. And good night, Jo."

"Good night, Reston."

Chapter Forty-Two

My mom stared at her book, pretending she'd been reading it while Reston and I were on the porch. When I shut the door behind me, she looked up, feigning shock to find me home.

"How was your date?" she asked.

I shook my head, wishing I could do as I had as a teenager, and simply walk past my mom without speaking to her.

"It was nice, thanks," I replied. "Thanks for your help with the girls."

"You're welcome. Did I hear you and Reston having a talk on the porch?"

"Definitely not."

"I could have sworn I did."

"Good night, Mom."

And then I stopped mid-step, blocking my mom from leaving.

"Do you think they'll stop talking about us eventually?" I asked, my words slow and deliberate.

"About you and Reston."

"Yeah."

"I don't know," she replied. "I'd like to think so, because we've all seen you and Reston together before, so it shouldn't be new or different."

"But things have changed since then."

"Yes."

"I don't know why they're judging me." Tears stung my eyes. "For moving on too fast? For moving on with someone I already dated? For moving on with someone I was close to while Steve was still alive?"

"I assume all of that, yes." My mom patted the space beside her on the couch.

I sat, and just like the night when I'd lost Steve, I lay on the couch beside her, my head in her lap, and let her comfort me. I'd had such a nice time with Reston, loved every minute of our date. And I hated that I'd loved it. I hated that I was happy and the boys were still gone. I hated how amazing it felt when Reston kissed me. I hated that I wanted him to kiss me again.

And I hated the guilt. I hated that I hated all of this. I was allowed to go on dates. I was allowed to kiss him. I shouldn't feel bad about it, but I couldn't stop the guilt. I couldn't stop the voice in the back of my head that told me I was supposed to spend the rest of my life miserable about what I'd lost. The voice that came out of the mouths of the people I knew in Haven. People who should have wanted me to be happy, and if they thought I was doing something wrong, wasn't I?

"If you're happy," Mom said, "then you are doing everything right."

"What about the girls?" I asked.

"If having Reston around was bad for your daughters, it's far too late now to fix that."

"What if it's someone else? What if Reston leaves, or things don't work out?"

"How little faith do you have in yourself, Jo?"

That stopped my tears. What was wrong with me? I had certainly never questioned how Steve and I would manage together. I'd always assumed everything would work out. I'd figure things out with Reston too. I would learn to ignore gossip. I didn't have to worry about how the girls would handle having him around, because he'd always been around, and he'd be around in the future, no matter what. If we went on a second date or a fortieth date and realized this wasn't for us, he'd be around forever, because he was Reston. He was a fixture in our family.

"No one thinks about this when they have kids," I said finally. "Or when they get married. No one goes into it thinking about what they'll do when it ends. No one thinks about the fact that it will end."

"You can take your time to figure this out. Is Reston pushing you?"

"He has never pushed me."

If anything, Reston had always been the cautious one. Four years into dating him the first time, he'd told me he was leaving. He'd never see me again, if things went according to his plans. He'd known that was coming, and when I thought about it later, it was clear from the time we'd started dating that he was preparing for that moment. I'd asked him out first. I'd been the first to tell him I loved him. And while we'd both been enthusiastic about our relationship getting physical as teenagers, he'd been even more diligent about birth control than I was. He was never going to let me keep him from what he wanted.

"You're doing a great job," my mom said. "You've figured out how to support your family. The girls are strong and healthy and coping well with all the changes that the world has thrown at them. You don't need to worry so much, Jo."

"I miss the boys."

"We all do."

"I'd give anything to have them back."

"Agreed."

"And I feel guilty for moving on."

"Of course you do. And moving on feels like a horrible term, Jo. You're continuing to live. There's no harm in that. It's not only what Steve would have wanted, but a completely normal thing that was always going to happen."

"True."

We sat in silence for a moment, my mother stroking my hair. Being happy shouldn't be so hard.

"Did I ever tell you," my mom began, "about how Reston's mom and I got in a fight when he came back?"

I sat up. "No! What about?"

"I never forgave him for leaving in the first place. You said you knew he was leaving and it didn't bother you, but it so clearly did. Miriam kept saying that you knew what you were getting into, and it felt so callous. When he came back, I told her that if he approached you, I'd set his house on fire."

I snorted. Had she threatened him in high school too? It would certainly explain his nerves around her.

"Oh, Lord, Mom. Tell me you didn't."

"I never thought he was good for you."

"Good enough, you mean."

"Yes, that too."

"What changed?"

"Reston."

I smiled, exhaling a breath of laughter. "That does feel...accurate."

"He always chafed at this town, but he doesn't now."

"He does. He hides it better. He does what he loves here, and it makes him love it here." I paused. "They'll let him coach again, right?"

"I haven't a clue, Jo."

My throat was tight around tears I didn't want to shed.

"I don't know if I could recover if he left," I admitted. "It's been so much."

"Life's not always going to be easy. That's not how it works."

"You mean I don't get a free pass on anything terrible ever happening to me again?"

"Wouldn't that be nice?"

"Truly, it would."

She patted my knee. "I'm glad you had a nice time with Reston tonight."

"Thanks. I appreciate you watching the girls."

"Anytime."

CHAPTER FORTY-THREE

The girls crawled into bed with me, and before I could open my eyes, they'd constructed an entire mythology around the previous night.

"How was your date?" Olivia asked.

"Did Uncle Reston kiss you?" Addy asked.

"Is he going to be our dad now?"

"My date was nice. We had a nice dinner," I replied. "Reston isn't going to be your dad. Leave me be."

"Cole says you and Uncle Reston have been dating for a long time."

I sat up straight, startling the girls, who jerked backward. "Cole said what?"

Obviously Natalie's son was a source of gossip.

Addy shrugged. "He said his mom said that you and Uncle Reston were finally going to be able to go out without hiding. How long have you been dating?"

"We haven't been." I shook my head. It was too early in the day for made up drama. "We did when we were kids. But we've both been sad since Daddy died. It didn't cross our minds until recently that we still like each other."

A half-truth, but believable.

"When you get married, do I have to wear a dress?" Olivia asked, reclining on a pillow, stretching her body to take up far more bed than a nine-year-old needed.

"If and when I get married again to whomever I choose," I replied, "you can wear whatever you'd like."

"Will Uncle Reston come live in our house?"

"Girls! It was dinner. No one is moving houses or getting married. Can we cool it with the questions?"

At least until I've had some coffee.

The questions didn't stop though, the girls chattering away and getting underfoot as I prepared breakfast. When was I going out with Reston again? When could the girls see Reston again? Did they have to start calling him Dad?

"What? Of course not," I replied. "I don't think anyone would want that, even if we were married. And we're not getting married!"

In high school, I'd pictured it, my and Reston's wedding. It had been very much a high school fantasy wedding with things like a horse-drawn carriage and multiple outfit changes. Not at all practical or within a budget. At seventeen, I'd never heard of a budget. I'd considered Reston the love of my life. While I still wasn't back to thinking like that, couldn't imagine thinking of him like that now, after the life I'd had with Steve, I let my mind wander. What would a future with Reston look like? Would he live here with me and the girls, or would we all prefer something else? I'd seen the previous night how Steve's memory hung over me, blocked me from considering an alternate future. Maybe that would change down the line, but for now, I'd stick to dinner dates and maybe some kissing on the front porch while my mom waited inside, high school all over again. Maybe that's why this felt okay: I was simply replaying an old life, one that existed before Steve. My relationship with Reston had been temporary then; maybe the transient nature then made things easier now.

"Do you love Uncle Reston?"

I paused. Man, this was complicated. It was just supposed to be dinner! Dating while parenting was going to be a bit more difficult to navigate than I'd hoped.

"Of course I do," I replied. "Not like I loved Daddy. Not even like I did a long time ago. But I'll probably always love Uncle Reston, because he's always been my friend."

The girls didn't know a life without Reston in it. He was even—somewhat reluctantly—Olivia's godfather. He was ever-present, a fixture in our lives, and I would never be okay with a life that didn't include him. Not now, after everything we'd been through together.

"I love Uncle Reston too," Olivia said through a mouthful of pancakes.

"Good to know."

"It would be okay if he was our dad."

"No, it wouldn't," Addy replied.

"He'll never be your dad," I said. "Even if he and I got married, no one could ever replace your father, not for me and not for you."

I wondered how much Olivia would truly remember Matt and Steve. How much did I remember about my life before I was nine? Sure, this was huge, and she wouldn't forget them. But how much would she retain in five, ten, twenty years? Would she remember how Steve doted on her, our baby? Would she remember how much Matt loved being her big brother, how patient and kind he was with her? Would she remember their voices, their laughs?

Would I?

It felt impossible that I'd forget them, and yet as if it were already happening. I'd kissed another man, had enjoyed kissing him. As if Steve never existed. It was normal, it was fine, but it didn't feel like it, and I wasn't sure it ever would. What if every time Reston kissed me, I pulled away in guilt? Neither of us would enjoy that.

Oh, God, did I need to break up with Reston? And how flighty did I sound, worrying that after one date, I needed to have some complicated conversation about what it all meant?

I didn't want to stop seeing him. I wanted to enjoy myself, wanted to find some measure of happiness moving forward, otherwise what was the point in going on?

I didn't want it to hurt my girls, though. I couldn't believe someone had the audacity to say I had betrayed my husband. Could I wait until it seemed more appropriate for me to date again, and did that time exist?

With the girls occupied—Addy with homework, Olivia with Lego—I mulled over what I wanted to say to Reston. He deserved to know what I was thinking.

I decided to text him, allowing myself the time to be diplomatic, should it come to that.

"I had a nice time last night," I wrote.

"The best I've had in a while," he replied. "When do I get to see you again?" I guess I took too long to answer him, because he responded for me. "At work tomorrow?"

Oh, goddammit, that was going to be awkward if this didn't work out.

"Absolutely," I replied.

"Do you mind if I ask what that pause was about?"

"I don't know," I typed. "Things are complicated."

"I hope you know that I understand what we're doing here."

"What, dating?"

"I'm getting a second chance with the one who got away. You're getting a consolation prize."

"That's not how I'm thinking about it."

I tried not to think about it. To think about how if Steve were still alive, I wouldn't even know that Reston had feelings for me. To think about how hard the last ten years must have been for Reston, watching me with my husband. He'd put himself through torture for a decade.

"Regardless," Reston wrote. "I know things are complicated. How could they not be?"

Speaking of complicated...

"Natalie is saying we were seeing each other before the accident. She's said it enough that my kids repeated it."

"I should have been ruder to her last night."

I couldn't help but laugh at that. "I don't know what to do, Reston."

"I don't feel qualified to weigh in," he replied. "You have to do what's best for the girls. I'll disappear, if that's what you need."

"I will never need you to disappear."

"I meant it more figuratively than usual."

"I'd hope so."

"Natalie's mad at me," Reston wrote. "She's taking it out on you. I don't know the best way to handle it. She still won't return my calls or speak to me. Last night was the first I've spoken to her since December."

I shook my head. We'd all been friends for years. All these lives lost and people were turning on their friends. Still.

"I'll see you tomorrow," I wrote. "And, God willing, every day after that."

"Good to hear," he replied.

Now I needed to deal with the Haven gossip mill.

CHAPTER FORTY-FOUR

I steeled myself, taking a deep breath before knocking on the door. And clearly Natalie did the same thing before speaking.

"Good morning, Jo."

"Hey, Natalie."

For someone who had been so brazenly rude to me the previous night, she seemed unsure of herself now. I waited for her to speak, refusing to bail her out by asking for the apology she owed me but didn't mean. I wasn't feeling charitable this morning.

"Is this about last night?" Natalie asked finally, glancing backward into her house.

"It is."

"I didn't mean anything by it. Harmless joking between friends."

"Yes, that's clearly how Reston and I interpreted your comments."

"Whatever, date who you want, it's not my concern."

"You seem to have made it your concern."

She rolled her eyes. "So you get to be the arbiter of everyone else's choices, but as soon as I make one comment about how it looks for you to be fucking your ex this soon after your husband died, and you lose your mind."

"I'm not fucking anyone. If I were, that would be none of your business. And who says I'm making myself the arbiter of people's choices?"

She put her hand on her hip, and if she rolled her eyes at me one more time, I was going to end up in jail for assault.

"I don't know, maybe Amanda?" she replied. "Whose actions haven't you questioned since December? As if you know anything about what she's dealing with."

My face went hot. "That's between me and Amanda."

"Not when she's calling me crying because you went off half-cocked at her again, telling her that she can't possibly be making the best choices for herself and her family because you would never do the things she's doing. As if you have any idea."

"I'm sorry I didn't want to sue the family of a dead old woman, okay?"

"God, Jo, that's not what this is about! It's about how judgmental you've become."

I narrowed my eyes. "I'm judgmental? Why have you stopped speaking to Reston?"

"Because he killed my son." She threw up her arms. "How do you act like he didn't kill yours?"

"He didn't. The accident report--"

"That report is bullshit. There is no way some lady in a sedan hit that bus and now they're all dead."

"Did you read the accident report?" I asked. I hadn't read it, taking Reston's word for what it said. Reston Tucker had never lied to me.

"I don't need to read the report. My son was here, Reston crashed the bus, my son is gone."

"I'm sorry for your loss." My voice was too hard, and I knew it.

"Are you? Because you don't seem to be sorry for anyone's loss but your own."

She acted as if I'd missed a single funeral. As if I hadn't sent food to every single one of them. As if I hadn't been there every time someone needed a shoulder to cry on.

"How do you know?" I asked. "Are you around me at all times, or do you assume you know because the Haven gossip mill never stops turning?"

"You think people don't talk to me about the things you say to them?"

"I think," I replied, "you thrive on drama. You did in high school, and you do now. I don't have the energy for that anymore. You want to hate Reston, even though you've known him for forty years. You know what kind of person he is, and you know he would have done anything for our boys. You want to hate me because you don't like how I've behaved sometimes while in the throes of grief, that's fine as well. You don't have to drag me into it. You can hate me quietly without spreading rumors that my daughters will hear."

"How are you not angry?"

For the first time, her voice was subdued, almost as if she was asking my advice instead of criticizing my behavior.

"I've moved past that step." I tried to take the anger out of my tone too.

"Who were you mad at? Clearly not Reston. Maybe not even Evelyn McCourt."

"I thought it was pretty obvious," I said. "Isn't that what all of this is about? I've been mad at Amanda."

She had everything I wanted. She had her husband and her son. She had somehow come out of this terrible accident with her life intact. And she took it for granted. It had been hard for me to look at her making her choices, to listen to her words, when I would have given anything to be her.

I knew it wasn't that simple, that I had been too hard on Amanda. And I was trying to be better.

"You look at Reston and you're angry he survived," I said. "But you don't look at Amanda and Vonda and get mad that their sons survived?"

"Honestly, no, it had never occurred to me."

I sighed. "I'm working on acceptance now, because I have to be. I can't be angry anymore."

"That feels impossible."

"All of it does. It's impossible that they're gone, and that life goes on anyway."

"You sound like you have it all figured out."

"I wish I did." I laughed. "We're all still in the middle of it, and that's why it bothers me when it feels like someone is pushing people away. That's why Amanda and I fought, and it's why your behavior is objectionable. Shouldn't you want to be friends? Shouldn't you want someone who knows exactly what you're going through to be around to lean on?"

"Amanda makes it sounds like you're not the most supportive post to lean on."

"And how did you react when she told you they were splitting up? When it turned out our prom king and queen didn't like each other anymore?"

"Okay, it required a bit of a shift in my mindset, sure."

I held out my arms in a gesture of see? "It caught me off guard. I've apologized to her. And for the record, my dating Reston has nothing to do with how much I loved Steve, or whether I still miss him, or who I'd leave to fend for himself in the proverbial burning building. It has everything to do with the fact that I can't have my husband back. Ever. No amount of sitting in my home dressed all in black will change that, no matter how much I wish it would."

She paused, and I worried about how awful her next statement was going to be if she was debating saying it.

"I can't ever trust Reston again," she murmured.

"No one's asking that."

"How do you trust him?"

"Because it's Reston. I've known him since we were babies. Not trusting him would be impossible. Don't you remember him the way I do? Don't you remember high school Reston?"

Natalie laughed. "He organized the senior prank, and no one suspected him somehow?"

"He should have been the prime suspect. I'll never understand why he wasn't."

"No one wanted to mess with his scholarship. Every teacher in that school knew he wanted out." She flushed. "Two months ago, I texted him just to say I wished he'd never come back."

I nearly laughed, although, God, was that awful.

"I'd imagine he feels that way too sometimes," I said.

"No one wanted me to be mad at the dead old lady, but plenty of people have been okay with being mad at Reston. When the lawyer said we could sue him too, some of us were willing to do that."

I wanted to be angry, but given the other things she'd said today, it seemed in line. "You're not mad that I'm dating him, you're upset that he's dating me."

She shrugged. "Given the lives lost on his watch, yeah, I'd like him to suffer a bit more."

"It would never be enough."

"No."

"I'll never understand the desire to see more suffering."

"No wonder we keep butting heads."

"I'll do my best," I said, "to be a bit more delicate with everyone. If you'd do me the same courtesy."

She sighed. "Seems doable."

"We all still live here. And we won't be able to avoid each other."

"I know. And of course that's part of the problem."

She was right about that. Hopefully we'd all learn to get along again.

CHAPTER FORTY-FIVE

I thought I'd never feel this way, but nine months in, my new life was starting to feel...normal. It wasn't easy to get the three of us out the door on time every morning, but we managed more often than not. I wasn't quite as organized as I needed to be, but I was learning, adapting.

I felt comfortable at school, finally. I wouldn't let myself think that Matt should have been in my class. If the accident hadn't taken my boys, I wouldn't be in the classroom. Isaiah returned to school, wheeling himself around a little faster than he probably should have, but no one ever stopped him. He would speed past my classroom, calling, "Hey, Mrs. G!" at me as he went, and I could only smile. Any sign that things might be the way they'd once been was a positive sign.

Landon still wasn't ready to come back, neither his mind nor his body cooperating yet. I checked in with Amanda, brought them food, and helped out with Elliot as often as I could. It never felt like enough. I wasn't sure that was possible—there was no fixing what had been lost. We couldn't replace the boys, couldn't fix Isaiah's body or Landon's brain.

All of us were embracing a new normal, a life with missing pieces. As strange as it felt to keep living, we had no other choice.

It was nice to run into Reston during the workday. Steve and I never taught together, so it was a new experience to walk down the hall and bump into the person I was dating. It shouldn't have; after all, Reston and I had done exactly that for four years as students.

Having someone to sit with at lunch, someone to stress over lesson plans with, it helped balance out how weird it felt to be dating again in my mid-forties.

I wasn't sure how to navigate dating. It was just Reston, and I'd never struggled with how to make plans with him. Suddenly, I was tongue-tied around him. Not about regular stuff, like work, but about us. About being a couple again, and going out, and what it meant. I wasn't sure what it meant. I couldn't think of it as anything serious, not this soon after losing Steve, and not with Reston gun-shy about staying in Haven. I had the girls to think about. They wouldn't understand if he left, especially if they expected him to be part of our family forever.

And yet when I was with him, I wanted to be with him more, wanted to know I'd see him again. That's why, during a lull in our lunchtime conversation, I blurted out, "Can I cook you dinner?"

Reston laughed, his dark eyes glinting. "You ask as if this is a new thing that you've never done before."

"Yes. The girls will be there. It's time you guys spent time together."

"You say as if this is a new thing—"

"Yes," I replied with an exasperated giggle.

"Sounds great."

"See you around five thirty?"

"You can see me now."

I laughed. "No, I have to get back to work now. See you tonight."

"Do you need me to bring anything?"

"I wasn't expecting to ask you over, so I definitely have everything I need."

He chuckled. "Good to hear. See you tonight."

The end of the day was always madness, and expecting company didn't help. I had to collect the girls from their schools, get them snacks, and supervise homework. I tried to leave my own work until after they went to bed, but sometimes things were urgent. I'd have messages from students or over-concerned parents. Or, like today, when I had ninety essays to grade, which would take weeks if I tried to get them done only when the girls were in bed.

After they'd eaten something, I sent the girls off to tackle their homework, while I set up at the kitchen table with my essays. I regretted this choice when Reston arrived and I learned that Addy had spent the intervening time watching TV instead of doing her homework.

"I thought you had homework," I said, noticing that her backpack was still where she'd dropped it by the door.

"I'll get to it," Addy replied.

"It's usually a good idea to do homework before TV," Reston commented.

I could see the words forming in Addy's brain before her lips started to move. I shook my head, wanting to stop them, ready to snap at her.

"You're not my dad."

Before I could react, Reston replied to her.

"That's a good point that I hadn't considered, Addy."

"So I don't really have to listen to you," she continued.

"Absolutely," Reston replied, nodding resolutely. "You do whatever you'd like, Addy. There will definitely be zero consequences."

"My homework will get done eventually."

"I'd hope so. Sixth grade doesn't learn itself."

"Sometimes it does. It's not that hard."

"I know. Remember, I'm a teacher."

Addy pursed her lips, then flicked the TV off. As she headed to the entryway to grab her backpack, Reston trailed after me into the kitchen.

"What are you making?" he asked.

I raised an eyebrow, but he merely shrugged.

"She was bound to say it at some point," he said softly.

"I'm making tacos. It's taco night."

"Ah, excellent."

"It's not over, is it?"

He glanced back at the living room, where Addy was now sprawled on the floor, a textbook open in front of her.

"Oh, never. And Steve would have been in for it too. I'll get through it." He paused, leaning toward me conspiratorially. "I don't know if anyone's told you this, but kids are kind of the worst."

"Are you giving me parenting advice?" I asked.

Reston wrapped his arms around my waist. "I'm full of parenting advice."

"Non-parents usually are."

"Do you need help with dinner? Should I be cutting tomatoes or something?"

"That would be more helpful than telling me how to raise my kids." I smirked.

"Kiss her."

The girls were huddled in the kitchen doorway, and when we looked at them, they scampered away. I couldn't help but laugh. They certainly pushed the idea of Reston kissing me these days.

I was a fan of that as well.

He obliged me and them, kissing me softly before pulling away.

"Where are these tomatoes you need help with?"

CHAPTER FORTY-SIX

"Hey, Jo! Are you free tonight?"

I was at my kitchen table, trying to get through my stack of essays while the girls were at a friend's house. Reston, apparently having let himself into my house, appeared in the doorway to my kitchen, his forehead creased, his eyes stormy. He had a scar on his forehead. How had I missed that all these months?

"What's up?" I gestured toward a chair. He wouldn't ask to sit, wouldn't admit that he needed to, so I offered it.

He settled in the chair across from me, his face relaxing almost imperceptibly. Getting off that leg seemed to help. He stubbornly refused to use the cane that made movement easier. "The school board is having a meeting about the team."

"Maybe they'll announce they're keeping you."

Reston shook his head, having none of my optimism. "No. If they were doing that, someone on the board would have reached out to me personally. They're going to announce that they're replacing me."

I wasn't sure what to say. It was garbage that they were taking Reston's job away from him. He was an excellent coach who cared about his players on and off the court. He didn't deserve this. He'd suffered some broken bones, and his left leg was weak, and he couldn't run or jump quite like he used to. But he was still an amazing coach, and he deserved the chance to show everyone. He coached a winning team, but more than that, he had a way of reaching his players to encourage them off the court too.

"I'm sorry," I said after a moment.

"I have…I've gotten some job offers. Coaching. At colleges."

"You're kidding."

He shrugged. "I wasn't taking them seriously, because I want my team back, Jo. But if they aren't going to let me have that…"

"Where have you gotten offers from?"

He returned to the doorway of the kitchen, where he'd dropped his bag. He pulled out a folder and set it on the counter. He began leafing through the papers. "NC State. UNC. Davidson. Duke."

"Duke? Are you serious?" I rose to join him at the counter, needing to see this for myself. That would be nearly impossible to turn down. Once Reston was resigned to coaching instead of playing, Duke should be the Holy Grail of coaching jobs, even though there was no way it was the head coaching job.

"I'd be so low on the totem pole. It feels like a publicity thing, knowing the media would love the story of the coach who lost his team being brought into this amazing program, but at least it would pad my résumé."

"And it's one of the best basketball programs in the country."

"Yeah. So I have that to consider."

I flipped through the offer letters, trying to wrap my brain around what he was telling me.

"Are you…Reston, are you leaving Haven again?"

"I can't watch someone else coach my team, Jo. I know I've only been the head coach at Haven for five years, but I've made that team mine. If they're going to take that away from me…there's nothing here for me."

"That's shocking to hear."

He sputtered, his face flushing. "That's not what I meant. I'm sorry."

"I understand, and if you have to leave, you have to leave. It's going to hurt though."

I couldn't look at him. Whatever we were doing was just for fun, and it wasn't serious, and it would be fine if he left. It was going to hurt, because it always hurt when Reston left. But I'd be okay, just like I was before. I'd find someone better, just like I had before.

"I promise you," Reston said, his hands on my upper arms, holding my back against his chest, "I'm not going to do that to you again. I won't abandon you."

"It sounds like that's exactly what you're doing. I understand."

And I did, because how could he watch someone else take over his job? How could he be just a history teacher, as if that would make him happy the way coaching did?

"You wouldn't come with me if I left," Reston said softly.

"Of course not."

"This is where you've always lived, where you've raised your family."

"The only home my children have ever known."

"I wouldn't ask you to leave, Jo."

"This is crazy," I said after a moment, turning to look at him. "This is all supposition. Maybe you'll keep your job."

The kitchen was too small, and we were too close together. He smelled warm and earthy, and my eyes drifted shut as I fought the urge to breathe him in. If I breathed too deeply, our bodies would touch. Who knew what would happen then?

His hands were on my arms, but drifted down, taking my hands in his. My mouth was suddenly dry, and I licked my lips. Reston wrapped his arms around my waist, pulling me against him. He pressed his lips to mine, squeezing me too tight, but I didn't mind. His tongue parted my lips, and I moaned against the invasion. His hands slid under the hem of my T-shirt, sliding up my back, my skin on fire under his touch.

My hands closed into fists, balling up the whisper-soft fabric of his T-shirt. I could feel his heart pounding. I tugged on his shirt, pulling it free of his jeans. He pulled back just enough to look into my eyes, and his gaze turned me into a puddle of lust, ready to rip his shirt in half.

"Where are the girls?" Reston asked, his voice tight.

"At a friend's."

"Do we have time?"

"I think so."

I had no idea what time it was, or how long we were going to be in bed, but I didn't care. I needed this right now, and I'd figure out the rest of it later.

Reston followed me to my bedroom, a room I was fairly certain he'd never entered, no matter how many times he'd been in this house. I swallowed hard as his hands went back to my waist, skimming up my sides, taking my shirt with them. I flushed, worried that he'd be disappointed by the changes in my body since the last time we'd gone to bed together.

We were sixteen the first time we'd had sex. I'd gone to his house to "study" while his mom was at work. I was sure my parents saw through that, but apparently they trusted me, at least to keep from getting pregnant. We'd done plenty of other stuff before that, but we were still clumsy and awkward with each other. It had been slightly unpleasant for me. It got better, but it wasn't like this.

This was different.

Reston unhooked my bra with one hand. That was new and exciting. Then he captured my nipple between his lips, and I forgot all about comparing things.

He unbuttoned my jeans, trying to tug them from my hips without relinquishing the hold on my breast. I pushed his hands off. His hands cupped my breasts as I wiggled my way out of the jeans. I wanted his shirt off too, but didn't want to break his hold on me, so I settled for getting his pants off instead. He still had a perfect, well-muscled athlete's body. My hands brushed over his ass, resisting the urge to cup what I'd revealed when I pushed his pants to his ankles.

He flushed now and stepped back from me.

"I have to sit," he said.

"I can work with that."

Before he sat, I snagged the waistband of his boxer briefs, pulling them off now that he was off his feet. I didn't know if it was his strength or his stamina that wouldn't allow him to stand on one foot right now, but I didn't care, as I sank to my knees at his feet.

This, I knew, I was much better at than I'd been twenty-five years ago.

Reston groaned as I took him in my mouth, his hands sliding into my hair.

"Oh, God, Jo."

My head and hand bobbed in time with each other, eliciting more groans. I wanted him to enjoy himself, but I also wanted him inside of me, so I took things slow and steady. I bathed him with my tongue and briefly reconsidered making him hold out.

Reston's voice was hoarse when he spoke again. "Come here."

He pulled off his shirt before lying back on my bed, positioning me above his head, his tongue hot and moist as it explored my folds. He moved as if he did this every day, knowing exactly how fast to tease me, where to focus his attention. It was the first time Reston had ever tasted me. He was good at this, too good, bringing me to my peak far faster than I'd hoped. I came loudly, collapsing forward, barely catching myself on the headboard.

Reston slid up the bed, his face beneath mine now. He grasped my hips, moving me over him, directing himself inside of me.

"Is this okay?" he asked. "I don't have protection."

"No need," I replied, thankful that he'd been considerate enough to worry about it, but several years past worrying about more children, and trusting him not to give me anything.

He pulled me down onto him, sinking into me slowly, deeply, both of us moaning as he did so. He knew what angle to keep me at, what speed, and he directed my hips slowly at first, until we were both gasping. I took over the rhythm, climaxing again, calling out his name, and a moment later I felt him explode inside of me.

I didn't want this to end. I wanted to keep him inside of me, to continue to explore his body, to relearn each other. I couldn't keep my hands still, stroking his biceps, the curve of his hips beneath my own. Reston panted beneath my hands, his eyes closed, his head thrown back. He took a deep breath and looked up at me, his dark eyes soft. His gaze slid down from my face, I assumed to look at my body. But his eyes clouded, his hands balling into fists. He slammed his fists down on the bed, then grabbed my hips too roughly. He moved me onto the bed beside him, turning away from me.

I knelt on the bed, frowning down at him. "What's wrong?"

Reston rolled over and flicked my necklace with his finger. The pendant that had once been my husband's wedding ring swung in an arc.

Oh.

"I'm feeling this…" He sighed and turned his back on me again. "This is why you stop me. This is why you pull away."

My skin prickled with goosebumps. I hadn't allowed that thought inside, for once, but apparently he'd taken care of that for me.

"Oh. Yeah."

"I just made love to my best friend's wife in my best friend's bed. And there's nothing wrong with that, but I still feel…awful."

"Yeah."

I wasn't feeling that, and it was nice to feel for once as if it was okay to move on, to be happy again. Yes, I'd felt it before, but today, this afternoon in my bed with the man I loved, I'd kept the thought of the other man I loved out of my head.

"I'm sorry I've made you feel like this," Reston said, his voice tight.

"You didn't. And it's fine. It's hard. But it's fine."

His fingers tangled in his hair, as he curled in on himself, pulling further away from me. "I can't believe I did this."

"Reston." I placed my hand on his shoulder. "Reston Tucker. I love you."

It had been a long time since I'd said those words. He rolled onto his back, staring up at me. It felt strange to say that to him, after all this time, in the bed I'd shared with my husband.

But it also felt right, like it was okay that I was going to put my life back together, even though Steve was gone.

I imagined it wasn't the last time this was going to happen.

"Love you, too, Jo," Reston finally replied.

"It's going to be tricky. We'll figure things out."

"Okay."

"What time is this meeting we need to go to?"

He laughed. "Oh, God, I'd forgotten about it. Six?"

"Let me get a sitter."

CHAPTER FORTY-SEVEN

I slid off the bed, turning my back as I scrounged for my clothes. I could feel Reston's eyes on me. I went hot, and hotter as I became sure that my entire body was flushed. Daytime sex was a luxury I hadn't experienced in many years, probably since I was a newlywed. And even if that was something Steve and I did, he knew my body. He'd watched every line appear, every new pound. Reston knew my teenage body, decades removed now. I couldn't bear the scrutiny.

"You look beautiful," he said.

I winced, knowing he'd noticed my shyness.

"Thanks," I mumbled. "I'll be downstairs. I have to call my mom."

I turned to face him, my fingers trying to right my tousled hair. I stumbled, stunned at the sight of him in my bed, lounging on top of the comforter as if he'd slept there dozens of times. He was exquisite. I resisted the urge to return to the bed, to relearn every inch of him, to explore the ridges and ripples of his muscles, to trace the scars.

"I wish you could linger," I said softly.

"Another time. A lot of other times."

Once I'd confirmed that my mom could stay with the girls, I returned to idly flipping through the job offers Reston had laid on my counter.

"Can we talk about these?" I asked as he entered the kitchen.

Reston pulled his T-shirt down over abs that were unfairly perfect after all this time spent rehabbing his injuries. "I didn't go looking for them. They came to me."

"Shouldn't you be looking for them? Do you want to coach high school forever?"

"I wouldn't be the head coach at any of these schools," Reston replied with a shrug. "I'd be a cog in someone else's program, and I don't know if that's for me."

I couldn't argue with that. He'd built Haven High into a perennial contender for the state championship. Stepping back and taking orders from someone else didn't feel like a fun prospect.

"The money though," I said after scanning the pages again.

"Yeah. It's, uh, a hard thing to say no to."

"You don't have to say no."

"And maybe I won't. There's a lot to consider, and I'm trying to weigh all of it. And despite what I said before, you are a large part of my consideration."

"You don't have to worry about me."

"Or your daughters?"

He wasn't committed to us. We'd barely started dating, and the last hour notwithstanding, this wasn't serious. I wasn't ready for serious this soon after losing Steve. I wasn't ready to promise the kids a stepfather, wasn't sure that was something that even appealed to Reston.

I shrugged. "Technically, no, you don't need to worry about them either."

Reston reached around me, closing the folder. "It will all be moot if I keep my team. That's the best-case scenario. As long as that's possible, I'm not going to worry about the rest."

"How are you going to get what you want from the school board?"

He shrugged. "I've got these bargaining tools. I'm going to present my case and cross my fingers."

"You're using the job offers as a bargaining tool?"

"I assume part of why the school board is threatening to take the team away from me is an effort to punish me. I need to show them that forcing me out wouldn't be a punishment."

I shook my head, still in denial that anyone would want to hurt Reston. "That can't be it."

"Look, Jo. I've been...campaigning a bit. I need to know that I'd have support if I tried to fight the school board. I have no illusions about how some people in this town feel about me now."

"It shouldn't be like that."

"No. But I told you on day one that those boys were lost on my watch. I will always be an easy scapegoat."

I crossed my arms in front of my chest. "Because blaming the woman responsible would be too easy."

"Apparently."

It should have surprised me that people had turned on a member of our community, but everything he was saying felt like the things that had chased him away from Haven in the first place. I wanted better for him, like I always had. I wanted him to be happy, and to not have to worry about what people were saying when they thought he couldn't hear.

"Take the job, Reston," I said softly, not looking at him, not wanting to see his reaction, for fear that it would be relief.

"What, at Duke?"

"Yes. Go out there and be amazing and don't look back at this town that doesn't know what it's missing without you."

He turned me around, tipping my head up to force me to meet his eyes. He shook his head and smiled softly. "For the first time in my life, I want to be here. I'm not going without a fight."

Reston pulled me against him, and I snuggled into his chest. I could smell myself on him, and debated sending him back upstairs to shower before the meeting. There wasn't time, now, before the girls would be back. I couldn't have them arriving home to a clearly freshly-showered Reston.

"Don't ever sacrifice your happiness for me again," Reston murmured into my ear.

"I'll be fine without you. I've done it before."

"And I'll do everything in my power to keep that from happening again."

"Until leaving is your only option."

"And then I'll figure something out. I want to spend my life with you, Jo. And I know you're not ready for that, and I shouldn't have said it."

I couldn't stop the laugh that forced back threatening tears. "I am definitely not ready for that."

That didn't mean it wasn't nice to hear. Once upon a time, I'd forced myself not to consider that option. Knowing that Reston was going to fight for me warmed my heart. With all that I'd lost, knowing that I wasn't going to lose him was a comfort.

"Do you need to pick up the girls?" Reston asked.

I shook my head. "Heather's bringing them back. Soon, though, she said four."

"Okay. Can I help you get dinner ready for them or something?"

"That would be nice."

"I know it's impossible," Reston said, "but don't worry about tonight's meeting. Leave that to me to worry about. Okay?"

I laughed. "Impossible indeed."

He gazed studiously into my eyes. "I should never have said anything to you about that day. About the accident."

My heart sped up thinking about that conversation from weeks ago. I wanted to know everything. I wanted to know nothing. I wanted that day to fade from my memory, and I wanted to talk about nothing else.

I chose my words carefully, not sure I wanted to keep this conversation going. "The idea that you and I are spending this much time together, that we...that we're together, and you might never bring it up is kind of ridiculous, Reston."

"I know. But my memories of that day are spotty. I was in and out of consciousness. I couldn't see any of them. It's all noise, and some of it's…kind of white noise, Jo."

"What do you mean?"

He sighed. "Screams and moans and rattled breathing, and some of it might be me, and some of it is my team, and then some of it is the people who were trying to help us. I don't remember hearing Matt or Steve at the time. And I tell myself that means they were gone before I was aware of what was happening. Maybe I couldn't hear them, maybe I couldn't recognize their screams, couldn't pick them out in the chaos. I don't know. I can't say anything to reassure you. Would it even reassure you if I could?"

I shook my head slowly. "I doubt it. None of it has been particularly comforting. They're still gone, and nothing will change that."

"I regret saying anything to you, and I hope we never talk about it again."

"You can talk to me about anything you want, Reston."

"Thanks. I have someone I'm paying to listen to me about this. It's not right for me to involve someone who is also in the middle of it."

"I don't like the idea of us having a black hole between us. Something we can never discuss."

He frowned. "Sure, someday, we can absolutely have that conversation, Jo. But I think right now, while this is still fresh, I don't even want to talk about it with my therapist. I definitely don't want to talk about it with my friends."

"I understand. And I honestly don't know if I want to hear more. But I will, if that's ever what you need."

"Thank you."

"What do you need from me for this meeting tonight?"

He sighed, running his hands through his hair. "I don't know. Be with me?"

"Always."

CHAPTER FORTY-EIGHT

Reston had been pacing for nearly an hour by the time my mom arrived to watch the girls so that we could attend the school board meeting. I tried to tell him things would be okay, but he was right. There was no way this meeting was happening so that the school board could publicly announce they were keeping him on. He was going to have to fight for his job.

I was ready to fight along with him. I hoped the rest of the town was as well.

At the door to the auditorium, where the meetings were usually held, we were rerouted to the gym. I was shocked by the crowd size and noise level. Everyone in town clearly had an opinion on the future of the team.

Reston had the folder full of job offer letters in one hand and my hand in his other, but when he saw the assembled crowd, he dropped my hand and sidestepped away from me. It was enough that he was getting ready to put on a performance for the school board. We didn't want to add to the gossip of the evening.

Amanda was front row center in the bleachers. She waved us over. I didn't think either of us wanted that much attention, but it seemed inevitable.

"Everyone's got your back, Coach," I murmured.

I wasn't sure that was true, especially given the conversation I'd had with Natalie, but certainly enough people did. It would be okay.

Carol Mills, the school board president, called the meeting to order. Beside me, Reston's leg twitched, his fight-or-flight response manifesting. I wanted to take his hand or put my arm around him, but he clearly wasn't ready for that level of public affection. Instead, I clutched Amanda's hand, wishing I could ask her what she thought about all of this.

"We had a bit more turnout than we were expecting," Carol said. "Thanks, everyone, for coming. As I'm sure everyone is aware, tonight we'll be discussing the Haven High boys basketball team, and how we'd like to move forward. I know some people think we put this off longer than we should have, but we're trying to be respectful of the grieving families."

"You haven't asked any of us what we want," a voice called from behind me. I was fairly certain it was Natalie, and it didn't surprise me that she was speaking up.

"First we'll be discussing the coaching search," Carol continued, ignoring the comment.

"The team has a coach," Amanda called.

"It is the school board's opinion that Mr. Tucker—"

"Excuse me." Now Amanda was on her feet. "What did you call him?"

"Mrs. Ellis—"

"Show Coach Tucker the respect he deserves."

"Coach Tucker is not medically capable of coaching this team."

"Because I couldn't win a foot race?" Reston asked.

"Our opinion is based on the physician's report we received."

Reston walked to the court baseline, his limp nearly concealed. He took a basketball from the rack, dribbled to midcourt, and casually tossed it toward the opposite hoop.

"I'm not coaching track," he said as the ball swished through. "I'm here to coach basketball."

It wasn't like Reston to show off like this. In fact, it felt very much like a Stephen Grant move, and I loved that Reston had adopted his swagger, if only for this moment.

"You can't coach alone."

"I'll coach with him."

The words were out of my mouth before I realized I'd spoken. What was I doing? How was I supposed to coach the boys' team? I'd never played a real game of basketball in my life, and I couldn't very well walk into the locker room.

"That's a kind offer," Carol started.

Oh, God, I had to argue my point. I had to help Reston try to save his job.

"I know the playbook," I started. "I know the conditioning routine. I'm on the faculty at the high school. I know this team."

"Mrs. Grant."

"Carol."

"You are hardly qualified—"

"I'm more qualified than anyone else here."

"It's sweet of you to support Coach Tucker like this, but—"

"Every single family who had a player on this team last season will put their support behind Jo and Coach Tucker," Amanda said. "If you truly want to honor our sons, this is how."

Several voices behind me called out in agreement with her. As tears blurred my vision, I reached over and grabbed Amanda's hand.

"That's out of the question," Carol said. "We're sorry, but the decision has been made."

"Then don't bother to attempt to field a team," Natalie called.

"Without our support, you will never have another team at this school," Amanda added.

My head was spinning. For so long, it had felt like people—especially Natalie and Amanda—genuinely didn't want Reston back. Now they were his biggest champions. He needed that. I needed that. Still, it was overwhelming to feel the classic Haven support.

"And can you imagine the headlines?" Reston approached the table where the school board sat. "School board ignores request of grieving families. Oh, the national news will love that story."

"Sit down, Mr. Tucker."

"Coach." He stared at her, holding her gaze as he continued. "Do not discount my contributions to this town, Carol. I won three state championships in five years. I've sent my kids to Division I schools. But if you don't want me, I have other offers." He retrieved the folder from me and laid it on the table in front of the school board. He began to casually flip through the letters, making sure the board saw the school logos on the top of each one. "I'd rather stay in Haven, but when Duke makes an offer, it's hard to say no. That's a heck of a coaching tree to get into. I want my team back. But if you won't give it to me, I'll get a new team."

He walked out of the gym, leaving a stunned silence in his wake. Gradually a low murmur rose behind me, and then the sound of people filing out of the bleachers.

Amanda took my arm. "Time to go," she whispered.

I glanced around us, mystified by the sheer number of people exiting the gym. Surely this was coordinated, but how? And how did they pull it off without me hearing about it?

"Was this planned?" I asked as we walked out of the school.

"Mostly. We weren't expecting you to volunteer to coach with him."

"I wasn't either."

"Does he really have an offer from Duke?"

I nodded. "Among other places."

"Oh, my God. Well, at least he'll land on his feet."

"I told him to take it. The job at Duke. He wants to stay here."

It seemed like the whole town was gathered in the parking lot, giddily chattering about the school board meeting. I caught Natalie's eye across the parking lot, and mouthed, "Thank you."

She nodded back. Reston gathered me to him, grinning like a mad man, as if there wasn't a crowd of people around us, most of them now staring at us.

"You're really going to coach with me?" Reston asked.

"Until you find someone who knows what they're doing, sure."

He kissed me, both of us smiling now. I tried to ignore the hooting that rose up from the assembled crowd. We were going to be the hot gossip for a while now.

"Welcome to the team, Assistant Coach Grant."

CHAPTER FORTY-NINE

The atmosphere at school on Monday was electric. There hadn't been a formal announcement from the school board. Reston was twitchy with anxiety on Sunday, bouncing around my house, trying to keep his mind occupied after Friday's performance. I was shocked he and Amanda had planned a walkout of the meeting in support of him keeping his job. I was glad they'd put the plan together, and I prayed it worked.

I didn't blame him for his nerves. Hell, I was barely keeping it together. What if the school actually let me coach with him? It would be disastrous. What did I know about coaching a basketball team?

And this morning the students buzzed about what Reston had done at the meeting. I knew he had their support too, though I couldn't imagine it carried much weight with the school board. It didn't matter to them that the entire town stood behind Reston.

It was a battle to calm down my class to start the day's lesson.

"Guys, we have to get started," I said, exasperated.

"Sorry, Coach Grant."

Okay, that was new.

I raised an eyebrow. "Books open, please."

It didn't stop happening either. Every time I greeted a student in the halls. When I called on students by name in class. They called me coach, and I was mystified.

"My students are calling me coach," I complained to Reston at lunch. "It's weird."

"It's what we want. The title helps it seem real. Especially since you're a woman. No offense."

"Some taken."

He glanced around the teachers' lounge, as if anyone here didn't know what was going on.

"The school board wants to meet with me privately." He lowered his voice.

"What do you think they're going to say?"

"If they have any sense, they'll let me have my job. And if they don't, then I figure out how I'm going to live here and work in Durham."

"That's a bit of a commute." My heart pounded in my chest. He was going out of his way to make our relationship work. After all these years, he might leave Haven, but he wouldn't leave me.

"It is," he replied. "I'll figure it out. I suppose I'll split my time between cities."

"They're going to let you have your team back, Reston."

"I hope so."

"How could they not after the show Saturday night?"

He stared at me for a moment, then stood up, making a point of his limp as he disposed of his trash.

"I can try to hide it all I want." He returned to his seat. "It's still there."

"And getting better all the time."

"One leg is shorter than the other, Jo. I will always have a limp."

"And is that going to keep you from coaching?"

"Nothing's going to keep me from coaching."

That certainly seemed true.

"You better have been serious," Reston said.

He'd appeared on my porch at far too late of an hour, the knock on the door coming as I was heading to bed. I couldn't read his face, even after I flipped on the porch light. Was it good news? Bad news? Could he at least smile?

"Serious about what?" I asked.

"You're going to coach with me, right?"

"I'll mostly be a body on the bench with you."

"I expect more than that from my assistant coach, you know."

"I know." I paused. "They gave you back your team."

"They gave me my team."

He grinned, and I couldn't help but smile back. It was nice to see him this happy.

I sagged with relief. "Oh, Reston. Thank God."

It was, truly, the best possible decision. I couldn't imagine a team at Haven High that wasn't coached by Reston, and I couldn't imagine Reston without his team.

"Sorry it's so late. The meeting went long."

"It's fine. I'm so happy for you."

"I mean it. I need an assistant. I don't need a warm body."

"I'll do everything I can."

"I've got tryouts scheduled for Friday. You'll need a sitter for the girls."

I winced. "Friday? I don't know if I can be prepared to assess players by then."

"You'll be fine." He took my face in his hands and kissed me. "Thank you. For everything."

"Always."

"Arrange yourselves into teams, we'll get a few five-on-five games going," Reston announced to the assembled students, mostly freshmen, but a handful of upperclassmen. "Coach Grant and I will keep an eye on things. Go ahead and get started."

"What am I looking for?" I whispered to Reston as the boys separated into groups.

"Whatever you want. I'll know what I'm looking for when I see it."

"Reston—"

"Coach Tucker."

"Coach Tucker," I repeated, amused, because of course he was going to make me call him that. "I don't know what I'm doing."

"I think you do, instinctively, and you'll know it when you see it too. Just observe, Grant."

There were three games going, two five-on-five and one four-on-four. Reston moved from court to court, watching each game for a moment before checking in on the next one.

"Little, Chamberlain, switch teams," Reston called out.

"They weren't playing the same position," I noted.

"No, they weren't. They needed to swap positions." He moved to the next game. "Hutton, that would have been a foul. Watch your hands."

I stood on the sidelines of the first game, watching the boys Reston had switched. Mason Little was smooth with the ball—what Reston called "good hands." His passes were in precisely the right spot, the balls perfectly arched toward the net. This kid was impressive.

Some of the others were, too. It wasn't like watching the old team, who had worked together for years. These kids were good, but not the well-oiled machine I was used to watching. I tried to pick out the ones I thought should make up the roster. How Reston was going to figure that out was beyond me. How had he and Steve done it, with the number of kids he usually had trying out.

I'd never watched him coach without Steve. It was weird and wrong, as if I was wearing a sweater that had shrunk in the wash. It looked similar enough, the basic parts where they should be, but uncomfortable, making me chafe against the change.

Reston started the players on drills, and stood next to me on the sideline, observing.

"I'm livid that Little's never tried out before," he murmured.

I cut my eyes toward him. "Seriously?"

"He's a junior, Grant. I could have had two years with him already. We could have another state championship."

I tried to muffle my laughter. Yep, that seemed like something that would bother him.

"Well, at least you'll have a head start on another one?" I replied.

"I need to stop watching him and pay attention to these other kids, but he's brilliant."

"Shane is too slow," I commented.

"Who?"

"Shane. Um, Simmons."

I still wasn't used to this convention, the sports way of only using last names. At least this mattered less than, say, if I picked up our play calls. I had a head start on those.

"Pick up your speed, Simmons," Reston called, then dropped his voice. "You're right about him."

"Slow is fine, if he can speed up. I don't think he can."

"I'll keep an eye on him. Nash, you're getting the move wrong. Stop for a second and watch the other guys."

He would normally be out there, demonstrating the exact moves, but for now he was relying on the players to guide each other. He'd be back out there, even if it wasn't with the dexterity he used to have. For now, though, he'd observe.

"I don't like the way Williams handles the ball," Reston murmured to me.

"Is it fixable? What can you teach him?"

He rubbed his chin for a moment. "Good question. Okay. Moving on!"

Drill after drill, Reston put the boys through their paces. I mostly observed, relaying my thoughts to Reston and weighing in on his opinions. We'd definitely be able to put together a dozen of these kids into a team.

And soon enough, it would be time for our first game.

It was inconceivable our boys had been gone long enough that they'd been replaced in a visceral way. I shook off the agonizing thought, trying to concentrate, reminding myself that no one could possibly replace them. That's not what this was. In a way, this was simply business, and if I thought of it that way, surely I could get through this.

There was no choice. I'd promised Reston I'd help him, and I wouldn't let him down.

Chapter Fifty

After tryouts, I picked up supplies, ready to figure out how to schedule the next few months of our lives. The piece of poster board took up half of my dining room table, and the six months' worth of calendars taped on top took up the entire poster board. I had a stack of flyers, my cell phone, and a handful of scribbled notes, plus assorted colored markers.

Let's do this.

I started with the school calendar, sketching in the girls' days off, my days off, testing days, when the class parties would be. Next was the remainder of Olivia's soccer schedule. Then Addy's dance stuff. Then basketball, the games and practices I'd thought would disappear from our schedule. I noted important birthdays, holidays, little things that might slip through my memory.

Now it was time to deal with the days when the things I'd written down overlapped.

I'd already signed up the girls for the after-school program, so they'd be occupied for those practices. I'd spent years trading care on the kids' days off school, so I texted some friends, calling in all my favors.

Things would come up, emergencies would happen.

But I had a plan in place for the next six months. I could do this.

My confidence only lasted a few hours. Addy had a dance recital—hot pink on my new calendar system. It was always a bit of a scramble to get her ready. We had to have dinner, Addy needed her hair and makeup done, then we needed to get out the door and to the studio with plenty of time for her to get dressed, stretched, and onstage.

"Addy!" I called up the stairs. "You've got ten minutes."

She didn't answer.

I finished the last few things on my list, hustling Olivia into her shoes. It wasn't like Addy to take this long to get ready.

But usually she had help.

She'd refused my offer to help her get ready, so I'd given her a wide berth. She was taking too long, though, and I jogged upstairs to check on her.

If she'd started on her makeup, her tears had washed it away. Her hair wasn't even combed, let alone pulled back. I couldn't be mad, but I was in a panic. We'd be lucky to make it to the theatre on time.

I took a deep breath. All that mattered was that she was okay. After that, I could worry about the recital.

"Hey, baby," I said softly.

"Hi, Mom."

"What's up?"

She collapsed onto the bathroom floor. Her words were hard to make out through her sobs, but I understood the gist. "Daddy's supposed to be here," came through pretty clearly, and then she said something that I was sure was, "I can't do this without him," which was honestly the most relatable thing she'd ever said to me.

"I miss him too," I said.

Addy said, "You don't understand."

I couldn't take her dad's place, but I was going to do the best I could.

Getting her ready for her dance recitals was her and Steve's thing, their special time together. It had taken some work for him to execute the perfect bun, but he'd taken such pride in it when he did. On recital or competition days, he'd toil endlessly to get every strand in place, while Addy applied her stage makeup. They'd talk during that time, catching each other up on their lives.

Should I have pushed her to let me help today? Should I have given her the choice not to participate in the recital? It was the first since the accident. Letting her skip this one would only make the next recital the first since the accident.

"Do you want to bail?" I asked.

Addy sat up, her face streaked with tears, her eyes red and puffy, and shook her head.

"Let's grab your stuff." I swept bottles off the counter and into her dance bag. "You can figure it out on the way."

But by the time we got to the auditorium, she hadn't so much as run a brush through her hair. I kept silent, turning her over to her instructor, mouthing sorry as I scrambled out front to find seats for me and Olivia.

I spotted waving arms near the front of the seats and exhaled in relief at the sight of Reston.

"I saved you seats," he said. "I was worried you weren't coming."

"Addy might not dance," Olivia said, while I merely shook my head.

"It's been a rough half hour," I said. "Thanks for coming."

"Of course! I'm dying to see her dance."

When the girls came out for their first dance, Addy was dressed identically to her classmates. But her hair hung loose around her shoulders, her face washed out in the stage lights. Reston made a soft aha sound, and I nodded.

She danced beautifully, if not technically perfect. Tears glinted on her cheeks as she moved, her artistry beyond anything I'd ever seen from her.

When the song ended, the girls left the stage to thunderous applause. They'd have a short break now to change costumes for the next piece.

"Is she okay?" Reston whispered.

"I have no idea."

From the beginning of this horrible time, I'd struggled to know if the girls were okay. Even with their counseling sessions, they had good days and bad. Today was one of the bad ones.

Clearly.

When the curtain rose for the second number, Addy's hair was secured in a tight bun, her lips crimson, eyelashes for days. Dance-mode Addison.

And this time her movements were technically perfect, every arm and leg going exactly where it was supposed to be.

Some of the emotional artistry was gone from her movements, and I wondered if that was intentional. Had she turned off her emotional response, wanting to stop the tears? Was she simply more focused this time, concentrating on getting the moves right?

Either way, she was beautiful, her dancing was beautiful, and I beamed, my cheeks burning against my too wide smile.

"You were amazing!" I exclaimed.

Addy's face was flushed, like it had been since Reston handed her the bouquet of roses that he'd brought her. "Thanks," she squeaked. "It was harder than I expected."

I wanted to tell her it would get easier. But it would also get harder again. And she'd be fine then too.

Her flush deepened, and she waved to someone behind us. I glanced over my shoulder, catching a glimpse of white blond hair as Dr. Banks slipped from the lobby.

I knew Addy was still seeing her, that Dr. Banks made periodic trips to the middle school to check in on Addy and a couple of the other kids. I'd imagine they'd talked a lot about this night over the past few weeks. I was glad she'd come to show her support. And Addy was too.

Dr. Banks was one of the few outsiders who had shown up to help, had stayed to help, after the accident. Somehow, that touched me more than all the neighborhood ladies dropping off casseroles.

Maybe it was because she was taking care of the most precious Haven residents.

Whatever it was, I was grateful she was here, and that she'd helped my girls.

CHAPTER FIFTY-ONE

Home from the dance recital and getting the girls settled for the night, I was struck by a compulsion to visit the cemetery. I hadn't been since the day of the funeral, but suddenly I needed to be there. I needed to feel Steve with me, more than anything. I needed to know that I wasn't screwing this up.

"Girls, will you be okay if I run out for a bit?"

"Where are you going?" Addy asked.

"Just out by myself for a bit. Can I trust you guys to get in bed and go to sleep?"

"Not really," she said, smirking a little, forever her father's daughter.

"Okay, then. I'll be back soon, I promise."

It was colder than I expected, and I shivered in my light fall coat. Luckily the cemetery was well-lit. I hadn't been sure I'd be able to find the boys after all these months away, but the lights helped me find my way.

Their headstones hadn't been here the last time. I traced the letters carved in the cold stone, their names, the familiar dates. My throat closed, trying to stop my tears, and I coughed to clear it. I sat on the grass six feet above my husband, the chill from the ground soaking into my body.

"I wish you were here to tell me I was doing okay," I whispered.

I didn't want Steve to be disappointed in me. I didn't want him in the afterlife watching me fumble around, botching our children.

He should be able to rest easy, knowing I'd do what's right, knowing I'd take the best possible care of them.

Today I failed at that. Addy had been so heartbroken, so lost, and I should have anticipated that.

"I'm sorry I never visit," I added. "I'm so busy, and I have so much to do, and...I don't like reminders that you're gone."

My pendant burned against my skin, the way it always seemed to when I was thinking about the boys. I didn't need reminders that they were gone. I always felt it.

"You're supposed to be here." My voice cracked as tears filled my eyes. "I need you."

I pulled my coat tighter around me, snuggling against Steve's headstone. I wanted my life back. I wanted the life I was supposed to have, the life I'd worked so hard for. I didn't want this life anymore, no matter how well I managed sometimes. I could do this fine—I could be the breadwinner and raise my daughters and have a life. But I didn't want it. I didn't want this if I could have my old life, my life before the accident.

The trick was convincing myself that I couldn't have that anymore.

"Oh, it's you."

I looked up at the voice. Reston was tucking his phone back into his pocket, dressed far more practically than I was, jeans and a heavy sweater under a jacket.

"I was about to report a vagrant," he said.

I scrambled to my feet, brushing off my rear end, hoping the ground hadn't made a mess of me. "What are you doing here?

"I'm hanging out with my team like I do every day," he replied matter-of-factly. "What are you doing here?" I gestured to the headstones behind me and to my left. "Right, of course. I've never seen you here before."

"I've never been here before. Do you come every day?"

"If I can."

"I didn't know that."

It made sense. His team was his life.

"I didn't mean to disturb you. I'll be over there and I'll keep my voice down. I won't listen to anything you're saying."

I narrowed my eyes. "You talk to them?"

He'd turned to go, but he turned back at my question. "Sometimes, yeah. Sometimes I come here to think, because it's quiet and being with my team helps. Weren't you talking to them? Isn't that half the point of coming here?"

"I'm not sure why I'm here, honestly."

"Because of the thing with Addy at her dance."

My face went hot. Yes, that was the obvious answer. But it wasn't as if this was the first time I'd felt like a failure. "Thanks."

"So you did know why you came."

"I knew why I was more upset than usual. But that happens plenty, and I never felt the need to be here before."

"You've wanted to stay away, because it hurts too much."

"How do you know all of this?"

"Do you still think you're the only one in Haven who's grieving?"

No, but I did sometimes forget that we weren't all grieving the same. Of course some people were coming here to be with the boys.

"How do you come here every day?" I asked. "How does that not hurt?"

"For months, I couldn't be here, I was stuck in recovery. I thought about what I would do when I could finally go where I wanted and do what I wanted, and I realized all I wanted was to be with them. So here I am."

"What do you talk to them about?"

"It depends on the day. Sometimes I tell them how everyone here is doing, so they know we're all okay. Sometimes I complain about how much bullshit it is that my left leg is shorter than my right leg now because it couldn't be bothered to heal correctly. I asked them if they were okay with me having another team. Normal stuff."

"Are they okay with you having another team?"

He shrugged. "They didn't tell me otherwise."

"And how were they supposed to do that?"

"A fair point." He looked away from me, his hands deep in his pockets. "Honestly, did you come here to tell Steve you're failing at parenting?"

"That wasn't exactly how I worded it."

"You're doing a great job."

"Thanks."

"It doesn't matter coming from me."

It did, but it wasn't the same. Reston loved my daughters, but he wasn't invested the way Steve was. Reston and I hadn't spent years learning how to parent together, propping each other up through imagined failures.

"It does," I protested. "It means…it's good to hear, Reston."

"Jo, you are magnificent. You figured out how to take care of your family, and you're raising two amazing daughters. Steve would be proud of you. I'm proud of you."

I glanced down at my feet, at the ground where my husband was buried. "You shouldn't talk to me like that here."

"It's okay, Steve knows about us. I told him everything."

I flushed at the implication of his words. "Everything?"

"Okay, not everything, this is still a public space, and Matt's here too."

"I can't believe you told him anything."

"Of course I did. He's my best friend, Jo. I tell Steve everything."

"That's going to make things a little weirder than I expected," I said, as if there hadn't been plenty of uncomfortable moments between me and Reston.

"It's okay, he's happy for us."

"I'm not sure how you know that."

"He hasn't told me otherwise."

My lips twitched into a near smile. "That's good to hear, I suppose. I should get home. I told the girls I wouldn't be gone long."

"Have a good night, Jo. Don't dwell on tonight. Remember all the other nights where you nailed it."

I smiled. "Have a good time with the boys."

"Always."

CHAPTER FIFTY-TWO

"All right, team meeting." Reston commandeered my kitchen table, spreading sheets of paper around the surface.

The girls were in bed, hopefully asleep, and I probably should have been too. But there were only so many hours in the day, and I had to give some to basketball.

"I appreciate that you were willing to come here for this."

"I'll come here for anything."

The silken tone of Reston's words had sent a shiver down my spine, but I couldn't stifle the yawn that burst out of me before I could reply.

"The days are long," I said by way of apology.

"Next time," Reston said, his voice a low growl in my ear, "don't volunteer."

I laughed, rejuvenated. "All right, Coach, tell me what we're up to tonight."

"I'm trying to figure out this roster," Reston said. "What do you think?"

I looked at his notes, the hastily scribbled, barely legible names that he'd sorted into groups on the paper. Why had I volunteered for this? Why did I think I knew enough to assist him in any real way? It was so much, and Reston was counting on me, and what if I let him down?

"I think I'm not going to be able to cut it," I said softly.

He looked up from the paper in front of him. "About the roster, Grant."

"Oh."

I'd never been part of this discussion when Reston and Steve worked together. Sure, I attended games, practices. Occasionally they'd discuss strategy. This seemed next level, and I wasn't quite sure what I could offer Reston.

"I wouldn't start Collins," I said finally.

"Good. Why not?"

"He hesitates. He sees the best move, and he questions it, every time. He needs another year before he'll get the confidence to trust himself."

"Excellent, Grant, thank you," Reston said, rearranging the names on the paper.

"Reston."

"You're going to be fine."

"What if I'm not?"

He sighed. "You caught something I missed. You noticed someone who needed to gain confidence. Perhaps, Jo, you need a year to learn to trust yourself. That's why you're not on your own."

"I don't want to hold you back."

"You couldn't possibly hold me back. I'm an unstoppable force."

I blinked at Reston for a moment, gauging how serious he was. It was hard to argue otherwise, of course. There was a reason they'd kept him on here. He was a coach who won games. And I knew that Steve contributed to that, but Reston was…skilled. He knew what he was doing.

"Are you scared about how this season's going to go?" I asked.

Reston shrugged. "I'm trying not to think about it. I'm trying to pretend there weren't these twelve other kids. Another team. I'm trying to focus on the day-to-day stuff with this team."

"Can you forget about the other team?"

I certainly couldn't. Knowing he went to the cemetery daily, he couldn't either.

"Never. I try to tell myself, you know, my teams always grow up. They always go away. Ashton and Julian were going to graduate last year anyway. I was already going to be missing them, even if this hadn't happened. It doesn't help. Losing that team is harder. Most of those kids were on my first team here. Matt, Landon, Gabe, they've been mine since they were babies, practically."

"Tell me about it," I replied.

"And I want Landon and Isaiah to be part of this team, however they can or want to be. But I don't know how to ask. I don't want it to look like pity. I want them to know that they were part of this family, and they always will be."

"Tell them that."

He was fidgety, not looking at me, pretending to concentrate on the papers in front of him. I knew it hurt him to talk about the boys we'd lost, but I couldn't stop thinking about them as we built a new team.

"Landon won't see me," Reston finally said.

"Then start with Isaiah," I replied, my voice gentle. "You see him at school, right?"

"You talk to him. That's why I have an assistant."

"No, it's not, and talk to him yourself."

Now he looked up at me. "You know I worry."

"That he blames you?"

"Yes. I don't want to rub it in his face, like I got better and everything's back to normal."

"Everyone knows it's not back to normal, Reston."

"Building this team," Reston said, gesturing to the papers on my table, "it feels like pretending that never happened."

"It's moving on, and it's normal, and it's what they would have expected and wanted."

"That sounds like something my therapist would tell me."

"It's what my mom told me about dating you."

He nodded, speaking slowly. "Steve wouldn't mind, because you're supposed to move on."

"Yep."

"Does it help you to hear that?"

"A little."

"I suppose the guilt's normal too."

"Seems like it."

None of what he said was wrong. He was only walking me through the same things I told myself.

Reston looked studiously at the papers for a moment, idly sketching in the margins of one sheet.

"I'll talk to Isaiah," he said finally.

"What do you mean Landon doesn't talk to you?"

"Seems self-explanatory."

"What happened?"

"Didn't you hear? There was this accident with the bus—"

"Reston."

"Landon's brain doesn't work anymore. I don't know if he blames me, or if he simply associates me with what happened, but he gets agitated when I'm around. So I don't go around."

"He'll get better." I needed to believe that was true.

"That's still unclear."

"Fair enough."

"What you said before, about how they would have expected us to move on, I worry that Landon doesn't. That he won't understand because he isn't capable of that."

"I suppose that makes sense."

He breathed deeply and straightened his body. "But I can't think about any of that. I have to focus." Reston looked resolutely back at the papers. "I think we're ready."

"I don't think that's possible," I replied. "But I'm excited to find out."

CHAPTER FIFTY-THREE

Reston waved his arm at me, but for the life of me, I couldn't remember what the signal meant. The crowd was too loud for me to hear any instructions from him, which was why I was supposed to have memorized the hand signals.

Now the signal was clearly "hurry up," and I scrambled.

"Dane," I said, grabbing one of the boys from the bench. "Get to Coach."

I hoped I'd grabbed the right kid.

It was strange, being on the bench instead of in the stands. It was our first home game, and it had started somberly with a moment of silence for Steve and Matt and the rest of the boys. Reston and I had stood at midcourt with the families, with Landon, who was agitated by the noise of the crowd, with Isaiah in his wheelchair. Addy and Olivia stood on either side of me, and I squeezed their hands as everyone in Haven thought about what we'd lost.

Now the game was heating up, and I needed to get my head straight. The score was close, and Reston's gestures became tighter, more tense. I did my best to keep up, but I wasn't quite hacking it yet. It was only the first game, but I knew he expected me to be better.

He expected the boys to be better too, but at least he was kind about it. I missed a lot of the postgame chat with the team, banned from the boys' locker room, but they left at the end of the night looking excited to come back. The fact that we won probably helped.

"You have to get better with the signals, Jo," Reston said as I drove us back to my house after the game.

"I know I do, Reston. I'm working on it."

"We got lucky tonight. We're going to have harder teams. You can't slow me down."

"I understand."

He was tough on me, but I needed that. If I was going to coach with him, I was going to have to be better. It'd been irrational when I volunteered, but it turned out I liked it. Now I just had to be good enough not to get in his way.

"Do you know any math tutors?" Reston asked.

Steve would have known someone. He probably would have volunteered himself.

"I can ask around."

"I need to find someone for Little. His grades aren't where they need to be."

"Is he going to get kicked off the team?"

"No, not even close. But his grades aren't good enough for the schools he wants to go to."

"I didn't know that was something you worried about."

"When I say I get my kids into D-I schools, I don't just mean by teaching them how to dribble. He wants schools that won't take a kid who's lucky to make Bs."

I pulled into the driveway, mulling over my words before speaking. "Did you ever do anything for Matt?"

"Matt didn't need me. His grades were acceptable for what he wanted to do after high school. He was going to be fine."

"What did he want to do?"

Reston followed me into the house, where the girls were already in bed, and my mom sat on the couch in the living room, reading a book. They'd left the game at halftime, the girls needing to get to bed.

"Hey, Mrs. Franklin."

She snapped her book closed, rising from the couch. "Hello, Reston. Hey, Jo."

"Mom. How were the girls?"

"They were perfect. How'd the game go?"

"We won by six," Reston replied. "Should have been twelve."

"We need more practice," I added, though I was genuinely pleased with how the game had gone. I didn't think I'd ever have expectations as high as Reston's.

"The team will keep getting better," Mom said.

"I'm sure. Thanks for watching the girls."

"Of course."

With my mom gone for the night, I reheated dinner while Reston set the table. I also warmed a heating pad for Reston. He'd never admit his leg was aching. I'd seen the grimaces he tried to hide, even from me.

"What did Matt want to do after high school?" I asked again while we were eating.

"He wanted to play basketball. He was going to be one and done and off to the pros."

"You think he could have done that?"

"I have no doubt."

"That's kind of you to say."

Reston shrugged. "I don't bullshit about my players."

"Good to know."

"Thanks for the heating pad."

"You're welcome."

"You can't get the hand signals down, but I don't have to speak for you to know exactly what I need at home."

I'd had far more practice with one than the other.

"I'll get better with the hand signals," I said.

"And I'll get used to spending this much time on my feet, and eventually I won't be in this much pain after a game."

"Jesse says physical therapy is going well."

"You shouldn't be talking to Jesse about my PT."

"Welcome to Haven, where everyone talks about everyone else."

He shook his head, chuckling to himself. "Fair enough. PT's going fine. Thanks for your concern."

"Hey, I can't be an effective assistant coach if I don't know how you're handling the work."

"Or if you can't learn my signals."

He wasn't going to let me live that down.

"I'll work on it," I said with a laugh.

"You're going to have to run laps after practice on Monday."

"Oh, no. I don't run."

"That's what happens when you aren't doing what you need to do for the team."

"Did you make Steve run laps?"

"Steve knew the signals."

I laughed. "Of course he did."

"Honestly, you're catching on great, for someone who had no idea what they were doing a month ago."

"Hey," I protested. "I knew plenty. It's not like you had to teach me the rules."

"Do you want me to help with the dishes?"

"Nah, I'll take care of it in the morning."

"Then I should get going."

"You know you're welcome to stay. The guest room is always ready for you," I added when he began to protest.

Neither of us wanted to complicate things for the girls. They knew Reston and I were seeing each other, but I didn't want to put too much importance on it, nor did I want them to feel like I was replacing their dad. Reston and I spent nearly every waking moment together, thanks to work, but we hadn't spent our sleeping hours together yet.

It would happen, eventually.

"Thanks for the offer," Reston replied. "Another time."

"Definitely."

"Good game tonight, Grant."

"You too, Coach." I took his face in my hands, kissing him gently. "Good night."

"Good night, Jo. I love you."

"I love you too, Reston."

I didn't know what was going to happen next, but I finally felt whole again. My family was still broken, but it was also still good.

And it could only get better.

www.ingramcontent.com/pod-product-compliance
Lightning Source LLC
Chambersburg PA
CBHW070740180626
46818CB00007B/2927